W9-BUB-470

Praise for Julie James's debut romance

Just the Sexiest Man Alive

"Witty banter and amazing chemistry between Taylor and Jason bring this delightful story to life." —*Chicago Sun-Times*

"Fantastic, frolicking fun . . . Read *Just the Sexiest Man Alive*, and you will be adding Julie James to your automatic buy list!" —*New York Times* bestselling author Janet Chapman

"In her debut novel, James shakes up the world of lawyers and celebrity romance, producing a captivating, beautifully written story. The fireworks between the characters fuel the plot and will keep readers flipping the pages at a dizzying pace." —*Romantic Times*

"James's familiarity with both the law and the film industry lends credibility to this fast-moving, contemporary romantic comedy between two strong-willed characters." —*Booklist*

"Witty and romantic." —*Publishers Weekly*

"*Just the Sexiest Man Alive* by Julie James is a laugh-out-loud funny read . . . It is nice to see such a down-to-earth heroine and a hero that has to work to get what he wants. Ms. James writes very human characters that, like we do, have communication problems . . . This is my first book by Ms. James, but it will definitely not be my last!" —*Fallen Angel Reviews*

"[A] smartly written contemporary." —*All About Romance*

"The sparks fly between the [hero and heroine] in this engaging romance . . . The supporting cast is great as well . . . Author Julie James has done an excellent job, giving us characters we really care about and an unlikely but realistic romance." —*The Romance Studio*

continued . . .

Practice Makes Perfect

JULIE JAMES

BERKLEY SENSATION, NEW YORK

THE BERKLEY PUBLISHING GROUP
Published by the Penguin Group
Penguin Group (USA) Inc.
375 Hudson Street, New York, New York 10014, USA
Penguin Group (Canada), 90 Eglinton Avenue East, Suite 700, Toronto, Ontario M4P 2Y3, Canada
(a division of Pearson Penguin Canada Inc.)
Penguin Books Ltd., 80 Strand, London WC2R 0RL, England
Penguin Group Ireland, 25 St. Stephen's Green, Dublin 2, Ireland (a division of Penguin Books Ltd.)
Penguin Group (Australia), 250 Camberwell Road, Camberwell, Victoria 3124, Australia
(a division of Pearson Australia Group Pty. Ltd.)
Penguin Books India Pvt. Ltd., 11 Community Centre, Panchsheel Park, New Delhi—110 017, India
Penguin Group (NZ), 67 Apollo Drive, Rosedale, North Shore 0632, New Zealand
(a division of Pearson New Zealand Ltd.)
Penguin Books (South Africa) (Pty.) Ltd., 24 Sturdee Avenue, Rosebank, Johannesburg 2196,
South Africa

Penguin Books Ltd., Registered Offices: 80 Strand, London WC2R 0RL, England

This is a work of fiction. Names, characters, places, and incidents either are the product of the author's imagination or are used fictitiously, and any resemblance to actual persons, living or dead, business establishments, events, or locales is entirely coincidental. The publisher does not have any control over and does not assume any responsibility for author or third-party websites or their content.

PRACTICE MAKES PERFECT

A Berkley Sensation Book / published by arrangement with the author

PRINTING HISTORY
Berkley Sensation mass-market edition / March 2009

Copyright © 2009 by Julie Koca.
Cover art by Tony Mauro.
Cover design by Rita Frangie.
Interior text design by Laura K. Corless.

ISBN: 978-0-425-22674-2

BERKLEY® SENSATION
Berkley Sensation Books are published by The Berkley Publishing Group,
a division of Penguin Group (USA) Inc.,
375 Hudson Street, New York, New York 10014.
BERKLEY® SENSATION and the "B" design are trademarks of Penguin Group (USA) Inc.

PRINTED IN THE UNITED STATES OF AMERICA

10 9 8 7 6 5 4 3 2 1

For Jackson

Acknowledgments

I would like to thank my literary agent, Susan Crawford, for this wonderful journey, and for all her guidance and enthusiasm. I also want to express my continuing appreciation to Dick Shepherd, for taking a chance on a lawyer from Chicago who said she had a good idea for a romantic comedy.

I want to thank my fantastic editor, Wendy McCurdy, and the entire team at Berkley, including Allison Brandau, Kathryn Tumen, Crissie Johnson, and Emma Stockton.

Special thanks to Chris Ernst, golf technical consultant; to Brian Kavanaugh, class action expert and web designer extraordinaire; and to Darren for vaguely, loosely, inspiring the idea behind this book.

I am forever grateful to my family for their love and support, and am also very lucky to have a great group of girlfriends who continually inspire me—the smartest, strongest, and funniest women I know.

Lastly, and most important, I want to express my deepest gratitude to my husband, Brian, for his endless encouragement, and to the newest—and cutest—little hero in my life, my son, Jackson.

Is not general incivility the very essence of love?

—JANE AUSTEN, *PRIDE AND PREJUDICE*

One

THE ALARM CLOCK went off at 5:30 a.m.

Payton Kendall lifted a sleepy hand to her nightstand and fumbled around to silence the god-awful beeping. She lay there, snuggled in amongst her cozy down pillows, blinking, rousing. Allowing herself these first, and last, few seconds of the day that she could call her own. Then—suddenly remembering—she jumped out of bed.

Today was the day.

Payton had a plan for this morning—she had set her alarm to wake her a half hour earlier than usual. There was a purpose for this: she had observed *his* daily routine and guessed that *he* got to the office every morning by 7:00 a.m. He liked being the first one in the office, she knew. On this morning, however, she would be there when he got in. Waiting.

In her mind she had it all worked out—she would act casual. She would be in her office, and when she heard him walk in, she would just "happen" to stroll by to get something from the printer. "Good morning," she would say with a smile. And without her having to say anything else, he would know exactly what that smile meant.

He'd be wearing one of his designer suits, the ones Payton knew he had hand-tailored to fit him just so. "The man *knows* how to wear a suit," she had overheard one of the secretaries say while gossiping by the coffeemaker in the fifty-third-floor break room. Payton had resisted the urge to follow up the secretary's comment with one of her own, lest she reveal the feelings about him that she had fought to keep so carefully hidden.

Moving with purpose, Payton sped through her morning routine. How much easier it must be to be a man, she reflected not for the first time. No makeup to apply, no hair to straighten, no legs to shave. They didn't even have to sit to pee, the lazy bastards. Just shower, shave, wham-bam, out the door in ten minutes. Although, Payton suspected, *he* put a little more effort into it. That perfectly imperfect, mussed-just-right hair of his certainly required product of some sort. And, from what she had personally observed, he never wore the same shirt/tie combo twice in the same month.

Not that Payton didn't put some effort into her appearance as well. A jury consultant she had worked with during a particularly tricky gender discrimination trial had told her that jurors—both men and women—responded more favorably to female lawyers who were attractive. While Payton found this to be sadly sexist, she accepted it as a fact nonetheless and thus made it a general rule to always put her best face forward, literally, at work. Besides, she'd rather hang herself by a pinky toe than ever let *him* see her looking anything but her best.

The "L" ride into the office was quiet, with far fewer passengers riding this early in the morning. The city seemed to be just waking up as Payton walked along the Chicago River the three blocks to her law firm's offices. The early morning sun glinted off the river, casting it in a soft golden glow. Payton smiled to herself as she cut through the lobby of her building; she was in that good of a mood.

Her excitement grew as the elevator rose to the fifty-third floor. Her floor. *His* floor. The door opened, revealing a dark office hallway. The secretaries wouldn't be in for at least two hours, which was good. If all went as planned, she had a few things to say to him and now she would be able to speak freely, without fear of the two of them being overheard.

Payton strode with confidence down the corridor, her briefcase swinging at her side. His office was closer to the elevator bank; she would pass it en route to hers. Eight years it had been since they had moved into their respective offices across the floor from each other. She could picture perfectly the letters on the nameplate outside his office.

J. D. JAMESON.

My, how the mere mention of that name made her pulse quicken . . .

Payton rounded the corner, grinning in anticipation as she thought about what he would say when—

She stopped cold.

His office light was on.

But—how? This couldn't be. She had gotten up at this ridiculous hour to get in first. What about her plans, her big plans? The casual stroll by the printer, the way she was supposed to smile knowingly and say, *Good morning, J.D.*?

She heard a familiar rich baritone voice behind her.

"Good morning, Payton."

Payton's pulse skyrocketed. She couldn't help it, merely hearing his voice had that effect on her. She turned around and there he stood.

J. D. Jameson.

Payton paused to look him over. He looked so quintessentially *J.D.* right then, with his suit jacket already off and his classically cut navy pinstripe pants and yes, that perfectly styled rakish light brown hair of his. He looked tan—probably out playing tennis or golf over the weekend—and he gave her one of his perfect-white-teeth smiles as he leaned casually against the credenza behind him.

"I said, 'Good morning,'" he repeated. And so Payton did what she always did when she saw J. D. Jameson.

She scowled.

The shithead had beaten her into work.

Again.

"Good morning, J.D.," she replied with that sarcastic tone she reserved just for him.

Noting her arrival, he checked his watch, then glanced up and down the hallway with deliberate exaggeration. "Wow—did I miss the lunch cart? Is it noon already?"

She *really* hated this guy.

I hardly get in at noon, Payton nearly retorted, then bit her tongue. No. She wouldn't stoop to his level and defend herself.

"Perhaps if you spent a little less time keeping track of my comings and goings, J.D., and a little more time working, it wouldn't take you fifteen hours to bill ten."

She watched with satisfaction as her reply wiped the smirk right off of his face. Touché. With a well-practiced cool and calm demeanor, she turned in her heels and headed across the hall to her own office.

Such a silly thing, Payton thought. This endless competition J.D. had with her. The man clearly spent far too much time focusing on what she was up to. It had been that way since . . . well, since as long as she could remember. Thank goodness she was above such petty nonsense.

Payton got to her office and closed her door behind her. She set her briefcase down on top of her desk and took a seat in the well-worn leather chair. How many hours had she logged in that chair? How many all-nighters had she pulled? How many weekends had she sacrificed? All in her quest to show the firm that she was partnership material— that *she* was the top associate in her class.

Through the glass on her door, she could see across the hall to J.D.'s office. He was already back at his own desk, in front of his computer, working. Oh, sure, like he had such important matters to tend to.

Payton pulled her laptop out of her briefcase and turned it on, ready to start her day. After all, she had very important things to focus on, too.

For starters, like how the hell she was ever going to get up at *4:30* tomorrow morning.

Two

"I SEE YOU broke your own record."

Payton peered up from her computer as Irma walked into her office, waving the time sheets Payton had given her earlier that morning.

"I get depressed just logging in these hours," her secretary continued in an exasperated tone. "Seriously, I need to be assigned to a different associate. Someone whose weekly time sheets aren't as long as *Anna Karenina*."

Payton raised an eyebrow as she took the stack of time sheets from her secretary. "Let me guess—another recommendation from Oprah?"

Irma gave Payton a look that said she was treading on seriously dangerous ground. "That sounds like mocking."

"No, never," Payton assured her, trying not to grin. "I'm sure it's a wonderful book."

At least four times a year Irma made the pilgrimage out to the West Loop to sit in the audience at Harpo Studios and be in the presence of Her Holiness the Winfrey. Irma took all recommendations from the TV maven—lifestyle, literary, and otherwise—as gospel. Any comments in the negative by Payton or anyone else were strictly taboo.

Irma took a seat in front of the desk as she waited for Payton to sign off on the completed time sheets. "You'd like it. It's about a woman who's progressive for her time."

"Sounds promising," Payton said distractedly as she skimmed the printout of the hours her secretary had entered.

"Then she falls for the wrong man," Irma continued.

"That's a bit cliché, isn't it? They call this Tolstoy guy a writer?" Payton quickly scrawled her signature across the bottom of the last time sheet and handed them back to Irma.

"This 'Tolstoy guy' knows about relationships. Perhaps you could learn a thing or two from him."

Payton pretended not to hear the comment. After years of working with Irma, the two of them had developed a comfortable, familiar relationship, and she had learned that the best way to handle her secretary's not-so-subtle remarks regarding her personal life was simply to ignore them.

"You've seen the evidence of my lack of free time," Payton said, gesturing to her time sheets. "Until I'm through with this trial, I'm afraid Tolstoy will have to wait." She pointed. "But if Oprah happens to know of a book about responding to subpoenas for corporate documents, *that* I would be interested in."

Seeing Irma's look of warning, Payton held up her hands innocently. "I'm just saying."

"I tell you what," Irma said. "I'll hold on to the book for you. Because after this month, I suspect you'll be able to give yourself a bit of a break." She winked.

Payton turned back to her computer. Despite Irma's repeated attempts to engage her on this subject, she didn't like to talk openly about it. After all, she didn't want to jinx things. So she waved aside the remark, feigning nonchalance.

"Is something happening this month? I'm not aware of it."

Irma snorted. "Please. You've only had this month highlighted in your electronic calendar for eight years."

"I don't know what you're talking about. And stop snooping around in my calendar."

Irma rose to leave. "All right, all right, I know how you are about discussing this stuff." She headed toward the door, then paused and turned back. "I almost forgot—Mr. Gould's secretary called. He wondered if you're free to meet in his office at one thirty."

Payton quickly checked. "Works for me. Tell her that I'll come by his office then." She began entering the appointment in her daily planner when she heard her secretary call to her from the doorway.

"Um, Payton—one last thing?"

Payton looked up distractedly from her computer. "Yes?"

Irma smiled reassuringly. "You're gonna make it, you know. You've earned it. So stop being so paranoid."

Despite herself, Payton grinned. "Thanks, Irma."

Once her secretary was gone, Payton's thoughts lingered for a moment. She glanced over at the calendar on her desk.

Four weeks left. The firm's partnership decisions would be announced at the end of the month. Truth be told, she was feeling fairly hopeful about her chances of making it. She had worked hard for this—long hours, never turning down work—and now she was in the homestretch. The finish line was finally in sight.

Payton felt her heartbeat begin to race as she gave in to the excitement for one teeny-tiny moment. Then, not wanting to get carried away just yet, she calmed herself and, as always, got busy with work.

A FEW MINUTES before 1:30, Payton gathered her notes and her summary trial file folder for her meeting with Ben. She wasn't sure exactly what he wanted to meet about, but she guessed it had something to do with the trial she was about to start next week. As the head of the firm's litigation department, Ben stayed on top of all cases going to trial, even those with which he wasn't directly involved.

As was typical, Payton felt slightly on edge as she prepared for the meeting with her boss. She never knew what to expect with Ben. Despite the fact that he had never given her any indication that he was disappointed in her work—to the contrary, he consistently gave her the highest marks in her annual reviews—she felt that, at times, there was some sort of awkward undercurrent to their interactions. She couldn't quite put her finger on it, she just got a weird vibe now and then. He ran hot and cold with her; sometimes he was fine, other times he seemed a bit . . . stiff. Stilted. At first she had assumed this was just part of his personality, but on other occasions she had seen him joking easily with other associates. Interestingly, all male associates. She had begun to suspect that Ben—while never blatantly unprofessional—had a more difficult time getting along with women. It certainly wasn't an unlikely conclusion to draw. Law firms could be old-fashioned at times and unfortunately, female attorneys still had a bit of an "old boy network" to contend with.

Nevertheless, because Ben was the head of her group—and thus a key player in the decision whether to make her a partner—Payton resolved to keep trying to establish a more congenial rapport between them. After all, she liked to think she was a relatively easygoing person. With one exception (and who really counted *him*, anyway?) she prided herself on getting along well with pretty much everyone she worked with.

Payton grabbed a pen and a legal pad, stuffed them in the file folder she carried, and headed out her office door. Irma's desk was right outside her office, and she turned to let her secretary know she was leaving. In doing so, she nearly ran right into someone coming down the hallway from the other direction.

"Oh, sorry!" Payton exclaimed, scooting aside to avoid a collision. She looked up apologetically and—

—saw J.D.

Her expression changed to one of annoyance. She sighed. She had been having such a nice day until now.

Then Payton realized: oops—they had an audience. With a glance in Irma's direction, she quickly adopted her most charmingly fake smile.

"Well, hello, J.D. How have you been?" she asked.

J.D. also cast an eye in the direction of the secretaries working nearby. As well practiced in this ruse as Payton, he matched her amiable expression with one of his own.

"My, how nice of you to ask, Payton," he gushed ever so warmly as he gazed down at her. "I'm well, thank you. And yourself?"

As always, Payton found herself annoyed by how damn tall J.D. was. She hated being in a position of—literally—having to look up to him. She had no doubt that J.D., on the other hand, quite enjoyed this.

"Fine, thank you," Payton told him. "I'm heading to Ben's office." She managed to maintain her pleasant grin. Meryl Streep may have her Oscars, but she could learn a thing or two from Payton. Best Pretense of Liking One's Assholic Coworker.

J.D.'s eyes narrowed slightly at Payton's reply, but he too kept up the charade. "What a nice surprise—I'm headed to Ben's office myself," he said as if this was the best thing he'd heard all morning. Then he gestured gallantly to Payton—*after you*.

With a nod, she turned and headed down the back hall-way to Ben's corner office. J.D. strode easily alongside her; Payton had to take two steps for every one of his to keep up. Not that she let *him* see that.

After walking together in silence for a few moments, J.D. glanced around for witnesses. Seeing they were safely out of earshot, he folded his arms across his chest with what Payton had come to think of as the trademark J.D. Air of Superiority.

"So I saw your name in the *Chicago Lawyer*," he led in.

Payton smiled, knowing he surely had a thing or two to say about that. She was pleased he'd seen the article the magazine had run in this month's edition. She had been tempted to send him a copy in yesterday's interoffice mail, but thought it would be better if he discovered it on his own.

" 'Forty to Watch Under 40,' " she said, referencing the article's title and proud of her inclusion in its distinction.

" 'Forty *Women* to Watch Under 40,' " J.D. emphasized. "Tell me, Payton—is there a reason your gender finds it necessary to be so separatist? Afraid of a little competition from the opposite sex, perhaps?"

Payton tried not to laugh as she tossed her hair back over her shoulders. Hardly.

"If my gender hesitates to compete with yours, J.D., it's only because we're afraid to lower ourselves to your level," she replied sweetly.

They arrived at the doorway to Ben's office. J.D. leaned against the door casually and folded his arms across his chest. After eight years, Payton recognized this gesture well—it meant he was about to begin another one of his condescending lectures. She gave it 95 percent odds that he'd begin with one of his pompously rhetorical questions that he had absolutely no intention of letting her answer.

"Let me ask you this . . ." he began.

Bingo.

". . . how do you think it would go over if the magazine ran an article called 'Forty *Men* to Watch Under 40'?" He took the liberty of answering for her. "You and your little feminista friends would call that discrimination. But then isn't that, per se, discrimination? Shouldn't we men be entitled to our lists, too?"

J.D. held the door open for her and gestured for her to enter. As she passed by him, Payton noted that Ben wasn't in his office yet, so she took a seat in front of his desk. As J.D. sat in the chair next to her, she turned to him, coolly unperturbed.

"I find it very interesting when a man, a graduate of Princeton University and Harvard Law School, sitting next to me in an Armani suit, has the nerve somehow to claim that *he* is the victim of discrimination."

J.D. opened his mouth to jump in, but Payton cut him off with a finger. Index, not middle. She was a lady after all.

"Notwithstanding that fact," she continued, "I submit that you men *do* have your so-called 'lists.' Several at this firm, in fact. They're called the Executive Committee, the Management Committee, the Compensation Committee, the firm's golfing club, the intramural basketball team—"

"You want to be on the basketball team?" J.D. interrupted, his blue eyes crinkling in amusement at this.

"It's illustrative," Payton said, sitting back in her chair defensively.

"What's illustrative?"

Payton sat upright at the sound of the voice. She glanced over as Ben Gould, head litigation partner, strode confidently into his office and took a seat at his desk. He fixed Payton with a curious gaze of his dark, probing eyes. She shifted in her chair, trying not to feel as though she was already under interrogation.

J.D. answered Ben before Payton had a chance. "Oh, it's nothing," he said with a dismissive wave. "Payton and I were just discussing the Supreme Court's recent decision in *Ledder v. Arkansas*, and how the opinion is illustrative of the Court's continuing reluctance to embroil itself in state's rights."

Payton glanced at J.D. out of the corner of her eye.

Smart-ass.

Although admittedly, that wasn't too shabby a bit of quick thinking.

The jerk.

Ben laughed at them as he quickly glanced at the messages his secretary had left on his desk. "You two—you never stop."

Payton fought the urge to roll her eyes. He really had no idea.

J.D. seized on Ben's momentary distraction to lean forward in his chair. He held the lapel of his suit out to Payton and whispered. "And by the way, it's not Armani. It's *Zegna*." He winked at her.

Payton glared, tempted to tell him exactly where he could stick that *Zegna* suit.

"Sorry to call you both down here on such short notice," Ben said. "But as you both may be aware, Gibson's Drug Stores chain has just been hit with a class action gender discrimination lawsuit."

Payton had indeed heard about the lawsuit—yesterday's filing of the complaint in a federal court in Florida had made all the national papers and had even been discussed on MSNBC and CNN.

"The complaint was filed yesterday, assigned to Judge Meyers of the Southern District of Florida," she said, eager to let Ben know she was on top of things.

"The claims were filed under Title VII—one-point-eight

million female employees of the company allege they were discriminated against in hiring, pay, and promotion," J.D. added with a sideways glance in Payton's direction. He, too, had done his homework.

Ben smiled at their eagerness. He leaned back, twirling his pen casually. "It's the largest discrimination class action ever filed. That means big bucks to the law firm that defends Gibson's."

Payton saw the glint in Ben's eye. "And who might that be?"

Ben laced his fingers together, drumming them against the back of his hands like a villain in a James Bond movie.

"Funny you should ask, Payton . . . The CEO of Gibson's, Jasper Conroy, hasn't decided yet which law firm will defend his company. He has, however, chosen three of the top firms in the country to meet with."

J.D. grinned. "Let me take a wild stab in the dark here: our firm is one of those three."

Ben nodded, proud as always that his group of litigators was continually ranked as being among the best in the world. "Nice guess. I got the call earlier this morning from Jasper Conroy himself."

He pointed at J.D. and Payton. "And here's where you two come in: Jasper was very clear about the type of trial team he's looking for. He wants a fresher image to represent the face of his company, not a bunch of stodgy old men in suits, like me." Ben chuckled, fully aware that at forty-nine years old he was actually quite young to be the head of litigation at such a prestigious firm. "Personally," he continued, "I think Jasper is just trying to avoid paying partner rates."

Like the good associates they were, Payton and J.D. laughed at the joke.

"Anyhoo . . ." Ben went on, "I told Jasper that this firm just so happens to have the perfect litigators for him. Two very experienced, very savvy senior associates. You two."

Through her surprise, it took Payton a moment to process what Ben was saying. A large pit was growing in her stomach, because this conversation was headed in a very bad direction.

If someone made her swear an oath under cross-examination—better yet, if Jack Bauer himself subjected her to the full array of interrogation tactics at CTU's disposal—Payton couldn't have said exactly *how* her war with J.D. had started. Frankly, it had been going on for so long that it simply seemed to be the way things always were.

Without ever saying a word, however, she and J.D. had implicitly agreed to keep their mutual dislike to themselves. Both wanting more than anything to be successful at work, they understood that law firms were like kindergarten: it wasn't good to get a "needs improvement" in "plays well with others."

Luckily, it had been relatively easy to maintain their charade. Even though they were in the same group, it had been years since they had worked together on a case. There were a few reasons for this: First, as a general rule, cases in the litigation group were staffed with one partner, one senior associate, and one or two junior associates. As members of the same class, there was little reason for both Payton and J.D. to work on the same matter.

Second, and perhaps more important, the two of them had developed specialties in very different areas of the law. J.D. was a class action lawyer. He handled large multi-plaintiff, multi-district cases. Payton, on the other hand, specialized in employment law, particularly single-plaintiff race and gender discrimination lawsuits. Her cases were typically smaller in terms of damages at stake but higher profile in terms of the publicity they garnered.

Thus far—whether by fluke chance or luck—there had been very little overlap in the niche practice areas she and J.D. had carved out for themselves.

Apparently until now, that is.

Payton remained silent as Ben continued his pitch, trying to refrain from displaying the growing apprehension she felt. She snuck a quick peak at J.D. and saw him shift edgily in his chair. From what she could tell, he appeared just as displeased as she by this development.

"Combined, your skills are perfect for this case," Ben was saying. "Jasper sounded very excited to meet you both."

"This is wonderful news, Ben," Payton said, trying not to choke on her words.

"Yes . . . wonderful." J.D. looked as though he had just swallowed a bug. "What is it you need us to do?"

"Jasper and Gibson's general counsel, and a few of their in-house attorneys, will all be coming to Chicago on Thursday," Ben said. "I want you two to work together and I want you to *bring them in*," he emphasized, tapping his finger on his desk. "Think you're up to it?"

Payton and J.D. eyed each other carefully, both thinking the same thing. Could they really do this?

Knowing what was at stake, in mutual understanding of how the game was played, they turned to Ben.

"Absolutely," they said in unison.

Ben smiled at them, the future of his firm. He leaned back in his chair, getting sentimental. Undoubtedly at the thought of the big bucks they would bring in.

"Ah . . . eight years," he said affectionately. "For eight years I have watched you two grow up at this firm, into the great lawyers you are. I'm excited by this chance to see you work together—you'll make quite a team. And it's perfect timing, too, because soon you'll both be p—"

He abruptly stopped speaking.

J.D. and Payton sat on the edge of their seats, nearly falling off their chairs as they hung on to Ben's last word.

Apparently realizing he had said too much, Ben waved this off with a coy grin. "Well, one thing at a time. Right now, you guys have a pitch to prepare for."

Seeing that Ben was finished discussing business, Payton stood to leave. But instead of following her, J.D. remained seated. Payton paused awkwardly.

"Is there something else we need to talk about, Ben?" she asked.

Ben shook his head. "No, that'll be all, Payton. I have something else I want to discuss with J.D., something that doesn't concern you." He gave her a curt nod of dismissal. There it was—he'd been friendly enough just moments ago, but now he was back to being all business.

With a nod of her own, Payton left Ben's office. As she turned into the hallway, she overheard him talking to J.D.

"So, Jameson," she heard Ben say jovially, "the rumor is that you were playing at Butler this weekend. What are you shooting these days, anyway?"

As Payton walked back to her office, she tried not to let it bother her, the fact that J.D. always had an easier time connecting with their boss on a personal level. To date, her attempts to establish a similar relationship with Ben had been largely unsuccessful. Movies? He didn't watch 'em. Television? He had once asked her if Seinfeld was "that chubby paralegal always hanging around the vending machines." When Payton had laughed at this, thinking he was joking, she'd been greeted with a blank stare and had immediately fallen silent. From that point, she had vowed that until she could wax poetic on whether trading So-and-So for What's-His-Face was a smart move by Team Who-the-Hell-Cares, it was probably best to keep the nonlegal chitchat with Ben to a minimum.

Team Jameson scores another point, Payton thought as she entered her office. He had an automatic advantage over her: she could just picture him and Ben right now, all buddy-buddy in Ben's office and chuckling their hearty man-laughs while trading tips on the best garage to have one's Porsche/Mercedes/Rolls-Royce/Some Other Fancy Car serviced at.

Not that it was a competition between them. Not at all.

That J.D. had, like Payton, seemingly devoted the last eight years of his life to the firm (perhaps the *only* thing they had in common) was wholly irrelevant in her mind to the question of whether she personally deserved to make partner. While it might have been something she had worried about back when she first started, her concern over being compared to J.D. had subsided as the years passed.

"There are no quotas or maximums," Ben had repeatedly assured her in her annual reviews. "Each associate is judged on his or her own merit." And from what Payton had observed in the classes before her, this statement appeared to be true: each year the associates who were ranked at the top of their class all made partner regardless of the total number of associates being considered that year.

So from where Payton stood, her chances of making it were pretty good, especially since she and J.D. were the only two litigators left in their class. According to her friend Laney, who also worked at the firm but was in the class below them, this was not coincidence: the gossip among the younger associates was that Payton and J.D. had scared off the other members of their class who hadn't been nearly as interested in keeping pace and working the same ridiculous hours as them.

Which was why it wasn't a competition between them.

Frankly, Payton would've disliked J.D. no matter what class he had been in. He just had this way about him that really, really irked her.

Payton got to her office and took a seat at her desk. She checked her computer and saw that she had received thirty-two new email messages during the brief time she had been in Ben's office. She refrained from sighing out loud in exasperation. *Four more weeks*, she reminded herself.

Plowing through the emails, she came across one from the firm's Executive Committee. Intrigued, Payton opened it and was pleasantly surprised by what she read:

*In order to honor its commitment to the policies cre-
ated by the Committee for the Retention of Women, the
firm is proud to announce that it has set a goal of in-
creasing the number of female partners by 10 percent
by next year.*

Payton sat back in her chair, rereading the announcement and considering the reasons behind it. Frankly, it was
about time the firm took some action—they were notori-
ous for having the lowest percentage of female partners in
the city.

She reached for her phone to call Laney, who she knew
would have a similar reaction to the news. Mid-dial, she
glanced across the hall and saw J.D. returning from his
male-bonding meeting of the Mighty Penis-Wielders with
Ben. Payton hung the phone up as she watched J.D. enter
his office—she had to see this.

J.D. took a seat at his desk. Just like Payton, he immediately checked his email. There was a moment's delay as
Payton waited in delicious anticipation . . . then—

J.D.'s eyes went wide as he read what Payton could only
presume was the email from the Executive Committee. He
clutched his heart as if having an attack, then snatched the
phone on his desk out of its cradle and dialed someone up
with a quickness.

His friend Tyler, Payton guessed. If she were a betting
woman, she'd wager that J.D. was just a tad less excited about
the email regarding the retention of women than she.

Score one for Team Kendall, Payton thought.

Not that it was a competition between them.

Not at all.

Three

"IT'S HORSESHIT!"

J.D. felt some satisfaction as he smashed the squash ball with his racquet. He'd been in a foul mood all day, ever since he'd seen that ridiculous email from the Executive Committee.

"A *ten* percent increase in female partners!" he raged on, his breath ragged with exertion. He was definitely off his game that evening. Tyler had barely broken a sweat while J.D.—normally the far better player of the two (if he modestly said so himself)—had been diving all over the court just to keep up.

Tyler returned J.D.'s volley easily. "Still only brings them to twenty-eight percent," he said good-naturedly.

"Who are you, Gloria Steinem?" J.D. glared at his friend for even suggesting there was any possible defense for the policy change the firm had announced today. "It's their decision, Tyler," he continued. "There is no glass ceiling anymore—these women choose to leave the workforce of their own volition."

"Ahh . . . the voice of equality rings out once more." Tyler laughed.

"Hey, I'm all for equality," J.D. said as he hit the ball with another gratifying smash. Frankly, his friend's lack of concern over the Executive Committee's email baffled him. After all, Tyler worked at the firm, too, and while he wasn't up for partner this year, his day soon would come.

"And anyone else who *allegedly* stands for equality should be against this policy as well," J.D. continued. "It's reverse discrimination."

Tyler shrugged this off. "It's only a commitment to make a ten percent increase. What difference does it make?"

J.D. couldn't listen to another word. With one hand, he caught the ball, bringing their game to an abrupt stop. He pointed his racquet at Tyler. "I'll tell you what my problem is."

Tyler set his own racquet down and leaned against the wall. "I sense that I should get comfortable here."

J.D. ignored the sarcasm. "The playing field isn't level—that's the problem. Now maybe you're comfortable accepting that, but I'm not. You know as well as I do that these days, if a man and a woman are equally qualified for a position, the woman gets the job. It's this socially liberal, politically correct society we live in. Men have to be twice as good at what they do to remain competitive in the workplace. Women just have to stay in the race."

Tyler eyed him skeptically. "Do you really believe that?"

"Absolutely," J.D. said. "At least in the legal environment. It's a numbers game. Because, percentage-wise, so few women stay at these large law firms—again by *choice*," he emphasized quickly, "when one woman who's halfway decent does come up for partner, she's a shoo-in. But do guys like you and me have it so easy?"

Tyler opened his mouth.

"You're right, we don't," J.D. finished for him. "No one from the Human Resources Department is telling the Executive Committee they need to increase the percentage of white males they make partner. So we"—he pointed—"have to fend for ourselves by making sure we don't give them any excuse not to promote us."

Tyler held up his hands. "All right—just take it easy. I know you're stressed out these days—"

"—I'm just saying that everyone should be judged solely on *merit*. No 'plus' factors for gender, race, national origin, or—"

"—what with the partnership decision coming up and all, I realize you're nervous—"

"—so that each person is given a fair chance—" J.D. stopped. He had just caught Tyler's last words. "Wait—you think I'm *nervous* about making partner?"

Tyler looked him over. "Are you saying you're *not* nervous?"

"Are you saying I have a *reason* to be nervous?"

J.D. glanced around and lowered his voice to a whisper. "Why, what have you heard? Do you know something? Wait, never mind—don't tell me. No, really—what?"

Tyler laughed. "Take it easy, buddy. I haven't heard a thing. The Executive Committee doesn't exactly let lowly sixth years in on their partnership decisions."

J.D. exhaled in relief. "Right, sure." Resuming his façade of nonchalance, he tossed the ball to Tyler. "Your serve."

The two played in silence for a few moments, the only sound being the repetitive *bounce-smash!* of the ball as they volleyed back and forth.

Finally, J.D. broke the silence. "For the record, I don't believe I'm 'stressed out.'" But if, for argument's sake, I am a little anxious, it would only be natural. After all, it's been eight years. It's my job, you know. It's—"

"—the only thing you've ever done without your father's

help and you don't want to screw it up," Tyler cut in. "I get that."

J.D. stopped dead in his tracks. The squash ball whizzed by, careened off the back wall, and bounced around the court until it finally rolled to a stop. He faced Tyler in stony silence.

Tyler smiled innocently. "Oops—was that one of those things we're not supposed to say out loud?"

J.D. still said nothing. As his best friend, Tyler understood that the topic of his father was distinctly off-limits.

"But I thought we were bonding," Tyler continued. "You know, one oppressed white male to another."

J.D. gave him a look. "Very cute. Laugh now, but we'll see who's laughing in two years when you come up for partner and they toss your ass out onto the street with nothing more than a 'thanks for your time.'" J.D. gestured to the court. "Now—if we're finished with your little personal insights into my psyche, do you mind if we play some squash here?"

Tyler bowed agreeably. "Not at all."

The two once again resumed their game. Silent. Focused. J.D. was just getting back into his groove when Tyler brought up another topic of conversation he had even less interest discussing.

"So I saw you walk by my office this afternoon with Payton," Tyler said. "You two looked chummy as always."

J.D. dove for the ball and narrowly missed it. Cursing under his breath, he picked himself up from the floor and walked it off. He knew Tyler was baiting him once again and was hardly about to give him the satisfaction of being successful at it a second time.

"Payton and I had a meeting in Ben's office," he replied matter-of-factly. He tossed Tyler the ball.

As their play continued, so did Tyler's taunting. "So . . . did you congratulate her on the *Chicago Lawyer* article?"

J.D. smiled, thinking back to his conversation with Payton

earlier that day. "Yes, as a matter of fact, I did. In my own way of course."

"You know, maybe you should run your whole 'women just have to stay in the race' argument by her," Tyler teased. "I'm sure she'd have a few thoughts."

J.D. scoffed at this. "Please—as if I'm worried about anything Payton has to say. What's she going to do, give me another one of her little pissed-off hair flips?" He flung imaginary long hair off his shoulders, exaggerating. "I'll tell you, one of these days I'm going to grab her by that hair and . . ." He gestured as if throttling someone.

Without breaking stride, he returned Tyler's serve. The two smashed a few back and forth, concentrating on the game when—

"Is violence always part of your sexual fantasies?" Tyler interjected.

J.D. whipped around—

"Sexual—?"

—and got hit smack in the face with the squash ball. He toppled back and sprawled ungracefully across the court.

Tyler stepped over and twirled his racquet. "This is nice. We should talk like this more often."

J.D. reached over, grabbed the ball off the floor, and hurled it right at Tyler.

J.D. HEADED HOME later that evening, still smarting from the squash-ball blow to the cheek. He didn't know what hurt more—his face or his ego. A very competitive player, he couldn't believe he had let Tyler distract him so easily. Taunting him about Payton, it was so . . . simplistic. But what could he say? As always, she brought out the worst in him. Even while playing squash, apparently.

Truth be told, however, on this particular occasion he had a bit more on his mind than Payton Kendall. As J.D. parked his car in the underground garage of the Gold Coast high-rise condo building where he lived, he felt tired. Really tired. As if all the nineteen-hour days he'd been putting in the last year were suddenly catching up with him.

Heading toward the garage elevators, J.D. pushed the remote on his key a second time to double-check that he had locked the doors. He knew he was overprotective of his car, but come on—who wouldn't be? As he had once joked to Tyler, driving a Bentley actually made a man wish he had a *longer* commute to work. While Tyler had laughed at the joke, his father sure hadn't when J.D. had said the same thing to him. In fact, it was that very car, the silver Bentley Continental GT, that had precipitated The Fight, the infamous argument between him and his father two years ago.

J.D.'s father, the esteemed Honorable Preston D. Jameson, had once again been trying to tell J.D. how to live his life.

"You have to sell the car," his father had said in no uncertain terms the day after J.D.'s grandfather's funeral.

J.D. had pointed out that his grandfather, the illustrious entrepreneur Earl Jameson, had specifically left J.D. that car in his will. This reminder had only further annoyed his father, who most definitely was not a "car guy," and who also had always been resentful of the bond between J.D. and his grandfather.

"But you can't drive that car to work—the partners don't want to see an associate driving a one-hundred-fifty-thousand-dollar car!" His father had tried appealing to what normally was J.D.'s weakness—his desire to be successful at the firm. But for the first (and to date, only) time, J.D. had other priorities—that car meant more to him than his father understood.

He had smiled thinly at his father, tired. The days surrounding his grandfather's funeral had been long and difficult. "Actually, Dad, it's more like a one-hundred-*ninety*-thousand-dollar car—what with the chromed alloy sports wheels and upgraded interior veneer. And yes, I *can* drive it to work, quite easily, in fact—see, I just take Lake Shore Drive south and get off at Washington Street . . ."

His father had not been amused.

"Do you know what people will say?" his father had ranted. "It's not dignified for a judge on the federal appellate bench to have a spoiled playboy son running around in some hotshot sports car!"

J.D. tried to hide his anger and not dignify the comment with a response. Sure, he was single and he dated, but "playboy" was a little extreme. Frankly, he put in too many hours at work to have anything above a moderately healthy social life. Besides, he knew what the real issue was—his *father's* reputation, not his. He figured his father could just add this to the list of other ways in which he had been a disappointment as a son: not being the editor of the *Harvard Law Review*, not being married, and then—worst of all—choosing to work at Ripley & Davis, the other of the top two firms in the city and direct competitor of the law firm his father had worked and been senior partner at before being appointed to the bench.

But what bothered J.D. far more than his father's disappointment or concern for his professional reputation (in thirty-two years he had grown quite accustomed to living under the shadow of those things) was the fact that his father had the audacity to call him spoiled. Sure, his family had money, a lot of money, but that shouldn't diminish that he had worked his ass off to get where he was. That was the very reason he had chosen not to work for his father's old firm: he didn't want any special treatment because of his last name.

Normally, J.D. would've ignored his father's refusal to acknowledge his achievements, but on that day, in the emotional wake of his grandfather's funeral, he simply couldn't. So he said some things, his voice growing louder and louder, and then his father said some things, and in the midst of their argument, J.D. declared that he didn't want another penny from his trust fund. From that day on, he vowed, he would survive on his own.

And from that day on, he had.

Okay, truthfully, this wasn't exactly a fiscally impossible task. By that time a sixth-year associate at the firm, J.D. was earning at least $300,000 per year, including his bonus. But that still was a helluva lot less than any Chicago Jameson of recent history had lived on. And for that, he was proud.

And he was also proud of that Bentley. Not only a sentimental link between him and his grandfather, it had become the symbol of J.D.'s Declaration of Independence from following in his father's footsteps. And beyond that—

He looked *really* cool driving it.

On the elevator ride up to his condo apartment on the forty-fourth floor ("Not the penthouse?" his mother had asked in abject horror when he'd first given her the tour), J.D. mulled over the comments Tyler had made during their squash game. Not that he'd ever admit it, but he had been growing increasingly anxious every day, waiting for the firm to make its partnership announcements.

Although certainly, J.D. thought as he walked the hallway to his apartment and unlocked the front door, his meeting with Ben that afternoon had stifled pretty much any lingering doubts that had been creeping into his head these past few weeks. He'd caught what Ben had nearly blurted out during their meeting, about J.D. and Payton soon being partners. J.D. had noticed that Payton hadn't missed Ben's slipup, either—he'd seen the gleam in those dark blue eyes of hers.

Probably the same gleam she'd gotten when she read the email from the Executive Committee, J.D. guessed. He tossed his briefcase and his gym bag onto the living room couch that faced the best feature of his apartment: floor-to-ceiling windows overlooking the famed Magnificent Mile of Michigan Avenue, and beyond that, the vast blue expanse of Lake Michigan. ("At least there's a view," his mother had sniffed reluctantly.)

Yes, indeed, J.D. had no doubt that the email from the Executive Committee had been the absolute highlight of Payton's day. She was clever—she never directly played the gender card with the firm's partners, but she also never missed a chance to flaunt her feminine status. Like that "Forty Women to Watch Under 40" article, for example. The only reason he'd asked her about it was to preempt any pleasure she'd get in bringing it up herself and rubbing it in his face.

Not that it was a competition between them.

Payton Kendall, Esquire, could be named in *ten* magazine articles for all he cared, she could have the entire firm wrapped around one of her little liberal feminist fingers—it concerned him not one bit. J.D. knew he was a good lawyer, very good, and once he made partner (even if *she* made it, too), and was in complete control of his own workload, he planned to make sure that he and Payton never worked together again.

Now, if he could just get through this business with Gibson's Drug Stores . . .

J.D. showered quickly. It was late, and he needed to get an early start tomorrow morning. Payton had very nearly beaten him into the office the other morning, and he needed to put a quick kibosh on that.

Not that it was a competition between them.

Not at all.

Four

PAYTON REVIEWED THE schedule of events for the Gibson's executives a second time.

To say she was displeased would be an understatement.

She had been swamped this week, preparing for both the Gibson's pitch and a sexual harassment trial that was set to start the following Wednesday. And J.D. had caught her at a particularly bad time when he stopped by her office yesterday to discuss the agenda for wining and dining Jasper Conroy and his in-house litigation team. She'd been arguing all morning with opposing counsel over last-minute additions to the exhibit list. She had hung up the phone, spotted J.D. standing in the doorway, and sensed her morning was only about to get worse. But instead, in a rare moment of apparent helpfulness, J.D. had offered to take the lead in setting up the Gibson's schedule.

And, in a just-as-rare moment of receptiveness to anything J.D. related, as her phone began ringing off the hook and she saw the familiar number of her opposing counsel on the caller ID and realized she was about to begin Round 137 with him, she accepted J.D.'s offer.

Big mistake.

Clutching the agenda in her hand, Payton looked up at her secretary with a mixture of frustration and trepidation.

"Is this really the agenda?" she asked.

Irma nodded in the affirmative. "J.D.'s secretary just dropped it off."

"Okay. Thanks, Irma."

Payton pretended to resume typing at her computer as Irma left her office. She watched as her secretary headed back to her desk, waited a moment or two more, then casually got up and walked across the hall to J.D.'s office.

J.D. peered up from his desk when he heard the knock on his door.

"Got a sec?" Payton asked pleasantly. One never knew who was watching.

"For you, Payton—anytime. How can I be of assistance?" he asked.

Payton stepped into his office and shut the door behind her. They both instantly dropped the charade.

She held out the agenda accusingly. "You told me we were having dinner with the Gibson's execs tomorrow evening."

J.D. eased back in his chair, gesturing to the agenda. "And as you see, we are."

"But you're also playing golf with them tomorrow afternoon. Why wasn't I invited?"

"Do you play golf?"

"No, but you didn't know that."

J.D. grinned. "Actually, I did. I overheard you mention it to Ben last summer."

Stunned by the overt snub, Payton opened her mouth to respond. She clenched her fist as she searched for some response, some insult, anything, and a moment passed, and then another . . . and—

Nothing.

J.D. smiled victoriously. "Tell you what—why don't you think about it for a while? Come back when you're ready— make it a good one." Then he ushered Payton out of his office and shut the door behind her.

She stood there in the hallway. Staring face-to-face with that stupid nameplate, J. D. JAMESON, which she was seriously tempted to tear off the wall and chuck straight at his face.

It was true, she didn't know squat about golf; she had never even swung a club. Her avoidance was purposeful. She had distinct opinions regarding the sport and, more important, those who played it.

Payton considered her options. On the one hand, she hated the idea of J.D. getting the better of her. And she *really* hated the idea of looking like a clueless novice playing golf in front of Jasper and the Gibson's team.

On the other hand, the thought of being left out for the entire afternoon was not appealing. With the partnership decision looming, she needed to ensure she was an integral part of the effort to land Gibson's as a client. And she simply didn't think she could stomach playing the part of the little woman sitting back at the office while the men talked shop at the twenty-fifth or whatever tee.

So as far as Payton could see, she had no choice.

Despite the fact that she was already worrying over how she was going to squeeze in a quick at-least-I-won't-look-like-a-total-jackass golf lesson that evening—she strode confidently into J.D.'s office.

He glanced up from his desk as the door opened, surprised by her sudden entrance. "That was fast." He leaned back in his chair and beckoned with his hand. "Okay, let's hear it, Kendall. Give me your best shot."

Payton saw the stapler near the edge of his desk and had to fight the urge to take him up on his offer.

"I'll do it," she declared. "Count me in for tomorrow's game."

J.D. appeared surprised.

Payton nodded in response to his silence. "Good. That's settled, then." She turned to leave, her mind already running in a hundred different directions. She needed to find a set of clubs; perhaps Laney had some she could borrow. And of course there was the matter of attire—should she wear shorts? A polo shirt? A jaunty little cap, perhaps? Were special shoes required? The details surrounding this event were—

"You can't go."

J.D.'s words stopped Payton right as she reached the door. She turned around to face him. "You can't be serious. You're *that* desperate to get some alone time with the Gibson's reps?"

"No, that's not it," J.D. said quickly. He hesitated, and for the briefest second Payton could've sworn he looked uncomfortable.

She put her hand on her hip, waiting for him to finish. "Then what, exactly, is it, J.D.?"

"We're golfing at Butler," he said.

Butler? Oh . . . of course, *Butler*, Payton thought sarcastically. That meant bubkes to her.

"And?" she asked.

"Butler National Golf Club?" J.D. said, apparently believing this should ring some sort of bell with her.

Payton shook her head. No clue.

J.D. shifted awkwardly. "My family has a membership there. Ben suggested it because it's a nationally ranked course. But, as it happens, it's a *private* club." He emphasized this last part.

Payton failed to see what the problem was. "But if you can get the Gibson's people in as guests, I don't see why I can't come, too."

J.D. cleared his throat uneasily. He shifted in his chair, then met her gaze.

"They don't allow women."

The words hung awkwardly in the air, drawing a line between them.

"Oh. I see." Payton's tone was brisk, terse. "Well then, you boys have fun tomorrow."

Not wanting to see what she assumed would be the smug look on J.D.'s face, she turned and walked out of his office.

"WILL I SOUND like a total crybaby if I say it's not fair?"

Laney patted Payton's hand. "Yes. But you go right ahead and say it anyway."

With a frustrated groan, Payton buried her head in her arms on top of the coffee shop table they had just sat down at moments ago.

"I hate him," she said, her voice muffled. She peered up at Laney. "This means he's going to get twice as much time with the Gibson's reps."

"Then you will have to be twice as good when you meet them for dinner," Laney replied. "Forget about J.D."

"Screw him," Payton agreed. She saw Laney's eyes cast nervously around the coffee shop at this.

"I mean, it's bad enough he plays this card with the partners," Payton continued. She lowered her voice, doing a bad male impersonation. "Hey, J.D.—you should come to my club sometime. I hear you shoot a two-fifty."

"I think that's bowling."

"Whatever." Payton pointed for emphasis. "The problem is, getting business is part of the business. It's like a ritual with these guys: 'Hey, how 'bout those Cubs' "—the bad male impersonation was back—" 'let's play some golf, smoke some cigars. Here's my penis, there's yours—yep, they appear to be about the same size—okay, let's do some deals.' "

When the woman seated at the next table threw them a

disapproving look over the foam of her jumbo-sized cappuccino, Laney leaned in toward Payton. "Let's use our inside voices, please, when using the p-word," she whispered chidingly.

Ignoring this, Payton took another sip of her vanilla latte. "In the business world, what's the female equivalent of going golfing with a client?"

Laney gave this some thought. Payton fell silent, too, contemplating. After a few moments, neither of them could come up with anything.

How depressing.

Payton sighed, feigning resignation. "Well, that's it. I guess I'll just have to sleep with them."

Laney folded her hands primly on the table. "I think I'm uncomfortable with this conversation."

Payton laughed. It felt good to laugh—she'd been very cranky since her encounter with J.D.; she couldn't believe he had managed to exclude her from the golf outing with the Gibson's reps by taking them to a club that didn't allow women. Wait, back up: what she really couldn't believe was that there was actually still a club around that didn't let women in. Once the existence of said club had been established, however, she had no problem believing that J.D. was its Grand Poobah.

But enough about J.D. already. Payton resolved not to let him ruin another minute of her day. Besides, she saw a prime opportunity to engage Laney in one of their "debates." The two of them couldn't have been more opposite on the social/political spectrum. Having herself been raised by an ex-hippie single mother who was as socially radical as one could get while staying inside the boundaries of the law (most of the time, anyway), Payton found Laney's prim-and-properness fascinating. And strangely refreshing.

"I didn't mean to make you uncomfortable, Laney. I guess being a conservative means you don't believe in free speech," Payton teased.

"Don't get on your liberal high horse—of course I believe in free speech," Laney said, toying with the heart locket she wore.

"Then I should be able to say anything I want, right? Even the word 'penis'?"

Laney sighed. "Do we have to do this right now?"

"You should try saying the word sometime."

"I'll pass, thank you."

Payton shrugged. "Your choice, but I think you'd find it liberating. Everybody could use a good 'penis' now and then."

Laney glanced nervously around the coffee shop. "People are listening."

"Sorry—you're right. Good rule of thumb: if you're gonna throw out a 'penis' in a public place, it should be soft. Otherwise it attracts too much attention."

The woman at the next table gaped at them.

Laney leaned over. "I apologize for my friend. She gets this way sometimes." She lowered her voice to a whisper. "Tourette's. So sad."

The woman nodded sympathetically, then pretended to make a call on her cell phone.

Laney turned back to Payton. "If you're finished with the First Amendment lesson, I thought maybe we could turn back to the subject of J.D. Because I do have a suggestion as to how you can solve your problem."

Payton leaned forward eagerly. "Great—let's hear it. I'm open to anything."

"Okay. My suggestion is . . ." Laney paused dramatically. ". . . learn how to play golf." She let this sink in a moment. "Then you'll never have this problem again."

Payton sat back in her chair, toying with her coffee mug. "Um, no." She brushed off the suggestion with a dismissive wave. "Playing golf is just so, I don't know . . . snooty."

Laney gave her a pointed look. "You know, when you

make partner, you'll have to get used to being around people who grew up with money."

"I don't have any issues with that," Payton said huffily.

"Oh, sure, right. You don't think that has anything to do with why you're so hard on J.D.?"

"I'm hard on J.D. because he's a jerk."

"True, true . . ." Laney mused. "You two do seem to bring out the worst in each other."

In *each other*? "I hope you aren't suggesting that I somehow contribute to J.D.'s behavior," Payton said. "Because if so, we really need to get this conversation headed in a *sane* direction."

"It's just kind of odd, because J.D. has lots of qualities that you normally like in a guy. A guy who maybe isn't quite so, you know . . ." Laney gestured, trailing off.

"So what?" Payton prompted.

"Rich."

Payton rolled her eyes. "First of all: please—like I said, I don't care about that. Second of all: What are these alleged other 'qualities' J.D. has?"

Laney considered her answer. "He's very smart."

Payton frowned and grumbled under her breath. "I changed my mind—I don't want to talk about this." She grabbed the dessert menu sitting next to her and stared at it intently.

Appearing not to hear her, Laney kept going with her list of J.D.'s supposed attributes. "He's also passionate about the law, interested in politics—albeit on the opposite side of the spectrum. Which, interestingly, doesn't seem to bother you about me."

Payton peered over the top of her menu. "*You* have charm."

"That's true, I do."

"It's quickly fading."

Laney went on. "And J.D. works hard, just like you, and he can be funny in that sarcastic kind of way that—"

"I object!" Payton interrupted. "Lack of foundation—when has J.D. ever said anything funny?"

"This isn't a courtroom."

Payton folded her arms across her chest. "Fine. *Total crap*—how about if I just go with that instead?"

"Gee, sorry, Payton—I didn't mean to make you so uncomfortable," Laney said with a grin. "I won't say anything else." She picked up her menu. "Let's see . . . now what looks good? That flourless chocolate cake we split last time was divine." She glanced up at Payton. "Except just one last thing on the subject of J.D.: he's totally hot."

Just in time, fighting her smile, Laney put her menu up to block the napkin that came flying at her face.

"Hot?" Payton nearly shouted. "That smarmy, prep-school-attending, pink-Izod-shirt-wearing jerk who's been handed his career on a silver platter?" She covered her mouth. "Well, look at that—maybe I *do* have one or two issues with money."

Laney nodded encouragingly, as if to say they were making progress. "But you're about to be named partner. I get why you've been guarded in the past, but you've made it. You don't have to keep trying so hard to prove that you fit in with these guys."

Payton was surprised by this. "You think I come across as guarded?"

"At work, you can sometimes . . . have a bit of an edge," Laney said carefully. "Like this thing with J.D., for example."

Payton tried to decide whether she should be offended. But as much as she might not want to admit it, a part of her knew that what Laney was saying wasn't completely off base.

"I suppose this 'thing' with J.D. has gotten a little out of hand," she sniffed reluctantly. "You're right—I should be the better person in this." She smirked. "That shouldn't be too hard in comparison to J.D."—she caught Laney's look—

"is *exactly* what Edgy Payton would've said. But the New Payton won't go there."

Laney tipped her coffee mug approvingly. "Good for you. To the New Payton."

"The New Payton."

Payton clinked her mug to Laney's, wondering what she was getting herself into.

Five

BE THE BALL.

J.D. focused intently. His eyes never left the tee.

Be the ball.

He pulled back, then—*swoosh!* His swing was effortless. With one hand raised to block the sun's glare, he watched as the ball landed on the green 240 yards away, within inches of the hole.

J.D. smiled. God, he loved this sport.

Hearing the whistling and clapping coming from behind him, he turned around to face his companions.

"Nice shot," Jasper called out in his lazy Southern drawl. "A man who bills three thousand hours a year shouldn't have time for a swing like that." Their three companions, representatives from Gibson's legal department, nodded in agreement.

J.D. walked over and took the beer Jasper held out to him. "Does this mean we're talking business?"

Jasper grinned. He had the bold smile of a man completely at ease with the power he held. He glanced down at his beer, then took in the beautiful tree-lined scenery of the eighth hole. "Tell you what. Wait till the fifteenth hole. Then we'll talk."

Following Jasper's lead, J.D. soaked in the warmth of the blue-sky summer day while admiring the view of the river that flowed just beyond the green. He tipped his bottle at Jasper. "Make it the seventeenth."

Jasper chuckled. "A man after my own heart. But are you sure you want to wait? I heard the back nine of this course brings a man to his knees."

"Maybe a lesser man, Jasper."

Jasper laughed heartily at this. "I like your style, Jameson."

Grinning, J.D. took a sip of his beer. So far, his afternoon with the Gibson's team had been going very well. He was comfortable here, in his element—which undoubtedly was one of the reasons Ben had chosen him for this assignment. J.D. had grown up around men like Jasper all his life and was familiar with the "good-ole boy" routine. He understood the lingo, the game, the role he was supposed to play. Ben wanted to do a little showing off—that's why he had specifically asked J.D. to bring the Gibson's team to this course. He was trying to impress them, but didn't want to look like he was trying to impress them. The fact that J.D. just so happened to have a membership at one of the most exclusive clubs in the country was the perfect way to accomplish this.

The only blemish on the afternoon was the nagging feeling he got whenever a vision of Payton sitting back at the office popped into his head. He kept trying to brush these feelings aside. Why should he feel guilty that she had been left out? After all, he was just doing his job, what Ben had asked him to do. And, had the shoe been on the other foot, he was quite certain Payton would've had no problem leaving him behind.

There was another image J.D. had a hard time shaking:

the look Payton had given him when he'd told her that the
club didn't allow women. For the briefest moment, he'd
seen something in her eyes he hadn't seen before. A slight
crack, a falter in her usual armor of confidence. For some
reason, it had bothered him, seeing that.

Realizing that one of the Gibson's lawyers was asking
him a question about the course, J.D. pushed all thoughts
of Payton from his mind. He couldn't be distracted right
now. He needed to be on, to be charming and professional.
And, no less important, he needed to mentally prepare for
the upcoming ninth hole—a ruthless par four that was one
of the narrowest holes he had ever played.

Besides, as he knew full well, Payton Kendall could
take care of herself.

PAYTON SAT AT the bar, waiting. She had agreed to
meet J.D. and the Gibson's team at Japonais restaurant at
seven thirty. She was familiar with the restaurant, as was
pretty much every other single woman in Chicago over the
age of twenty-five. Trendy and expensive with a modern,
ambient-lit decor, it was one of the most popular locales in
the city for a first date.

Not that she'd had all that many first dates lately. It took
time to meet people. It took time to date them, to get to
know them, to figure out whether you liked them and
whether they liked you. And time was something she didn't
have a lot of these days. So unless the mythical Perfect
Guy fell out of the sky and landed smack-dab on her doorstep, dating was something she needed to put on hold until
after she made partner.

Payton swirled her wineglass as she sat at the bar, thinking back to the last first date she'd had, with an investment
banker she'd met at a local wine tasting. It had been at this
very restaurant, in fact. Her date had polished off eight of
the restaurant's Mukune sakes by ten. By ten fifteen he'd

fallen over in his chair while standing up to go to the bathroom and by ten fifteen and fifteen seconds—when Payton
ran over to help—he'd slurringly confessed that he was having "a bidge of trupple" weaning off of his manic-depressive
medication.

Nice.

"And *these* are the guys who are out there," she had
later groaned to Laney. Her friend had no such troubles,
having of course married her frat-boy college sweetheart.

It was as a result of that disastrous last first date that
Payton had vowed to temporarily cease all dips into the
dating pool. At least until her professional life was in order,
that is. It was kind of funny, and maybe a tad pathetic: she
had realized earlier that evening as she'd been getting
dressed that it was the first time in weeks she'd worn something other than a suit outside of her apartment. Not wanting to look too formal—or as if she was trying too hard to
impress the Gibson's reps—she'd ditched her standard suit
jacket and gone instead with a fitted button-down shirt,
pencil-thin skirt, and heels.

Having by now polished off her drink, Payton checked
her watch and saw that her dinner companions were twenty
minutes late. Truth be told, she was a bit worried about this
dinner with the Gibson's reps. She had done plenty of pitch
meetings before, and she was sure J.D. had, too, but because their practices rarely overlapped, she and J.D. had
never done one together. *Alone* together. These meetings
required a certain finesse and cohesiveness between the
lawyers doing the pitching—they needed to present a united
front.

Unity.

Cohesiveness.

These were not exactly qualities that she and J.D. pos-
sessed together. Hence the slight jitters of apprehension
she felt that got worse with every moment she sat alone at
the bar.

When five more minutes passed, Payton reached into her purse for her cell phone. She figured she should check her voice mail, just to make sure J.D. hadn't left a message. She was mid-dial when she looked up—

—and saw J.D. standing in front of her.

For a second, Payton was struck by the fact that something about him looked different. She realized that like her, he had dressed more informally for the evening. Instead of his customary suit and tie, he wore an open-necked black pin-striped shirt and perfectly tailored charcoal gray pants.

It was strange, because for whatever reason, what popped into her head at that very moment were Laney's words from the other day about how good-looking J.D. was. Payton had seen J.D. pretty much five days a week for the past eight years, but right then she found herself looking him over more closely. She tried to see him the way a stranger might. Someone who hadn't ever actually spoken to him or anything.

He was tall (as previously mentioned, all the better to look down on people), he had light brown hair with warm golden streaks (probably highlights), his build was lean (undoubtedly from all that tennis or whatever else he played at his I'm-so-cool sexist country club), and he had blue eyes that, um . . .

. . . Well, fine. There wasn't really anything negative Payton could say about J.D.'s eyes. Speaking in a purely objective sense, she kind of liked them. They were a brilliant, bright blue. Such a shame they had to be wasted on *him*.

Having finished her assessment, Payton supposed that, if pressed, in that upper-crusty, Ralph Lauren–y, sweater-thrown-over-the-shoulders, have-you-met-my-polo-pony kind of way, J.D. was pretty damn good-looking.

Misinterpreting her look, J.D. cocked his head and pointed to her phone. "Oh, I'm sorry, Payton—I didn't mean to interrupt you in the middle of your important business," he said with just that right tinge of mocking.

Deciding it was better to go about with the business as usual of ignoring J.D., Payton turned her attention to the group of men he had arrived with. She immediately recognized Jasper from the pictures of him she had found on the Internet while researching his company and the lawsuit.

She stuck out her hand in introduction. "Payton Kendall. It's very nice to meet you, Jasper," she said warmly. With a firm handshake, she greeted the other members of the Gibson's team—Robert, Trevor, and Charles—being sure to look each man directly in the eyes.

"I hope you haven't been waitin' long, Ms. Kendall," Jasper said. "It was Charlie here's fault—how many strokes did you take on that last hole?" He turned to Charles, who clearly was the most junior member of the trial team. "Fourteen? Fifteen?"

"I'm not much of a golfer," Charles admitted to Payton. She liked him instantly.

"I'm a bit of a novice myself." She smiled. Then she turned back to Jasper. "And please, call me Payton."

"Like one of my favorite quarterbacks," Jasper grinned.

"Only with an *a* instead of an *e*. And slightly fewer yards in passing," Payton said. Damn—now she'd already blown one of the three measly sports references she knew in the first two minutes.

Jasper laughed. "Slightly fewer yards in passing—I like that." He turned to J.D., gesturing to Payton. "Where have you been hidin' this girl, J.D.?"

Luckily, J.D. was saved from choking on any polite words he was expected to utter by the hostess who appeared and asked to escort the group to their table.

Once seated, the group chitchatted through the standard business dinner preliminaries: Had Jasper and the others ever been to Chicago before? Where were they staying? Were Payton and J.D. from Chicago? They hit only the slightest bump in the road when Trevor, Gibson's general counsel, asked Payton if she lived in the same neighborhood as J.D. and she realized that despite having worked with him for the past eight years, she had absolutely no idea where he lived. In fact, she pretty much knew nothing about J.D.'s nonwork life. Assuming he had one, that is.

Payton glossed over the question, telling Trevor instead how Chicago was a relatively compact city, how close everything was, et cetera, et cetera. She saw J.D. watching her out of the corner of his eye as he spoke with Robert, the head of Gibson's in-house litigation department. Presumably, he had overheard her say his name to Trevor and was checking to make sure it wasn't being taken in vain.

Thankfully, no other questions arose during dinner that required any sort of knowledge of anything personal related to J.D. When their entrees arrived, Payton began to talk about the firm and the strengths of its litigation group. J.D. joined in, highlighting some of the group's recent legal victories, when Jasper cut him off with an impatient wave of his glass of bourbon.

"I know all about your firm's achievements, Jameson. That's why Ripley and Davis is one of the three firms we're considering. Your firm's successes are what got me here to this table tonight. But my understandin' is that you two"—he pointed to J.D. and Payton—"will be the leaders of this trial team, should your firm be chosen to handle the case. So I want to know more about you."

"Of course, Jasper. I'd be happy to tell you about my—"

Jasper cut him off. "Not from you, Jameson. I'm sure you and Payton both have pretty little prepared speeches you can rattle off about yourselves. But that's not how I like to do things." He turned to Payton, commanding. "Ms. Kendall, why don't you tell me—what's so special about J.D.?"

Payton nearly choked on the wine she was sipping. Clearly, she needed to buy a moment before answering.

"Well, Jasper . . ." She cleared her throat. Ahem. Ahem. "Wow—there are just so many things I could say about J.D. Well . . . where should I start?"

She was stalling. And as she did, Payton could see across the table to where J.D. sat. When she hesitated, he looked down and fiddled uncomfortably with his silverware.

Feeling four sets of eyes on her as the Gibson's people waited, Payton quickly forced herself to think: What would an *objective* person say about J.D.?

"See, Jasper, the thing about J.D. is . . ." Payton tried to buy another moment. What was "the thing" about J.D.? She had worked with him for eight years, and in many ways she knew him better than anyone. And in many ways she didn't know him at all.

Be objective, she told herself. The thing about J.D. was . . .

He was good. *Really* good.

Don't get her wrong, he was still a jerk. But he was a jerk who was *driven*. As Payton knew full well, J.D. was in his office every morning by 7:00 a.m., and—as much as she might not want to admit it—his hard work had paid off. Over the past eight years he had accomplished a tremendous amount for an attorney his age. Laney was right— he was smart and talented. He was a threat. And if she was being honest with herself, *that* was one of the main reasons she didn't like him.

Payton turned to Jasper. "The thing about J.D. is that he is one of the most successful class action attorneys in this city, probably even in the country. He's won every opposition to class certification he's filed—not once has a class been certified in a case he handled. He's been the lead attorney in multimillion-dollar cases for Fortune 500 corporations since his sixth year. He knows the strategies involved in class action practice better than attorneys twice his age. He's brilliant at what he does."

Payton leaned forward in her chair. "And here's the thing, Jasper: your company is being sued in the largest discrimination class action ever filed. No attorney has ever handled a case of this type and magnitude—so while experience definitely should play a role in your decision, that's not the only thing that matters. You need someone with raw natural talent. Someone with the right legal instincts, someone who will be your best shot at attacking this case on class grounds. I can tell you this on no uncertain terms—that person is J.D."

Payton sat back in her chair when she was finished. She saw Jasper grin. He swirled his glass and tilted his head as if carefully taking in everything she'd just said. Then, slightly self-conscious for having been so forthright in her praise, she stole a glance over at J.D. to catch his reaction.

He looked speechless.

Even from across the table she could see the expression of shock on J.D.'s face. She saw something pass through his eyes and his expression changed as he held her gaze.

His look made Payton pause. Because she remembered that look—she had seen it once before, a long time ago.

Jasper's voice felt like an interruption.

"All right, Payton," he said. "I like what I've heard so far. Although, I suspect I'm gonna hear similar pitches from the other firms we're interviewing." He grinned. "But admittedly, yours was quite good."

Payton pried her gaze away from J.D. and smiled at Jasper. "Why don't you just tell me the other firms you're considering, and I'll save you the time. I can tell you exactly what they'll say. Better yet, let me guess." She paused, thinking of the other two firms they were likely interviewing.

"Baker and Lewis," she guessed.

Jasper looked over at his general counsel, needing confirmation. Trevor nodded.

"And Sayer, Gray, and Jones."

Trevor nodded again. "You know your competition well."

"Those are good firms," J.D. interjected. "But they're not right for your case."

"Why? What does your firm have that they don't?" Jasper asked.

"Other than higher rates," Robert joked. Everyone at the table laughed. Except for J.D., who remained serious.

"They don't have Payton."

Jasper got comfortable in his chair. "All right, Jameson—it's your turn. Tell me about Ms. Kendall here."

Payton held her breath, hoping that J.D. intended to play as fair as she had. He certainly appeared very confident as he began.

"Payton was being very modest a moment ago, in describing your need for an experienced class action attorney. While that certainly is true, what is just as important—if not more so—is that you hire an expert in the field of employment discrimination. That's where she comes in.

"I'm sure you saw the article about Payton in the *Chicago Lawyer*," J.D. continued, "so I don't need to repeat everything you already know about her significant accomplishments. But I would be remiss if I didn't point out that, despite the fact that she's only thirty-two years old, Payton has tried over *forty* employment discrimination cases. That's more trials than many lawyers have during their entire careers. And do you know how many of those trials she's won? Every single one."

J.D. picked up his glass. "Now I'm sure Payton would be modest about these facts; she'd probably tell you that she's been lucky to get cases that are winners. But the truth is, she's a natural in the courtroom. She has incredible instincts as a trial lawyer, and that's exactly what your company needs—someone who can guide your company through the litigation process from start to finish." He paused. "Plus, she's a woman."

Jasper raised an eyebrow, as if unsure how to react to that. "Does that make a difference?"

J.D. looked across the table to Payton, who had been busy trying to appear as though she heard him say things like that about her every day. "Payton?" he said, indicating she should take it from there.

She knew exactly where he was going. "J.D. is right, Jasper. Your company is being sued for gender discrimination. One-point-eight million women claim that your company doesn't give a damn about treating them fairly. The press is going to have a field day. And if you stand in front of a jury with a trial team of men, you will lose this case."

As she spoke, Payton tapped her finger on the table, underscoring her seriousness. "You need a woman to be the face of your company. You gain instant credibility if you have a woman arguing that you don't discriminate."

"And trust me, Jasper," J.D. jumped in, "I've seen Payton when she argues. She's a force to be reckoned with."

As Jasper chuckled good-naturedly, Trevor jumped in. "I have a question." He pointed between J.D. and Payton, as if to say he wasn't fooled. "How many times have you two done this routine of yours? It's quite good."

J.D. shook his head. "There's no routine here. With Payton and I, what you see is what you get."

"No fancy legalese and no beatin' around the bush," Jasper agreed. "Now that I like." With a grin, he raised his glass in toast. "To the best pitch I've heard so far. No bullshit."

As the group laughed along with Jasper, clinking their glasses in toast, Payton's eyes caught J.D.'s across the table. With a subtle grin, he tipped his glass to her. She nodded back in acknowledgment. In that one moment at least, they shared the same thought.

Victory.

If only the evening had ended there.

Six

AFTER DINNER, JASPER suggested that the group head downstairs, to the restaurant's outdoor lounge that overlooked the Chicago River.

"I'm not signing any papers just yet, but I think a celebratory cigar might be in order," he declared.

Payton told the group she'd meet them outside and headed to the ladies' room. She didn't smoke cigars and didn't figure now was a good time to try it out. She stalled for a few minutes in the bathroom, then stopped at the bar, thinking she could kill a little more time by ordering a drink.

"I'll have a glass of the Silver Oak cabernet," she told the bartender. She'd already had a drink at dinner and anything stronger might make her tipsy. While she waited— feeling more than a tad conspicuous standing there, by herself, a lone woman at the bar—she accidentally caught the eye of a man wearing a silk shirt unbuttoned nearly to his navel.

Oh, shit—she immediately looked away, but her split-second glance apparently was all the encouragement Mr. Sizzle Chest needed. He made a beeline straight for her.

Payton had no choice. With a feigned reluctant look, she shook her head. "Sorry," she told him. "Lesbian."

Sizzle Chest raised an interested eyebrow, liking the sound of *that*.

Again, Payton shook her head. "Not that kind."

Disappointed, Sizzle Chest moved on to more promising conquests. Payton took a sip of the wine the bartender set down before her. She heard a familiar voice behind her, amused.

"Lesbian?"

Payton turned around and saw J.D. standing there.

Maybe it was the wine. Maybe she was basking in the glow of their successful pitch to Gibson's. Maybe it was her promise to Laney to be the "New Payton," or maybe it was a combination of all those things. But Payton actually found herself *smiling* at J.D.

"It's just an excuse, the lesbian thing," she said.

J.D. joined her at the bar. He gestured for a drink as Payton shrugged mock-innocently. "Unless you count that one time in college."

J.D. knocked over a nearby stack of shot glasses.

Payton giggled at his reaction. "Sorry—Laney would kill me if she knew I just said that."

J.D. did an about-face. "It was with *Laney*?"

Payton laughed out loud at the very thought. "No, no," she explained, "I was joking. I just meant that Laney is always lecturing me about saying things like that."

"Oh. Right." J.D. nodded as he threw some bills down for his drink. Watching him, Payton cocked her head, curious. "What are you doing here?"

J.D. eased back against the bar, having recovered from his momentary fluster.

"Well, see, Payton, you and I are here to pitch to Gibson's, remember?" he said as if speaking to a child or deranged person. "We just finished dinner and—"

"That's not what I meant, smart-ass." Payton gave him a look. "I meant why are you inside with me, instead of outside smoking cigars with Jasper and the other *boys*?" She put mocking emphasis on the last word.

"Well, I figured Jasper and the other *boys*"—he emphasized the word, too—"could get along without me for a few minutes. I didn't want you to have to be in here by yourself."

Seeing her look of surprise, he shrugged nonchalantly. "But I can go." He pointed across the bar to Sizzle Chest. "Maybe you'd like another minute to see if he'll come back and ask for your number?" He and Payton watched as the Sizzle worked his near-naked navel toward another poor unsuspecting woman.

J.D. shook his head sadly. "Uh-oh, look at that . . . What a shame. You two would've looked so cute together."

Payton rolled her eyes. "You know, J.D.—" She was about to say something sarcastic, probably something that included a profane word or two, when the woman on the other side of Payton leaned over.

"Excuse me—could you slide down?" The woman gestured at the open space between Payton and J.D. Payton glanced around and noticed that the traffic around the bar had picked up in the last few minutes. Having no choice, she moved closer to J.D.

"You were about to say something?" J.D. prompted her. He crossed his arms over his chest, readying himself for the expected insult.

But instead of taking the bait, Payton remembered her promise, the whole "New Payton" thing. Darn Laney and her "let's be nice to people" scam. Did J.D. really even count as a person, anyway?

Payton decided—what the hell—to give it a shot. This way, when J.D. was a jackass to her, she could shrug, say she tried, and carry on with business as usual. Hating him.

The problem was actually coming up with something non-insulting to say to J.D. Payton felt like an idiot, just standing there, so she blurted out the first thing that came to mind.

"So, um, what I was about to say was . . . how was your golf game? Did you have a nice time?"

WELL.

J.D. certainly hadn't been expecting her to say *that*. Something so . . . innocuous. Pleasant, even.

He peered down at Payton, caught off guard by her tone. Or rather, the fact that there wasn't one.

"It was . . . nice." J.D. paused. "Thanks." Then he looked her over, curious about something. "You know, I'm really surprised you've never learned how to play."

"Why? Because everyone who's anyone plays golf?" she asked sarcastically.

J.D. shook his head. "No, because I think you in partic-ular would like it. You seem like you enjoy a challenge."

Payton cocked her head, studying him. She appeared to be trying to decide whether he meant that as a criticism or compliment. He wasn't so sure himself.

A look of uncertainty clouded her dark blue eyes. "Did you really mean those things you said?" she suddenly asked him. "The things you told the Gibson's reps at dinner?"

"Did you?" J.D. fired back.

Payton shook her head at his return question, as if she had expected him to say exactly that. It was at that moment that someone joined the woman standing on the other side of Payton, crowding her even more. Making room, she moved closer to J.D., so that they now stood just a few inches apart. For some reason, it occurred to him right then that in nearly eight years, this was probably the longest conversation he and Payton had ever had without being engaged in some sort of political/social/work-related debate. And it certainly was the closest, in terms of physical proximity, that they had ever been.

She was beautiful. J.D. knew that, he had always known that—just because she was an argumentative, defensive pill didn't mean he couldn't objectively see that she was gorgeous. He normally didn't like blondes, but she had the whole Jennifer Aniston–ish long, straight dark blonde hair thing going for her. She had deep blue expressive eyes that showed every emotion (apparently anger and/or annoyance ruled the day, from what he could tell) and—what J.D. had just noticed for the first time—a scattering of freckles across her nose that—had she been anyone else—he would've described as "cute."

Payton peered up at him and opened her mouth as if to say something. Then she seemed to change her mind.

"Yes, I did mean it," she said almost defiantly. "You're a very good lawyer, J.D. I would've been lying if I had told Jasper and the others anything else."

She looked at him pointedly. "Now it's your turn to say something nice."

J.D. tried to hide his grin. "Well, I suppose I could say that this restaurant serves the best vodka tonic in the city—"

"That's not what I meant."

J.D. gazed down at her in all seriousness. "You know you're a great attorney, Payton. You don't need me to tell you that." There. Fine. He had said it. Now what? This was new territory for them.

He shifted nervously. Then he saw the corners of Payton's eyes crinkle with amusement.

"What?" he asked, immediately going on the defensive. "Is there something funny about what I said?"

Payton shook her head, studying him. "No, it's . . . I just noticed that your nose is sunburned from golfing." And she fixed those deep blue eyes on his.

It was the way she was looking at him.

Really looking at him.

J.D. would never admit it to another soul, but he knew what he was thinking right then.

It was her eyes. No, her smile—she never smiled at him. At least not genuinely, anyway.

Normally, J.D. was pretty damn skilled at reading female body language. Meeting women was not exactly a problem for him. He was a good-looking guy, he actually knew how to dress himself, he had a great job, and he came from a very wealthy family. He wasn't bragging, just stating the facts. Whether any of those things should matter was a debate for somebody else.

Except for the part about knowing how to dress, that is. He took great pride in his attire. Call him old-fashioned (something *she* constantly seemed to hold against him), but he thought there was a certain civility lacking in his generation. Whatever had happened to the days when men wore jackets to dinner? When women carried pocketbooks and excused themselves to "powder their noses"? (And no, snorting cocaine off a toilet seat in the ladies' room did not suffice here.)

At least Payton seemed to implicitly agree with him on this point. Again, not caving on the argumentative, defensive pill thing, but the woman always looked good. J.D. suspected that she made a point of this—almost as if she was trying to prove something. Although who she was trying to prove something *to*, he didn't know. Because Payton Kendall certainly had a way about her that impressed almost everyone.

Not that he had particularly noticed the slim cuts of her skirts, or the way her legs looked in those three-inch heels she snapped to and from court in. Nor had he noticed the fact that, tonight, her shirt was unbuttoned right down to that could-I-sneak-a-peek? point . . .

Suddenly feeling how warm it was in the restaurant, J.D. reached up to loosen his tie. Then he remembered he wasn't wearing one.

Maybe he'd better lay off the vodka tonics.

Regrouping, J.D. tried to make his face impassive and nonchalant as he gazed down at Payton. He didn't know what sort of game she was playing—being friendly to him and all—but he was not about to be played for a fool.

Payton tilted her head at his silence. "Is something wrong?"

J.D. tried to think of something he would normally say, something that would regain him the upper hand.

"Everything's fine," he assured her, lest there be any doubt about it. "I was just wondering whether your fellow feministas would approve of you using your sexuality as bait."

Payton pulled back. "I'm sorry?"

She appeared pissed. Good—*this* he knew.

J.D. pointed to the could-I-sneak-a-peek? V-neck of her shirt. "Planning on showing off the girls tonight, are we? Is that how you plan to impress the Gibson's execs?"

He regretted the words the moment they came out of his mouth.

He saw the flash of hurt in Payton's eyes, but she quickly looked away to cover it up. When she turned back to him, her gaze was icy.

"We're asking Gibson's to give us twenty million dollars in legal fees," she said coldly. "If you think my *boobs* are going to land this deal, then they must be even more spectacular than I thought. Now, if you'll excuse me . . ." She brushed past him in a hurry.

J.D. tried to stop her. "Payton, wait. I didn't mean—"

"Well, there you are! We were startin' to wonder what happened to you two!"

Payton and J.D. turned at the sound of Jasper's voice.

Payton quickly regained her composure. "Jasper—we were just coming to join you," she said calmly. "Did you save one of those cigars for me?" With her head held high, she followed Jasper to join the other men out on the terrace.

She didn't look once at J.D. for the rest of the night.

DURING THE RIDE home, Payton's mood was subdued. Tired and lost in thought, she'd barely realized that the cab had stopped, arriving at its destination, until the driver glanced over the partition and asked if there was somewhere else she wanted to go. After quickly paying the fare, she hurried up the front steps of the quaint two-flat row house she had bought and rehabbed three years ago. It was a cozy place, nothing extravagant, but the mortgage was in her budget and the place was within walking distance of the "L." Most important, it was all hers. To her, home ownership was about stability and investment, and definitely not about hot trendy neighborhoods for which one paid a premium.

Payton let herself inside, tossed her keys on the side table by the front door, and headed back to her bedroom. Her heels clicked on the restored oak hardwood floors.

She didn't know why she let it bother her so much, what J.D. had said. Yes, it was insulting of him to suggest that she was playing up her sexuality to entice the Gibson's reps. The comment had come way out of left field—she had never done anything even remotely unprofessional to deserve such an attack on her character. But what bothered her even more was the fact that she had been completely unprepared for the insult. Normally she had her guard up around J.D., but tonight she had thought they were getting along—or at the very least, that they were tolerating each other, that they had put away the boxing gloves for the evening in the spirit of working together.

Boy, had she ever been wrong about that.

An oval full-length mirror stood in the corner of her bedroom, an antique she had inherited from her grandmother. Before changing out of her clothes, Payton paused before the mirror. She self-consciously fingered the neckline of her button-down shirt. It wasn't that low-cut, was it?

She stopped herself right there and stared defiantly in the mirror.

The hell with him.

FOR HIS PART, J.D. was not exactly in a celebratory mood when he got home, either. Over and over, his mind ran through the same debate.

He could call her, to apologize.

She'd hang up on him, no doubt.

And why should he bother, anyway? So she was pissed at him . . . big fucking surprise there. She *lived* to be pissed at him. In fact, it probably had made her night, what he'd said. With his comment he had single-handedly given her the logs of legitimacy to fuel her fire.

But still.

He had crossed the line. Over the years the two of them had traded innumerable barbs and insults, but he knew he had gone too far that evening.

So J.D. settled it in his mind. He would call her.

He looked up Payton's phone number in the firm directory. This certainly had been a night of firsts for them, all starting with the complimentary things they had said about each other to Jasper. And now he was going to call her? They'd never even spoken on the phone before, outside of work.

Sighing to himself—not relishing this task he was about to undertake—J.D. reached for the phone. It was then that it occurred to him that he was about to call Payton at *home*. He tried to picture her in her . . . apartment? Condo?

House? He wondered what it looked like, the place she lived.

Then he wondered why he wondered that.

Mere curiosity, J.D. assured himself.

He pictured her place as being a tad . . . plebian. That probably wasn't the most politically correct way to say it. What word did liberals prefer nowadays? Granola? Organic?

In reality, however, Payton was none of those things. In fact, if she never spoke, one might actually think she was quite normal.

Then a second thought suddenly occurred to J.D.

Maybe she didn't live alone.

He should know things like this, shouldn't he? He should at least know the basics, have some inkling of what her life was like when she wasn't busy being *her*.

Realizing he was stalling, trying to avoid apologizing to Payton, J.D. grabbed the phone. He was about to dial her number when he noticed that he had a new message. He entered the code to access his voice mail, then heard a familiar deep voice as the message began to play.

"J.D., it's your father. I thought I'd check in and see if there's any news on the partnership front. I'm guessing no, otherwise we would've heard from you already." There was a preemptory disappointed sigh. "I suppose if you don't make it, I can always call my old firm. But maybe you're going to surprise me for once, son. Although—no offense—I bet your mother a new mink that you'll be calling me to bail you out by the end of the month, ha-ha. And that woman *really* does not need another fur coat."

When J.D. heard the beep, signaling the end of his father's message, he hung up the phone. He sat there, in the leather armchair in his living room, staring out the windows and their sweeping view of the city at night, but not seeing.

After a long moment, he put the phone receiver back in its cradle.

This thing with Payton was a distraction. And he certainly did not need any distractions right now. It would be best if he put her out of his mind entirely. He simply needed to stay on track for the rest of the month, doing everything exactly as he had done for the past eight years.

If anything, it was a good thing Payton was giving him the silent treatment. Ha—if that's all it took, he should've been a rude bastard years ago. Maybe now he'd finally have some peace at work. No more pissed-off hair flips, no more covert you're-such-a-wanker-J.D. glares, no more secret arguments in back hallways over feminist and right-wing agendas.

These were things J.D. certainly would not miss.

Not at all.

Seven

"**I FOUND THE** *perfect* guy for you."

Payton barely looked up as Laney strolled into her office and plunked down in one of the seats in front of her desk.

"Hmm, that's nice," Payton said distractedly. "Can we talk about this in say . . ." She checked her watch. "Three weeks?" Putting aside partnership issues, she had a trial starting in two days.

"I'm excited about this, Payton. Don't ruin the moment with sarcasm."

"Oh, well, then." Payton pushed aside the mound of files on her desk with a grand flourish. "By all means—continue."

Laney looked at her pointedly. "Career or not, a single woman in her thirties cannot neglect her personal life forever."

"Sorry, Laney, you're right. I had forgotten that we'd *traveled back in time* to 1950."

Another look from Laney. "May I continue?"

"Does Mr. Perfect have a name?"

"Chase."

"And what makes the Perfect Chase so perfect?" Payton asked.

Laney leaned forward, eager to share the details. "He was in Nate's fraternity in undergrad," she began, referring to her husband. "He just moved here a few weeks ago. He's a lawyer, too—and you'll love this—he does pro bono work with the Chicago Legal Clinic. He went to Harvard Law School, he was president of both the Harvard Law chapter of the ACLU and the Harvard Law Advocates for Human Rights—"

Payton raised a skeptical eyebrow at this. "Harvard Law School?" She already knew one Harvard Law graduate and that was one too many.

Laney held up a hand. "I checked it out. He went there on scholarship and paid the rest with student loans. And he's good-looking, too. Nate and I met him for dinner last night, and I subtly learned that he's looking to meet someone."

"How did you learn that?"

"I asked him if he was looking to meet someone."

"That *is* subtle." Payton shook her head. "You married people are always trying to set us single people up."

Laney nearly jumped right out of her chair. "That's exactly what he said! See—you two are perfect for each other." She paused deliberately. "So? Should I tell him to call you?"

The timing wasn't exactly the greatest, but Payton found her friend's enthusiasm hard to resist. And the Perfect Chase did sound somewhat promising. Career-driven. Interested in politics. Passionate about his beliefs. True, these were all things she found attractive in a man. And she certainly wouldn't hold being good-looking against him.

"Okay," Payton agreed. "Tell him to call me."

"Good. Because I already gave him your number."

Payton mulled things over. "Harvard Law, huh?" She couldn't help it; she glanced across the hall to J.D.'s office. They hadn't spoken since the night of the Gibson's pitch.

Over the last few days, to the extent possible, she had avoided walking by J.D.'s office and had been using the internal stairwells for all trips under five flights (normally two up, three down was her limit in heels) in order to minimize the risk of being stuck in the elevator with him. Because as far as she was concerned, she was *done* with J.D.

Not to suggest that she had ever *begun* with J.D., of course.

The way she saw it, she had put herself out there the other night at the restaurant. She had made an attempt to be friendly and—to put it mildly—he had not reciprocated. She had allowed herself to be caught off guard, to be momentarily vulnerable in front of him, and she would not make that mistake again. And now she just wanted to forget the whole thing.

It had been a foolish thought, anyway, her thinking that they could ever get along. At least the Gibson's pitch was over, putting an end, albeit perhaps temporarily, to their work together. And if the firm did indeed land Gibson's as a client, she and J.D. would likely both be partner by the time they started working on the case and she would find some way to staff it so that they encountered each other as little as possible.

Of course, there was that small part of her, the teeniest, tiniest part of her, that was disappointed J.D. hadn't apologized. If anything, he seemed to be avoiding her, too, and that Payton couldn't understand. She may have had her faults, but at least she owned up to her mistakes. He apparently didn't feel the same way. Unless he didn't think he had made a mistake, in which case she had even bigger problems with him.

Not that she had spent any time thinking about these things.

Payton turned her attention back to Laney, who was already thinking ahead to where she and the Perfect Chase should first meet.

"It should be drinks, not coffee," Laney was saying. "Too much caffeine makes you quippy."

Payton looked over, offended by this. "Quippy?"

They were interrupted by a knock at her door, and Irma poked her head into the office. "Your mother's on my line. Should I transfer her over to you?"

"Why is my mother on *your* line?"

Irma cleared her throat awkwardly. "She said she had been thinking about me and, um, wanted to discuss something before I transferred her over to you."

"What did she want to talk to you about?" Payton asked.

"She wanted to ask whether I had ever considered trying to unionize the secretarial staff."

Payton rolled her eyes. Her mother had done the *Norma Rae* routine on her a million times. Apparently Irma was her newest victim.

Payton waved to Laney, who was already on her way out, and told Irma to put her mother through. She picked up the phone, bracing herself. "Hi, Mom."

"Hey, Sis," came her mother's familiar greeting. In Lex Kendall's mind (formerly Alexandra, but that name was too bourgeois), all women were sisters under the same moon.

"How's my girl?" Lex asked.

"Fine, Mom. I hear from Irma that you're trying to rally the troops against The Man."

"See, I knew you'd get all uptight if I called her."

"Yet still, you did it."

"I just thought that she and the other laborers at your firm might want to know that they have rights. Not everyone there makes a six-figure salary, Payton."

Payton sighed. Her mother was the only person she knew

who was *disappointed* that her child was financially successful. "Irma could get in a lot of trouble, if the wrong person overheard your conversation and misunderstood. You forget that I'm a labor and employment lawyer."

"No, I haven't forgotten," her mother said, as if recalling some heinous crime her only child had committed years ago. And in Lex Kendall's mind, Payton's sin was egregious indeed.

She had become a yuppie.

Payton had been raised to "live and think freely"—a sentiment that sounded great in theory, but, as she discovered by a very young age, actually meant she was supposed to "live and think freely" exactly the way her mother told her to.

Barbie dolls were sexist. ("Look at her vacant expression, Payton—Barbie doesn't care about anything other than shopping.") Fairy tales—in fact, most of children's literature—were also sexist. ("Look at the message in these picture books, Payton—that beauty is the only important quality of a woman.") Even Disney movies were the enemy. ("I know that Lisa's mother lets her watch *Cinderella*, Payton. Lisa's mother obviously has no problem teaching her daughter that women must wait passively for a man to bring meaning to their pathetically lonely lives.")

Yes, Lex Kendall had a reason to protest just about everything.

It wasn't that Payton didn't agree with her mother's principles. She did agree with some of them, just not to the same degree. For example, she was absolutely against people wearing fur coats. Which meant that she *personally* did not wear one. It did *not* mean that she stood outside Gucci on Michigan Avenue throwing buckets of red paint on exiting shoppers. (Oh, yes, her mother had, several times, in fact, and had even twice gone to jail for her renegade artistic endeavors, necessitating several of young Payton's many overnight stays with her grandparents.)

In her mother's eyes, Payton knew, she had sold out. In fact, when Lex had found out that Payton planned to defend Corporate America as part of her law practice, she had refused to speak to her daughter for two straight weeks.

Ah . . . Payton still recalled those two weeks fondly. It had been the most peaceful 336 hours of her life.

"Can I call you back later this evening, when I get home?" she asked her mother. "I'm pretty busy at work these days."

"With the partnership thing," her mother stated in a tone that was, at best, disinterested.

"Yes, the partnership thing." Payton bit back the urge to say anything further. Was it really that difficult for people to understand what she was going through? Did no one get the amount of stress she was under?

"You don't need to call me back," her mother told her. "I can hear the tension in your voice. Are you keeping up with your yoga practice? You probably need to liberate your chakras."

Payton put her head on her desk. Yes, of course—the tension in her voice had *nothing* to do with the fact that she hadn't taken a vacation in nearly four years. The problem was that her chakras were unliberated.

She could hear her mother rambling on through the receiver she held in her hand.

". . . talk more when I come into town later this month—"

At this, Payton sprung back to life. "You're coming to Chicago?"

"Steven plans to visit Sarah and Jess in L.A. for Father's Day," her mother said, referring to Payton's two stepsisters. "I thought I'd come to Chicago so we could spend the weekend together."

Payton peered over at her calendar. She had been so busy she'd completely forgotten about the upcoming holiday.

And, despite the rocky start to their conversation, she suddenly felt a rush of affection toward her mother. Lex Kendall could be a difficult woman no doubt, but she had never once let Payton spend a Father's Day alone, not even after she and her husband Steven had married and moved to San Francisco several years ago. Though they'd never discussed it openly, Payton knew it was her mother's attempt to compensate for the fact that Payton hadn't heard from her father in years.

"I'd like that, Mom," Payton said. They discussed briefly what they might do that weekend. Keeping her fingers crossed, Payton hoped she might have some good news to share by then.

After a few moments of chatting, Payton saw her other line ringing. Through the glass door of her office, she watched as Irma intercepted the call, nodded, then got up and signaled for her attention. Payton wrapped up the call with her mother, sensing it was something important.

"What is it?" she asked when Irma stepped into her doorway.

"That was Ben's secretary, Marie. He wants to see you in his office." Irma lowered her voice. "Marie says she heard him on the phone earlier this morning, with Tom Hillman from the Partnership Committee. She heard him tell Tom that he wanted to give you and J.D. *the news* early."

Payton felt a thrill of excitement run through her.

This was it.

With a faint smile on her face, Payton got up from her desk and thanked Irma for the message.

Then she headed out the door to Ben's office.

Eight

WHEN PAYTON GOT to Ben's office, she found J.D., alone, sitting in front of the partner's desk. He had his back to the door, unaware she stood there. She noticed that his leg bounced anxiously as he waited.

She cleared her throat. J.D. immediately stopped bouncing his leg and watched her take a seat in the chair next to him.

"Ben's not here yet?" Payton asked coolly.

J.D. shook his head. "Marie said he should be in shortly."

An awkward silence fell between them.

Payton glanced around the room. She suddenly was very aware of her hands; she tapped them against the arms of her chair, then stopped, then folded them in her lap.

More silence.

And then . . .

Still more silence.

"It's this job, you know."

Payton had been gazing out the window. She turned her head to J.D.

"We argue with people—that's what we do. We strategize against them, we try to get the upper hand. Sometimes, I find it hard to break away from that." He turned to face Payton and looked her straight in the eyes.

"I was very rude to you at the restaurant. I owe you an apology."

Caught off guard, Payton said nothing at first. Direct and unwavering, J.D. held her gaze.

He really did have the most amazing blue eyes.

Payton had no idea why she just thought that.

She nodded. "Okay."

J.D. seemed to have been bracing himself for something far worse. "Okay," he said, and Payton thought she saw him exhale in relief. Then he smiled. Genuinely.

"So . . . do you know why we're here?"

"I have a guess," Payton said.

J.D. leaned forward in his chair, his eyes lit excitedly. "What's the first thing you're going to do when you make partner?"

Payton hesitated, still feeling superstitious. Then she thought—what the hell—why not enjoy the moment? They both knew why they had been called to Ben's office.

"Sleep," she said. "For a week."

J.D. laughed. "And no voice mail."

"Or email."

"No BlackBerry."

"No cell phone."

"No *laptop*," J.D. said with a wink, knowing there was no way she could top that.

Payton thought for a moment. "Actually, I think I'll take a few weeks off. I'd like to travel."

"Where?" J.D. asked.

"Bora-Bora," she decided.

"Why Bora-Bora?"

Payton shrugged. "I don't know. It just sounds like someplace I'd like to go."

J.D. grinned, and it occurred to Payton that she was babbling on about Bora-Bora when someone like J.D. had probably vacationed in places like that his whole life. Hell, his *servants* probably vacationed in places like that. She must've sounded very unworldly to him.

But if he thought that, he didn't say it.

"Bora-Bora sounds great," he agreed, easing back in his chair. Then he snuck another glance at her. "You know, Payton, now that this is all over, I was hoping we could put aside our d—"

At that moment, Ben walked into his office.

He sat down at his desk. "Sorry to keep you guys waiting," he said. "My lunch ran later than I had expected."

Ben sat upright in his chair, hands resting firmly on his desk. "So. I have great news. Jasper Conroy called me earlier this morning. He's chosen our firm to represent Gibson's. He told me he was very impressed by you both. I knew you two would deliver." He paused. "Which brings me to some other news."

Payton held her breath. Out of the corner of her eye, she saw J.D. inch forward in his seat.

"It goes without saying that you're both aware the firm makes its partnership decisions at the end of this month," Ben said.

"The Partnership Committee's policy has always been that no one is supposed to leak early information about its decisions. But, in light of your stellar performance in landing the Gibson's case—and, in fact, the stellar work you've both done throughout your careers here—I think you've earned the right to a little advance notice. I know how eagerly you both have awaited this."

Payton's heart began to race. Holy shit—this really *was* it.

Ben cleared his throat. "Which is why what I'm about to say is going to come as a surprise."

Payton blinked. Surprise? That wasn't the word she wanted to hear right then.

"You both are aware of the EEOC's age discrimination lawsuit against Gray and Dallas," Ben said, referring to another of the top law firms in the city. "And as you know, one of the claims in that lawsuit is that the firm chases out older partners in favor of younger ones."

Ben looked to Payton for help. "You're an employment lawyer. You know how closely all the other firms in this city have been watching that case. Including us."

Payton answered him cautiously. "I'm familiar with the case, Ben. What I'm trying to figure out is how it has anything to do with me and J.D."

Ben chose his next words carefully. "The Partnership Committee has decided that we need to strategically leverage ourselves in order to avoid similar intrusions from the EEOC. We simply can't afford to have too many partners under the age of forty. Now, we obviously aren't going to take away the shares of anyone who already is a partner . . . so instead there will be cutbacks in the number of associates made partner this year."

J.D.'s jaw was set tensely. "You still haven't answered Payton's question. What does this have to do with us?"

Ben paused to look at each of them. "We've decided to name only one litigation partner this year. Only one of you will make it."

It was as if all the air had been sucked out of the room.

Only *one* of them.

Her or him.

Payton finally spoke. "Is this a joke?"

Ben shook his head. "I'm afraid not. You two are lucky you're hearing this from me now." He pointed to himself as if expecting gratitude. "*I* insisted on that. I wanted to give the one of you who won't make it at least some warning."

"The decision hasn't been made yet?" J.D. asked, his tone incredulous.

Ben—the cocky bastard—actually had the audacity to laugh. He held his hands out before him. "What can I say? You're both just so good. You have no idea how hard this is on us."

Hard on you? Payton nearly leapt out of her chair and strangled him.

J.D. appeared no less furious. He stared Ben down coldly. "This is bullshit. Just last week you were practically promising that Payton and I were both locks."

Ben shrugged this off, far too dismissively in Payton's mind. After all, this was only her *life*—and J.D.'s—that they were talking about.

"So I embellished a bit . . ." Ben conceded with a self-satisfied grin. "We're lawyers, that's what we do."

"How convenient that you tell us this *after* we land the Gibson's case," Payton said. "You used us, Ben."

Ben held up a finger, point of fact. "Technically, I only used one of you. Because one of you is still going to make partner, and that person will lead the Gibson's trial team as promised. As for the other of you, well . . ." he trailed off pointedly.

Payton didn't need Ben to finish. She, like every other lawyer there, knew about the firm's unwritten "up or out" policy. Associates who did not make partner were quickly transitioned off their cases and given a short grace period to "voluntarily" resign and find another job.

"I know this news probably comes as a shock to you both," Ben said. "And it is extremely unfortunate that circumstances have caused things to end this way, but that is the Partnership Committee's decision. I want to emphasize, however, that the choice between the two of you has not yet been made. It's going to come right down to the wire. So for what it's worth, I urge each of you to give it all you've got for these remaining couple of weeks."

Payton resisted the urge to laugh bitterly at that. Give it all she's got? What more could she give? A kidney? Her firstborn?

She glanced at J.D., sitting next to her. He looked over and met her gaze, and Payton could tell from the look in his eyes that they shared the same thought.

Only one of them would make it.

After eight years of practice, they were now truly adversaries.

J.D. MANAGED TO maintain an expression of unconcern the entire walk back.

When he got to his office, he stepped inside, shut the door behind him, and immediately began to pace. He was having trouble thinking straight. He took a seat at his desk, ignoring the blinking message light on his phone.

Merely ten minutes ago while sitting in Ben's office and joking with Payton, he would've put his chances of making partner at about 99.99 percent.

Suddenly, those odds had plummeted. To 50 percent. *At best.*

He'd been torn, on the one hand wanting to yell at Ben, wanting to tell him what a chickenshit weasel he was, and on the other hand—cognizant of the fact that the decision had not yet been made and that he had not yet definitively lost out on making partner—he had felt pressed to continue playing along, to continue being the good little associate he was.

But the truth of the matter was, he couldn't fucking believe this was happening.

Through the glass on his door, J.D. could see Payton hurrying into her office. He watched as, like him, she immediately shut the door behind her. It provided him no consolation that she had obviously been as stunned by Ben's news as he.

After eight years, it had finally come down to this.

Him versus her.

The buzz of the telephone intercom, his secretary's call, momentarily startled him.

"Yes, Kathy," he answered in a clipped, brisk tone. He needed a few moments alone to think.

"Sorry to bother you, J.D.," came Kathy's voice through the speakerphone. "Chuck Werner asked that you call him as soon as possible to discuss next week's deposition schedule."

J.D. pinched between his eyes. He felt a headache coming on and was not at all in the mood to deal with his opposing counsel. "Thanks, Kathy. I'll get back to him."

"And one other thing," Kathy added quickly, seeming to sense his eagerness to get off the phone. "Your father called and asked me to give you a message. He said you would understand." She spoke slowly, confused by the message. "He said to tell you that he heard the firm was making an announcement today and wanted to know whether your mother just got her new mink coat."

J.D. closed his eyes. His headache had suddenly gotten much worse.

PAYTON LEANED AGAINST her office door with her eyes shut. She slowly breathed in and out, trying to steady herself.

She wasn't in her office five seconds before her phone began to ring. She tried to ignore it.

Then her second line rang.

Payton opened her eyes and headed to her desk. Glancing over at her computer, she saw that she had twenty-five new email messages.

There was a knock at her door. Without hesitation, Irma popped her head into the office.

"Oh, good, I thought you were here—you have Mr.

McKane holding on line one, and Eric Riley waiting for you on line two. He wants to talk about the Middleton trial."

Payton couldn't breathe. She felt as though the walls were closing in around her. A third call came in, and the ringing of her phone seemed deafening.

She needed to get out.

Now.

She slid past Irma. "Tell everyone I'll call them back. I . . . have to take care of something. An urgent matter."

With that, she took off in a hurry toward the elevators.

THE FIFTY-FIFTH FLOOR housed the firm's law library. With grand cathedral ceilings and sunlit stained-glass windows, the library's grandeur befitted a different era, a time when—egads—lawyers consulted *books* for information. In the post-Internet days of online research, however, it was rare to find a living soul amongst the library's elegant two-story mahogany bookshelves—save for Ripley & Davis's lone librarian, Agnes, who had been with the firm since its inception.

Nearly six years ago, getting lost while looking for the accounting floor, Payton had stumbled upon the law library (it wasn't even included in the new associate tour anymore) and had been charmed by its quiet calm. It was an oasis of serenity amid the chaos and bustle of the firm's other floors.

Truthfully, it was also pretty much the only place in the entire building to which an associate could escape without being called, emailed, beeped, sent for, paged, or otherwise hounded by ne'er-do-well partners trying to pawn off emergency TROs at 4:00 on a Friday afternoon. Not that Payton—the highly industrious associate she was—had ever personally utilized the library for such nefarious purposes.

She could just *surmise* that the library would be great for hiding out, if one so happened to be inclined.

Payton burst into the library, relieved to see that it was empty as always. She hurried past the librarian's desk en route to her favorite "thinking" spot: the Archives shelves in the far back corner of the library.

"Hello, Agnes," she said politely as she breezed by.

Agnes turned at the sound of Payton's voice. Eighty years old if a day, the librarian's vision wasn't the greatest. She smiled and waved in the wrong direction, addressing the air.

"Hello, Ms. Kendall!" Agnes called out. "Come to practice another opening statement?" It was the excuse Payton had given her years ago, to explain what she did while hanging out by herself amongst the library stacks.

"I won't be long today," Payton said over her shoulder. She just needed a minute or two to collect herself. Ben's news had come as a shock. All of her anger was bubbling up to the surface and if she didn't get a moment to herself to calm down, she might explode.

Payton headed to the Archives section, and when she was safely tucked out of sight, she came to a stop. She leaned against the bookshelves and took a deep breath. And another.

Keep it together, she told herself. It wasn't the end of the world. Yet. She still had a chance of making partner. She still—

Oh, *hell*. Before she could stop it, tears of frustration welled up in her eyes. She looked up at the ceiling. No, no, no, she would *not* do this. Not here, not now.

It was at that moment that Payton heard Agnes call out in greeting to someone else. She peered through the bookshelves and saw—shit!—J.D. standing at the entrance of the library. Payton watched as he headed over to Agnes's desk, saying something she couldn't hear.

Payton glanced around, hoping to spot another exit out of the stacks. She *really* couldn't deal with J.D. right then. Unfortunately, there was no other way out. Peering through the books, she saw Agnes point to the Archives section where she was hiding. J.D. nodded, then began walking straight toward her.

Payton quickly brushed away the tears from her eyes, praying that her mascara wasn't smudged. She needed a cover—fast. She saw a nearby step stool and climbed up. She grabbed the first book she saw off the shelf and cracked it open just as J.D. rounded the corner.

"Payton," he said.

She feigned disinterest, peering up from her book. "Doing a little research, J.D.?"

"Of course not," he said. "And neither are you. I followed you here." He glanced around. "Strange—I thought this was an accounting floor."

Payton climbed down from the step stool, still striving for nonchalance. "You followed me here? Any particular reason?"

J.D. seemed embarrassed by the question. "I saw you run out of your office. After our meeting with Ben, I thought that maybe you, well . . ." he trailed off awkwardly.

Great, Payton realized. Exactly what she needed—J.D.'s pity. She suddenly felt tears threatening once again.

"I'm fine," Payton said, turning her back to him. "Really."

She felt J.D.'s hand on her shoulder. "Don't do this, Payton," he said in a soft voice.

It was too much, hearing J.D. speak like that. She needed to make him stop. She forced herself to look indifferent as she turned around. "What do you want, J.D.? Because I was thinking, for once, that maybe you could just *back off.*"

J.D.'s face hardened at her words, which unfortunately had come out sounding harsher than she'd meant them to.

He pulled back and folded his arms over his chest. "Well, somebody sure seems a little tense. You wouldn't be worried about this decision, would you?"

Payton feigned confidence. "No."

"No?"

She raised her chin stubbornly. "No."

A look of worry crossed J.D.'s face. "You know already," he stated woodenly. "You know they're going to choose you."

"I know that if the firm goes by *merit*, they'll pick me," Payton said.

J.D. narrowed the gap between them in one stride. "You really think you're that much better than me?"

Payton stood her ground. "Yes."

His eyes narrowed. "Please—if the firm picks you, we both know the reason."

Payton smirked at this. "What reason is that? My 'girls'?"

J.D. shrugged. "You said it."

"Bullshit," Payton said. "You, Ben, and pretty much every other man at this firm are all one big team—you all went to the same Ivy League schools; you're all members of the same country clubs. And tell me, J.D.—how many of Daddy's CEO friends did you promise you could bring in as clients? I bet the members of the Partnership Committee are just foaming at the mouth at the thought of the money you'll bring in with your connections. Or your father's connections, I should say."

She was being mean, really mean, and she knew it. But Payton couldn't seem to stop herself—the floodgates had opened and all the emotions of the last twenty minutes were pouring out.

She saw J.D.'s eyes flash with anger. "Oh, but what about what *you* can give them, Payton?"

"This should be good. Enlighten me."

"Diversity. If they chose you, the Partnership Committee can pat themselves on the back for hiring the right demographic."

With a loud slam, Payton threw the book she had been holding onto the shelf next to her. Dust flew everywhere, including onto the sleeve of J.D.'s jacket. "Diversity?" she repeated incredulously. "Why don't you look around this firm sometime—everyone here is just like you, J.D. White with a penis."

Ignoring this, J.D. pointed to the dust on his sleeve. "Take it easy on the suit, cupcake. This was hand-tailored in London."

"Oh—I'm sorry. I guess you'll just have to pick up another one the next time you visit Her Majesty for tea. Isn't she another friend of the family?" Angrily, Payton shoved J.D. out of her way and stormed through the stacks.

J.D. followed after her. "Are you saying I don't deserve this?" he demanded. "I've billed over twenty-nine hundred hours for the past eight years!"

Payton whipped around. "So have I! And the only difference between you and me is that statistics say you're more likely to keep it up. The firm doesn't worry that one day you'll decide you want to leave at five to kiss your kids good night."

J.D. stepped closer to her. Then closer again, literally trapping her against the bookshelves.

"Spare me the feminist rant, Payton. It's getting a little tired. I've had to work my *ass* off to get where I am, while you had your ticket written from the minute you stepped into this firm."

Payton felt her face flush with anger. "Really? Well, you know what *I* think, J.D.?" She jabbed his chest with one of her fingers. "I think that you are an uptight, pony-owning, trickle-down-economics-loving, Scotch-on-the-rocks-drinking, my-wife-better-take-my-last-name *sexist jerk!*"

J.D. grabbed her hand and pulled it away. "Well, at least I'm not a stubborn, button-pushing, Prius-driving, chip-on-your-shoulder-holding, 'stay-at-home-mom'-is-the-eighth-dirty-word-thinking *feminazi*!"

He had her pressed against the bookshelves, his body against hers, her hand pinned to her side as he glared down at her. She glared up at him right back.

He was furious. So was she.

Neither of them moved. And in that moment, the strangest thought popped into Payton's head.

She had the feeling that J.D. was going to kiss her.

And—even stranger—she had a feeling that she just might let him.

J.D. must have read the look on her face. Payton saw his eyes flash—but not with anger this time—and she felt his hand suddenly reach for the nape of her neck, the strength of his arms pulling her in, his head bending down to hers, and even as she cursed him for thinking she would ever, ever allow it, she closed her eyes and parted her lips and—

"Excuse me."

The shock of the voice hit Payton like a cold bucket of ice.

She blinked as if coming out of a fog, and both she and J.D. turned their heads to see Agnes standing at the end of the aisle, waving at them. Payton could only imagine how it looked, the two of them wild-eyed and pressed up against each other.

But the amiable librarian was either extremely discreet or more likely—given the Coke-bottle-sized glasses perched high atop her nose—extremely blind. She smiled at them as they stood there, frozen.

"I just wanted to remind you that we close in ten minutes," she said pleasantly.

"Thank you, Agnes," Payton said, her breath ragged. Perhaps if they didn't move, the octogenarian couldn't see them. Like T. rex.

"We'll be just a moment longer," J.D. said. His voice sounded husky. Sexy.

Payton had no idea why she just thought that.

Agnes nodded, then left. As soon as she was out of sight, Payton angrily shoved J.D. off her.

"Stay away from me, Jameson," she said, her voice still a little shaky. She cleared her throat and hoped she wasn't blushing.

J.D. straightened up and adjusted his suit indifferently. "Not a problem. In fact, it's my pleasure." With a nod, he stepped out of her way.

Payton moved past him, eyes facing forward. But when she got to the end of the aisle, she couldn't help it—she turned and looked back.

"Oh, and by the way"—she flung her hair back confidently—"that partnership spot is *mine*."

J.D. looked her over. "Don't bet your Prius on that." With a haughty wink, he brushed past her and coolly walked out of the library.

TEMPORARY INSANITY.

That was her defense.

The stress of finding out she might not make partner had momentarily made her lose it, all the marbles, gone.

Not to mention the high-altitude sickness. Her body simply wasn't used to the lower oxygen levels of the fifty-fifth floor.

But all that had now passed.

Payton thankfully was once again clearheaded and focused. She had come this far, she would not lose now, she would not let these last eight years all have been for nothing. In other words—

This was war.

She called Laney during the cab ride home from work. She told her best friend everything. Everything about her meeting with Ben that is, about the Partnership Committee's decision to name only one litigation partner. She did not, however, see any point in discussing her argument with J.D. Whatever that little blowout was, it was over. She had a career, one potentially in jeopardy, to focus on.

At the end of the conversation, Payton checked her voice mail and discovered—to her pleasant surprise—that she had a message from the Perfect Chase, asking to meet her for a drink later that week.

Payton decided to meet him. She needed the distraction.

By the time she arrived home, she had managed to convince herself that the only thing she needed distracting *from* was work.

J.D. WAS THE last person to leave the office that night.

About twenty minutes ago, he had glanced up from his computer and seen Payton packing up her briefcase for the evening. She hadn't once looked in the direction of his office as she left.

Good, J.D. thought. He preferred it when they weren't talking. Things were much simpler when they weren't talking.

He still didn't understand why he had followed Payton to the library in the first place. Clearly, that had been a mistake.

Stay away from me, Jameson.

As if he ever had any intention otherwise. Sure, their argument in the library had gotten a little out of hand. And there was that moment when . . . well, that was *nothing*. And even more important, in light of her reaction, he most definitely would not be interested in ever trying *nothing* again. He—J. D. Jameson—could easily find more amiable trysts to divert his attention than that angry shrew of a woman.

Oh, and by the way . . . that partnership spot is mine.

Hmm . . . let's think about that. He was one of the top lawyers in the city, she had said so herself. Should he be scared? Should he throw in the towel, toss eight years of hard work down the drain and cede the partnership all because of some woman in a fitted skirt and high heels?

Not bloody likely.

Nine

PAYTON ARRIVED AT the restaurant ten minutes late.

She blamed this primarily on Laney, who had been micromanaging the date ever since Payton had spoken to the Perfect Chase and set it up two days ago. Thankfully, Laney had approved of her choice in locale, SushiSamba Rio, which was upscale ("no feminist BS, Payton—let him pay") although not overtly flashy ("but don't order anything over twenty-five dollars; you don't want to look like a materialist hussy") and had a separate lounge and dining area. This way, Payton figured, she and Chase would start with drinks and, if things went well, could stay for dinner.

Now anyone who has ever been on a blind date is well familiar with "The Moment"—that moment where you first walk into the bar or restaurant or coffee shop and scan the crowd and suddenly your heart stops and you say to yourself: *oh, please—let it be him.*

And then you immediately think, wait—it can't be *him,*

why would anyone who looks like *him* be on a blind date? But you allow yourself to hope anyway, until—inevitably— some equally gorgeous woman comes back from the rest-room and sits down at his table, and you realize that—lucky you—*your* date is the schmoe at the bar with the lame blue button-down shirt and high-waisted khaki pants who obviously just finished his shift at Blockbuster.

Which explains why, when Payton first walked into the restaurant that evening, she immediately noticed the guy at the bar in the dark shirt and jeans, but then just as quickly turned her attention elsewhere, having written him off as far too delicious.

Seeing no other likely prospects, Payton figured the Perfect Chase was at the very least not so perfect by running even later than she, so she took a seat at the bar to wait. She hadn't even had the chance to order before she felt someone tap her on the shoulder from behind. Payton turned around and had to stifle her gasp.

Sweet Jesus.

It was The Delicious in the dark shirt and jeans.

"Payton, right?" The Delicious asked with a friendly smile. "Laney asked Nate to call and tell me what you were wearing. That girl thinks of everything, doesn't she?"

Wow.

Laney—that sneaky little Republican—had knocked it out of the ballpark with this one.

Payton grinned. "You must be Chase." As she extended her hand in introduction, she took the opportunity to give him a more thorough once-over.

He had dark wavy hair and warm brown eyes. Very Patrick Dempsey/McDreamy-esque. Good build, not terribly tall, maybe only five-ten-ish, but since Payton measured in at exactly five-three and one-third inch, she could work with this.

Chase took her hand. His grip was firm. "It's a pleasure, Payton," he said, still with an utterly genuine, easy smile.

Uh-oh. Payton's bullshit radar went on high alert. He was *too* nice. She eyed him cautiously as he took a seat next to her at the bar.

But as they talked and ordered drinks, Payton began to have a sneaking suspicion that Chase's nice-guy routine wasn't a routine at all. He seemed genuinely friendly and—even more shocking for a blind date—completely normal.

"So, Laney tells me you're a lawyer as well," Chase said as the bartender set their drinks down in front of them, a French martini for her, a Tom Collins for him. Payton made a mental note to ask what was in his drink they next time they ordered. (Oh, yes—she had already decided there would be a second round.)

Payton nodded. "I do labor and employment litigation." She told him a little about her practice, then asked about his.

"I just moved here to be the new general counsel for the Chicago Legal Clinic," Chase said. "Perhaps you've heard of us? We're a private not-for-profit firm that provides legal services to individuals who meet the federal poverty guidelines."

Payton was impressed. How altruistic of him. Her mother would love this guy. "General counsel? Laney hadn't mentioned that."

Chase grinned. "It sounds like a much more important position than it really is."

In her profession, it was rare for Payton to meet someone actually *disinclined* to brag. And as their conversation continued, she was pleasantly surprised to discover that Chase seemed just as modest about his other accomplishments. When they got around to the subject of law school (a subject two lawyers will always get around to), she liked that he referred to his education as "going to school in Boston" rather than identifying Harvard by name. And when she asked what he had done prior to coming to Chicago to work for the Legal Clinic, she'd nearly had to pry it out of him that he had been the assistant chief of staff for a certain senator who had run for president in the last election. He didn't like to name-drop, he told her, mildly embarrassed.

After a while, they moved to a private table in the back of the bar for their second round of drinks. (A Tom Collins, Payton had since learned, consisted of gin, lemon juice, soda, sugar, and—hmm—a maraschino cherry.)

As Chase finished telling a story about the coed softball league he and Laney's husband played in, Payton cocked her head curiously. "I hope you don't take this the wrong way, but you really don't seem like the typical Harvard Law type."

Chase laughed good-naturedly. "That's what I said myself, every day, right up until I mailed in my acceptance." He leaned in toward her, his brown eyes dancing with amusement. "Laney warned me about this, Payton, and I just have to say for the record that we're not all total assholes, us Ivy Leaguers. Some of us actually go there for the education—not just to be able to brag that we went to Harvard."

Payton couldn't help but smile. Point taken. "Now what am I supposed to say to that? I hate it when you Harvard boys are right."

"Then I promise to screw up plenty on our second date—*if* there is a second date," Chase added with a wink.

It was the wink that made Payton think of J.D.

More specifically, of her and J.D. in the library. The haughty way he'd told her not to count on making partner. How angry he'd been when they'd argued. The way he'd furiously backed her against the bookshelves. And the way he'd looked at her right before she'd—ahem—been stricken with the high-altitude sickness.

Payton pushed the memory from her mind. She was on a *date*. It was bad enough she had to deal with J.D. at work—there was no way she was going to let him intrude on her personal time, too.

So Payton rested her chin in her hand and looked at the handsome man sitting across the table from her with a blatant come-hither smile.

"*If* there is a second date?" she asked coyly.

Over the light of the candle that flickered in the center of their table, Chase returned the smile.

"*When* there is a second date."

"SO BASICALLY, YOU acted like a total trollop."

"Laney!"

"A man isn't going to buy the cow, Payton, if he can get the milk for free."

"We didn't even kiss!" Payton protested, not bothering to hide her laugh. The things that came out of her friend's mouth sometimes.

They were talking at work, in Payton's office. She had gotten home too late to call Laney the night before, having done three rounds of drinks with the Perfect Chase. The two of them had talked so much they hadn't noticed when the restaurant's kitchen closed. Hence, Payton hadn't had anything to eat with her three rounds. Hence, the slight headache and nauseous feeling she'd been battling since waking up. She was quickly remembering why she didn't like going out on weeknights, especially when she had to be in the office by 7:30 a.m.

"Wait, you didn't kiss him?" Laney's tone suddenly changed and she eyed Payton suspiciously. "What's wrong? Don't you like him?"

Payton dug through the stack of jury instructions on her desk. "Oh—look who wants to gossip now."

"Tell me, Payton," Laney demanded. "Nate tells me Chase is a really great guy. I've already had visions of the seven of us barbecuing on Sundays."

"The seven of us?"

"There are the children, of course."

Payton nodded. "I see. And . . . seven?"

"Nate and I have twins—a boy and a girl."

"Of course you do."

Laney fidgeted in her chair impatiently. "So, come on then—did you like him?"

"Of course I liked him," Payton said. "I mean, what's not to like? He's good-looking and nice and successful . . ."

"But?"

"Well, he ordered a drink with a cherry."

Laney sighed. "I see. Okay, whatever. I tried."

"What does that mean?" Payton asked, going on the defensive.

"Clearly, you're trying to find something wrong with him," Laney said. "His beverage selection? Come on, that's ridiculous."

Payton took issue with this. "Wait a second—why would I try to find something wrong with Chase?"

"Good question. You tell me."

"There's nothing to tell. As we already established from the 'trollop' comment, he and I are going on a second date."

"I'm just putting it out there that you really might want to give this guy a chance," Laney lectured.

"I told you, I like him!"

"Good."

"We have a lot in common—we talked for hours."

"Glad to hear it." Laney said nothing further; she just stared at Payton with the faint trace of a smile.

"You are just all over me with this," Payton said, semi-annoyed.

"I know. I'm really bored with work these days."

"I'd be happy to assign you a few of my cases, if you need things to keep you busy," Payton grumbled.

"As if any lawyer could ever handle your cases as skill-fully as you," Laney declined smoothly.

Payton sniffed at this, partially mollified. How true.

"Let's hope the Partnership Committee agrees with you on that," she said.

"Any further word on that front?" Laney asked.

Payton shook her head. "No. Just that Ben said that J.D. and I should give it all we've got these next few weeks." She gestured to the stack of files on her desk. "For starters, I better win this trial." She sighed, resting her chin in her hands. "I can't lose this, Laney."

"You won't," Laney told her matter-of-factly. "You've never lost anything."

Payton glanced through her window to J.D.'s office across the hall. She could see him working diligently, as always.

"I know. But neither has he."

FOR THE NEXT two days, Payton had little time to worry about J.D., so engrossed was she in the final prepa-rations for her trial. She and Brandon, the junior associate working with her on the case, bunkered down in her office from dawn till dusk, running through the trial from jury selection to closing arguments. The trial was scheduled to last just under two weeks, which meant it would be essen-tially the last assignment upon which she could be judged by the Partnership Committee before they made their deci-sion. A victory would be a tremendous feather in her cap; a loss would be disastrous.

Payton knew that J.D., too, had a lot on his plate. At their monthly litigation group luncheon, she overheard him men-tion to Max, a senior partner who "just happened" to be on the Partnership Committee, that he was juggling two class certification oppositions, both of which he was confident he would successfully wrap up by the end of the month.

Standing nearby, Payton was certain J.D.'s comment was primarily for her benefit. So she turned to Helen, another senior partner who also "just happened" to be on the Partnership Committee, and said she had heard that Helen's daughter was applying for law school at the University of Illinois, Payton's alma mater.

"It's a wonderful school, and such a good bargain with in-state tuition," Payton said.

Helen nodded, agreeing with this. "I'm just keeping my fingers crossed that she gets in. She didn't do quite as well on the LSAT as she had hoped."

"I'd be happy to write your daughter a recommendation," Payton offered.

Out of nowhere, Laney was suddenly at Payton's side.

"You definitely should take her up on that, Helen—they *love* Payton at that school. She's too modest to tell you this, but did you know that Payton graduated first in her class *and* set a new record for the most perfect scores earned on final exams by any one student?"

Payton could've kissed Laney right there.

"Wow," said Helen. She turned to Payton. "I *am* impressed. Maybe we could have lunch sometime this week, Payton? We could talk about that recommendation for my daughter. And who knows? Perhaps someday soon I'll be able to return the favor . . ." She winked.

A few moments later, after Helen walked away, J.D. sauntered over to Payton and Laney. He clapped sarcastically.

"Well played, ladies." J.D. looked Payton over. "But I wouldn't book that flight to Bora-Bora yet, Kendall. It's going to take a lot more than the vote of the one female on the Partnership Committee to win this." He smiled. "I had already conceded that one to you, anyway."

With that, he turned and confidently strolled out of the conference room. Payton and Laney watched him go.

Laney shook her head. "Unbelievable."

Payton gestured. "See—I *told* you."

"That man has such a great butt."

"Laney!"

"What? I'm conservative, Payton, not blind."

SOMEWHERE AROUND FIVE, the evening before her trial began, Payton reached her saturation point. She had prepared all her direct and cross-examinations, had practiced her opening statement, reviewed and taken notes on every witness's deposition transcript, and had thoroughly prepared her client's own witnesses for their testimonies. Now there was nothing left for her to do except to accept the fact that there was nothing left for her to do. Not an easy task, considering what she felt was riding on the outcome of this trial.

She needed a distraction. Left to her own devices, she would either drive herself crazy, worrying over insignificant minutiae, or she would start calling Brandon with questions, thus driving *him* crazy.

Laney was busy, Payton knew. Tonight, unbeknownst to Nate, her friend had prepared a PowerPoint presentation for her husband—complete with estimated income graphs, cost of living analyses, and a fertility projection—logically detailing all the reasons why they needed to start trying to have a baby *now*. And as for her other friends, Payton knew better than to call them—nothing was more annoying to a nonlawyer than to be stuck with one the night before a trial. Every sentence tended to start with, "So, if you were a juror on this case, what would you think if . . . ?"

There was, however, somebody who would be perfect company for the evening. She picked up the phone on her desk.

"Hi," she said when he answered. "I know it's short notice, but I thought I'd see if you happened to be free for dinner tonight."

AN HOUR LATER, Payton waited in the lounge at DeLaCosta restaurant. She'd managed to score a bar table along the window with a view overlooking the canal.

She smiled as the Perfect Chase walked in, looking very dashing in his light summer sweater and dark brown pants.

He returned the smile as he took the seat across from her. "Sorry—my cab got stuck in traffic."

The waitress approached to take his drink order.

"A Tom Collins," Chase told her. "But, please—make sure there is absolutely *no* cherry in it."

Payton nearly died of embarrassment right there. Oh, my god, she was going to kill Laney.

Chase laughed at the sheepish look on Payton's face. "It's okay, Payton. I don't get offended easily." He reached across the table and took her hand in his, lightly stroking his thumb across her fingers. "I'm just glad you called."

Payton relaxed. It was pretty much impossible *not* to like Chase. He was so low maintenance, being with him felt . . . comfortable.

"I'm glad you could make it," she told him. After all, comfortable was good.

Wasn't it?

The waitress brought Chase his cherry-less drink and asked the two of them if they'd like to order appetizers.

Payton asked for a moment. She skimmed the menu, quickly searching for things without meat. She never looked forward to this part of her first dinner date with a guy; she hated coming off as fussy.

She saw Chase peeking over at her, seemingly a bit self-conscious himself. "In light of the whole cherry debacle, I almost hate to say this, but I should let you know that I'm a vegetarian."

Payton set her menu down on the table in disbelief. "So am I!" She laughed. Funny coincidence.

"How long for you?" Chase asked.

"Since birth. My mother's doing."

"Fish?"

"Nope. 'Nothing with a face,' as my mom used to say."

"Nothing with a face," Chase repeated. "I like that."

After they decided what meatless appetizers to try, Chase signaled the waitress and placed their order. As Payton watched him, she couldn't help but think: if she had created him à la *Weird Science* at build-a-date.com, had him packaged, wrapped up in a red bow, and shipped right to her front door, she couldn't have found a guy seemingly more perfect for her than Chase Bellamy.

So why was there something nagging at her?

She was just out of sorts, she assured herself. She was feeling anxious and under pressure with the looming partnership decision. Nothing else.

She heard Chase ask her a question; he wanted to know about her trial. He said he'd love to drop by the courthouse one day to watch her.

Payton brushed aside her misgivings.

After all, it would be a silly woman indeed who disliked a man simply because he liked her.

Ten

IT ALL STARTED innocently enough.

Payton was in the second day of her trial, and things were progressing well. Her client, a Fortune 500 wireless carrier, had been sued for sexual harassment stemming from an incident that occurred at one of its sales offices. According to the plaintiff, a female sales representative, she had accepted a ride home from her male manager after the company's annual boat cruise and after pulling into her driveway, the manager had—one might perhaps say—sexually propositioned her.

Or—one might perhaps also say—he unzipped his fly and asked whether she wanted to "test-drive his love stick."

Whether or not the incident had occurred was not in dispute, as the plaintiff had been thoughtful enough to snap a photo of said love stick with her cell phone, which had now come to be known as "Exhibit A" of the trial.

"Fire the guy," Payton had advised her client in no uncertain terms when the incident had first come to light a little over a year ago. "And tell him to get a better line. That's just embarrassing."

Firing the manager, however, had not been enough to satisfy the plaintiff, who had slapped the company with a two-million-dollar lawsuit. Because no one disputed the incident had occurred, Payton's job at trial was to establish that the company had efficiently and appropriately responded to the incident, thus absolving it of any liability under the law.

Step one of her defense strategy started on the first day of trial, with jury selection. In light of the infamous Exhibit A (which the plaintiff's attorneys had blown up to ridiculously gargantuan proportions and undoubtedly planned to display throughout the entire course of the trial), Payton had avoided selecting any juror she felt had what one might call "delicate sensibilities." Someone who perhaps tended toward what one might describe as a "conservatively moralistic" viewpoint; one who could possibly be outraged by the conduct of the defendant's ex-employee and want to ease that outrage in the form of dollars thrown in the direction of the plaintiff.

In other words, no Laneys.

Nobody who would take one look at a six-foot color photo of a half-mast penis popping out of a Dockers button-fly (hello!) and promptly ask how many zeros are in a gazillion.

From there, step two of Payton's defense strategy was to set the right tone for the trial in her opening statement: sympathetic, but firm. Understanding and in complete agreement that managerial love sticks should be kept firmly tucked behind closed zippers, but rational and logical in guiding the jury to understand that her client, the employer, was not financially liable to the tune of two million dollars for the actions of one rogue *ex*-employee.

Payton hoped she had accomplished that task this morning. J.D. had been right when he'd told Jasper that she had

quite a bit of trial experience under her belt, and with that
she liked to think she was fairly skilled at reading jurors'
body language. She had started her opening statement by
gesturing to Exhibit A, the six-foot half-mast penis photo,
that plaintiff's counsel had displayed front and center during his opening statement.

"Wow," Payton had said, eyeing the photo as she turned
to the jury to begin. "If the courthouse coffee wasn't enough
to wake you up, seeing that at nine a.m. sure will."

The jury had laughed.

Now, any day that a person delivers an opening statement while standing in front of a six-foot billboard of
semierect male genitalia is clearly a bit of an unusual day.
But that was just the tip of the iceberg of events that spi-
raled out of control over the next forty-eight hours.

Payton returned to the office during her lunch break;
she and Brandon planned to use the time to review the
cross-examinations of the plaintiff's witnesses that would
begin that afternoon. When she got to the office, however,
she found Irma in a frantic state, digging through the files
on Payton's desk.

"Thank god you're here," Irma said as soon as she saw
Payton walk through the door. "Marie called—she's been
looking everywhere for the receipt for your dinner at
Japonais with the Gibson's reps. She needs to submit it before the close of the billing cycle—Accounts Payable won't
process any of the expenditures for your pitch until they
have all the receipts in hand."

Payton frowned. "J.D. paid for the dinner, not me. He
should have the receipt."

Irma looked at her helplessly. "I know, and I told that to
his secretary, but she couldn't find it in his office."

"So tell her to simply ask J.D. where it is."

"He's in a conference room upstairs, preparing for a
court hearing he has this afternoon. He told Kathy he'd
look for the receipt later." Irma sighed apologetically. "I'm

sorry, Payton, I know you're busy, too—I don't mean to bother you with this. It's just that Ben is on Marie's back about this, which means that she's on mine."

Payton checked her watch. She wanted Irma to type up the trial notes Brandon had taken that morning before she headed back to court at one thirty. The faster she could resolve this business over the receipt, the better.

She handed Irma the notes. "Here—take these and start typing them up. I'll look in J.D.'s office and see if I can find the receipt."

Irma nodded and hurried off. Payton headed across the hall and let herself into J.D.'s office.

How very unlike J.D., she thought, to overlook something as basic as submitting a receipt. If anything, it was an indication of the pressure he'd been under since Ben had dropped his bombshell that only one of them would make partner.

Good. She was glad to see she wasn't the only one who was on edge these days.

Payton looked first on top of the credenza that ran along the wall of J.D.'s office, searching for the receipt or any sort of file related to the Gibson's matter. Finding nothing there, she moved on to his desk.

At first she saw nothing. Then—almost having overlooked it—she saw the edge of a smallish piece of paper peeking out from under the desk calendar that sat on top of J.D.'s desk. Wondering if that could be it, Payton hastily reached over to lift up the calendar and—

Shit!—somehow managed to knock over a Starbucks cup perched near the edge of J.D.'s desk. Coffee poured out the lid. Payton immediately reacted, she grabbed the cup, but not fast enough as coffee spilled over the edge of J.D.'s desk and onto his chair—

And right onto his suit jacket, which he presumably had nicely set out over the arm of the chair to prevent wrinkles.

Payton swore under her breath as she scrambled; she looked around for a napkin, Kleenex, anything to wipe up the coffee, which was quickly setting into J.D.'s suit. Not seeing anything, she grabbed the jacket—maybe she could run it under cold water or something—in doing so she happened to notice the label, it had been tailor-made in London. She smirked; *of course* it had been. She remembered back to their fight in the library and the smug way J.D. had said—

"What the hell are you doing?"

Payton froze at the sound of his voice.

She immediately knew how it must've looked, her holding a coffee cup in one hand, his stained suit in the other. And a smirk on her face.

Payton looked and saw J.D. standing in the doorway with a very pissed-off expression. He held his briefcase, as if he was prepared to leave for court, and of course he was impeccably dressed in a tailored shirt and pants that fit him perfectly.

She had no idea why she just noticed that.

Moving on.

She turned to J.D. to explain. "I was looking for the receipt for the Gibson's dinner."

J.D. ignored her. He pointed. "Is that *coffee* on my jacket?"

"Yeeee . . . s."

He folded his arms across his chest. "Oh, I see. Maybe you thought I stashed the Gibson's receipt in a Starbucks cup?"

Payton went for a joke. "It's not my way of filing things, but . . ." she trailed off.

He was not amused.

J.D. took her in with a mocking tilt of his head. "That's awfully passive-aggressive for you, isn't it?"

Payton stared at him. Of course he thought she did this on purpose.

Now *she* folded her arms across *her* chest. "You've got to be kidding." She had been about to apologize, but now, well . . . screw him. She didn't feel like it anymore.

"So, what is this, your feeble attempt at sabotage?" J.D. asked scornfully. "Let me guess—you heard I'm in court for a hearing this afternoon, so you thought you'd make me look like a jackass."

"You don't need any help from me there."

J.D.'s eyes narrowed angrily.

"And I hardly need to resort to sabotage to be the one that the firm makes partner," Payton added.

"Actually, I think you must be *really* worried, if you're willing to stoop to this level." J.D. held up a finger, victorious. "But luckily, *I* keep a spare suit in my office."

J.D. shut his door, gesturing to a garment bag that hung on the back of it. He unzipped the bag and proudly pulled out a second suit, one that was just as expensive-looking. He draped the suit over one of the chairs in front of his desk and stared at Payton smugly. Ta-da.

She rolled her eyes at him. "You know, I was going to explain, but now it's not even worth it." She brushed by J.D. to leave his office, momentarily forgetting she still held both his jacket and the coffee cup.

"An easy cop-out."

Payton stopped at his words.

Cop-out?

Cop-out?

Payton Kendall did not *cop out*.

She turned around to face him.

With a cocky grin, J.D. took a seat at his desk. He leaned back, folding his hands behind his head. "Something you'd like to say before leaving, Payton?"

He was baiting her, she knew it. She considered letting it go. She could turn around and walk out of his office without another word. In two weeks, one way or the other, she would never have to deal with him again.

J.D. mistook Payton's pause for hesitation.

"In that case," he said, nodding at the suit jacket she still held, "I'll expect you to get that dry-cleaned at a decent place. Just make sure you have it back to me before they boot your ass out of here." Dismissing her, he turned back to his work.

Payton sighed. Oh, well. She had tried.

"No problem, J.D.," she said good-humoredly. "And while I'm at it, how about your second spare suit? Does that need to be dry-cleaned, too?"

J.D. looked up from his computer, confused. "I don't have a second spare suit."

"Oh. That's a shame." And with that, Payton tore the lid off the Starbucks cup and promptly dumped the remaining coffee all over the suit he had so neatly laid out over the chair.

J.D.'s mouth dropped open. He slowly peered up at her. "Oh. No. You. Didn't."

Payton looked down at the suit. Holy shit, she *had*, she really had.

She covered her mouth to mask her own look of shock. Whoops. But it was too late to turn back now.

"You can bill me for the dry cleaning, J.D. And, um, for the cup of coffee, too." With that, she delicately set the now-empty coffee cup on his desk.

Then did a quick about-face à la Road Runner and got the hell outta there.

Payton hurried across the hallway, flying by J.D.'s secretary's desk, then Irma's. She had just reached the doorway to her office when she heard J.D. shout her name.

"Payton!"

Stopping in her doorway, she turned around.

J.D. stood in his doorway with what had to be just about the most furious look she had ever seen on any human being's face.

They faced off across the hall, like two Old West gunslingers readying for a draw. Payton could practically see the tumbleweeds blowing by.

With a sly look, she glanced over at Irma and Kathy, who sat at their desks curiously watching her and J.D. Then she turned back to him with her eyebrow raised.

"Yes, J.D.?" she drawled coyly. All these years they had fought in secret . . . she knew he wasn't going to blow their cover now.

J.D. looked around, aware that his shout had garnered much interest from others around the office. He paused, then gave Payton a curt nod.

"I just wanted to wish you good luck in court this afternoon."

Payton smiled from the sanctity of her office. "Thanks, J.D., that's so sweet. And good luck to you as well." With an exaggerated nod of her own, a slight curtsy, she turned and headed into her office.

Payton shut the door behind her. She leaned against it, the smile remaining on her face. In some senses, she thought, it really was a shame J.D. had to go.

She would almost miss this stuff.

WITH EACH STRIDE, every step he took as he walked the three blocks to the courthouse, J.D. grew more and more furious.

He had been cutting it close as it was; he'd run later than he had meant to, going through his oral argument one last time in the conference room, wanting it to be perfect.

And now, perfect was *definitely* out of the question.

He could throttle her.

Maybe, he told himself, the stain wasn't as bad as it had been the last time he looked. Maybe some of the coffee had evaporated on the walk to the courthouse. He glanced down hopefully.

Fuck—it looked even worse than he remembered.

Wearing his spare suit had been out of the question, Payton had effectively seen to that by pouring more than half of a venti coffee all over it. Seeing how he didn't have time to go home and change, or even buy another suit, he was therefore stuck wearing the one she'd "accidentally" first spilled coffee on—a conservative dark gray suit that unfortunately wasn't nearly dark enough.

He looked like an idiot.

He could only hope that the lighting in the courtroom would be dim, and that the judge, who sat fifteen feet away from the podium he'd be arguing at, would somehow not notice the grapefruit-sized mocha splotch plastered across the left side of his chest.

J.D. arrived at the Dirksen Federal Building and hurried inside. He had to take his coat off to get through security, and was momentarily tempted to leave it off for his oral argument, but decided in the end that appearing jacketless in court was not only disrespectful, but also far more likely to attract negative attention from the judge.

The elevator was packed during J.D.'s ride up to the twenty-third floor. He waited until the last minute to slip his jacket back on, doing so right before he walked into the courtroom. He immediately headed to the front and took a seat in the galley while he waited for his case to be called.

J.D. had never before felt self-conscious about his appearance in court (or ever really, come to think of it) and he hated feeling that way now. He had an image to uphold, after all: he was a corporate defense attorney—he got paid hundreds of thousands of dollars to defend multimillion-dollar corporations. His clients expected, and paid for, perfection. They did not pay to have their uber-important opposition to class certification motions argued by some jackass who looked like he'd spilled his Dunkin' Donuts Coffee Coolatta all over himself while driving in from the suburbs in his Ford Taurus.

J.D. shuddered at the mere image.

His case was third on the docket. When the clerk called the case, he stood up, straightened his tie, and forgot about everything else. He had a job to do.

He got up to the podium and nodded to his opposing counsel, who approached from the other side of the courtroom. If the plaintiffs' attorney noticed the stain on his jacket, he didn't acknowledge it, and J.D. was immediately grateful for the courtroom's softer lighting.

The plaintiffs' attorney argued first. J.D. listened attentively, watching carefully for the points where the judge interrupted and making mental notes to address those issues. When the plaintiffs' ten minutes were over, J.D. stepped front and center at the podium. Opposition to class certification motions were of crucial importance in the cases J.D. handled and luckily, they were his forte.

J.D. began.

"Your Honor, today is the day the Court should put an end to Mr. DeVore's six-year class action charade. By asserting a breach of contract counterclaim and seeking nationwide class certification, Mr. DeVore has literally made a federal case out of what should have been a simple foreclosure proceeding. Whatever this Court makes of the mortgage contract and the provisions Mr. DeVore challenges, one thing is certain, no class can be certified in this case because Mr. DeVore is not an adequate class representative. He perjured himself in his deposition . . ."

It was at about this point that J.D. noticed the judge leaning forward in his chair. He peered down curiously from the bench, trying to get a better look at something.

The judge suddenly held up a hand to stop him. "Counselor," he asked J.D. with a quizzical brow, "did you get *shot* on the way over here?"

The judge leaned down farther from the bench. He squinted at J.D.'s chest, trying to get a better look at the stain.

"What *is* that?"

J.D. could only stand there at the podium, while the courtroom deputy, the clerk, the plaintiffs' lawyer, and now pretty much everyone else in the whole damn courtroom fixated on the softball-sized mark on his suit.

So much for scraping by unnoticed.

AND THEN IT got worse.

Of course, John Grevy, a partner in the litigation group at J.D.'s firm, would happen to have a motion before the same judge that afternoon.

"That's why we tell associates to keep a spare suit in their offices," he hissed disapprovingly as J.D. passed him on his way out of the courtroom.

Really, John? he wished he could say. *No shit.*

And then still, it got worse.

Once outside the courtroom door, J.D. set his briefcase down, hurrying to get the splotch jacket off as quickly as possible. He heard a familiar voice behind him.

"Are you trying to embarrass me, or just yourself?"

J.D. closed his eyes. Brilliant. Exactly what he needed right then.

He turned around, taking in the grave-faced man standing before him.

"Hello, Dad. Imagine running into you here," he said, although it actually wasn't that much of a surprise. As a judge on the Seventh Circuit Court of Appeals, his father's chambers were in this very building.

The esteemed Honorable Preston D. Jameson looked upon J.D. with much disappointment. It was a look J.D. knew well.

"Margie saw your name on this morning's docket," his father said, referring to his secretary. "She watches out for your cases. Since your mother and I haven't seen you in a while, I thought I'd stop by and watch your oral argument."

Preston took a step closer, his gaze fixated on his son's suit coat. J.D. braced himself for the inevitable.

"You look ridiculous," his father told him. "You really should keep a spare suit in your office."

"Thanks for the tip, Your Honor," J.D. said sarcastically. He grabbed his briefcase and stepped into the elevator that had just opened up.

"Tell Mom I said hello," he said tersely as the elevator doors closed shut.

Inside, J.D. stared ahead as the elevator descended. He had only one thought on his mind.

Revenge.

It would soon be his.

Eleven

HIS CHANCE CAME a few hours later.

J.D. sat in his office that evening, lying in wait for just the right moment. It came when Laney dropped by to pick up Payton for their yoga class.

He sat at his desk, pretending to work, stealing glances across the hall. For a moment, he thought he might have to abort his mission, as Laney apparently had a hard time getting Payton to leave.

"You know you're prepared," he overheard Laney tell her. "Come on, the class will help you relax."

J.D. was familiar with their routine; she and Laney went to this class every week—not that he paid any attention to Payton's whereabouts or anything—and tonight was no exception. She changed into her little downward-facing-some-other-hippie-crap yoga outfit, leaving her work clothes behind in her office.

J.D. watched as she and Laney left. For the briefest second, he thought he saw Payton glance over in the direction of his office, but he was probably just being paranoid.

When they were gone, he waited, then waited a few moments more just to be safe. He had about an hour to accomplish his task, which was fine. He would need only a few minutes.

J.D. stealthily crept across the hall. He was prepared, carrying an accordion folder in his hand—should his mission be compromised and he became in quick need of a cover story, he could always say he was in her office to drop off a file. Really though, he was being overcautious: it was already mid-evening and the vast majority of the office had gone home. He could go about his business deliciously unobserved.

Restraining the urge to let out an evil laugh, J.D. checked, saw he was in the clear, opened the door to Payton's office, and let himself in. A quick look around and he spotted what he was looking for on the floor in the corner of her office.

Her shoes.

His motive was simple: if she wanted to get down and dirty in this race for the partnership spot, so be it. She made him look like an ass in court, so now . . . well, payback was a bitch.

J.D. grabbed one of her shoes, a three-inch, skinny-heel black sling-back number à la one Mr. James Choo. And she had the nerve to call *him* a clothing snob. The skinny heel would most certainly prove to be to her detriment tonight, even if it did make her legs look amazingly fantastic.

He had no idea why he just thought that.

Realizing he was in danger of losing his focus, he stuffed the shoe in the accordion folder and hurried out of Payton's office to the supply room.

THE PAPER CUTTER did an amazing job.

Really, that blade just sliced right through, mid-heel, without leaving a mark.

A little invisible glue—just a light coat—to paste the heel temporarily back together and—presto.

Revenge was sweet indeed.

PAYTON FELT HORRIBLE.

The high from her victory that afternoon had lasted about twenty minutes before the guilt had set in.

Yes, J.D. was unbelievably, frustratingly arrogant and smug. He deliberately had been trying to push her buttons and she doubted she would have too many problems convincing a jury of her peers that he deserved it. But still.

She felt horrible.

Cycling through the events of the day, she now wondered whether she should've been searching through his office in the first place. She didn't know why she had felt comfortable taking such liberties, given that he was her sworn enemy and all.

And then there was the small matter of the—ahem—coffee.

As a litigator, she knew how much appearances mattered in court. To make matters worse, she had heard through the firm grapevine (i.e., Irma) that one of the partners had seen J.D. in court and reprimanded him for the stain on his suit. For that she felt particularly bad.

So, now came the hard part.

She needed to apologize.

Before leaving with Laney for their yoga class, she had glanced in the direction of J.D.'s office and momentarily had been tempted to do it in person, but, well, this wasn't exactly easy for her.

So instead, she lay in bed that night, having decided to apologize first thing in the morning before she headed off to court. But sleep eluded her. Frustrated, Payton rolled over and grabbed the phone sitting on the nightstand next to her bed.

She looked at it for a long moment, debating. Then she dialed.

THE MESSAGE WAS the last thing J.D. heard that night.

Per usual, he checked his work voice mail one last time before going to sleep and was surprised to discover that someone had called just before midnight.

The automated voice mail indicated that the call had come from outside the office. The caller did not identify herself; she just started right in as if they were in the middle of a conversation. But J.D. recognized the voice right away.

"So I know you're probably going to think that this is a cop-out, too," Payton's message began, "but it's late and maybe you're sleeping and I suppose I could just say this in the morning, but now *I* can't sleep and I'm just lying here so I might as well get it over with, and well . . ."

There was a long pause, and for a moment J.D. thought that was how the message ended. But then she continued.

"I'm sorry about this afternoon, J.D. The first spill honestly was an accident, but the second . . . okay, that was completely uncalled for. I'm, um, happy to pay for the dry cleaning. And, well . . . I guess that's it. Although you really might want to rethink leaving your jacket on your chair. I'm just saying. Okay, then. That's what they make hangers for. Good. Fine. Good-bye."

J.D. heard the beep, signaling the end of the message, and he hung up the phone. He thought about what Payton had said—not so much her apology, which was questionably mediocre at best—but something else.

She thought about him while lying in bed.

Interesting.

LATER THAT NIGHT, having been asleep for a few
hours, J.D. shot up in bed.

He suddenly remembered—her shoe.

Oops.

Twelve

J.D. RACED INTO the office early the next morning, eager to get there before anyone else. A quick look around told him he was the first one on the floor. He headed straight for Payton's office, and a hurried search revealed what he feared would be the case.

The shoes were gone.

He hadn't received any death threats that morning, so either the heel he had tampered with had held up on her way home from work last night, or she had simply left her yoga shoes on after class.

Fine. No problem. He would wait for her to come in. Not that he had any fucking clue what he was going to say when he saw her. "Hi, Payton, thanks for the apology, that was nice. Did you see they've got muffins in the break room? Oh, by the way, I sliced off one of your heels and shoddily glued it back together hoping it would break off in court and leave you hobbling about like a drunk one-legged prostitute. Have a nice day."

Somehow, he had a feeling that might not go over so well.

When nothing else came to mind, J.D. decided he would wing it. He was good at thinking on his feet.

So he waited in his office. He looked up from his desk every time somebody walked in, expecting to see Payton at any moment.

When 8:00 a.m. rolled around, then 8:30, he grew a bit concerned. By 9:00 he was in a full panic, thinking of the worst-case scenario. What if she wore the shoes on her way into work and the heel suddenly snapped and she fell and broke her ankle? Should he retrace her route into the office? Wait—she rode the "L" into work. What if she had tripped while getting on, sprained, maimed, or separated something, and was now trapped inside one of the train cars, calling for help, riding endless circles around the Loop?

J.D. decided to check with Payton's secretary. Maybe she had heard something.

He walked up to Irma's desk, where she typed steadily away at her computer. He oh-so-casually leaned against her credenza, being careful to appear as nonchalant as possible.

"Good morning, Irma, my, that's a lovely brooch—is it a seagull? Nice weather outside, isn't it? Hey—by any chance have you heard from Payton this morning?"

Irma paused her typing for a brief moment, looked J.D. over, then resumed her work.

"It's a kangaroo, not a seagull; actually it was quite cloudy when I walked in, and yes, she left me a message, she went straight over to the courthouse this morning."

Straight to the courthouse? Son of a—

Fighting to maintain his façade of disinterest, J.D. idly fingered the leaves of the plant sitting on top of Irma's desk.

"So, by any chance did Payton say what she was wearing this morning?" He picked imaginary lint off his suit.

"More specifically, did she happen to say anything about her, um, shoes?"

Irma stopped her typing and slowly peered over at him. J.D. knew he needed to say something quick by way of explanation.

"I just want to make sure she's, you know, accessorizing appropriately."

Irma folded her hands politely.

"Mr. Jameson. Whatever this is, I don't have time for it. If you have questions about Payton's attire this morning, I suggest you take a stroll on over to the courthouse and check it out for yourself. She's in Judge Gendelman's courtroom."

J.D. nodded. Yes, yes, fine, thank you. Nice attitude, by the way. Like boss, like secretary.

But always a gentleman, he smiled and thanked Irma for the information. He stopped by his own secretary's desk and told her that he had an errand to run.

Then he hurried out of the office and headed straight for the courthouse.

BY THE TIME J.D. walked into Judge Gendelman's courtroom, court was already in session.

He quietly closed the door behind him and slipped into the back row of the galley, wanting his presence to go unnoticed until he figured out what he was going to say to Payton.

J.D. took a seat. As he tried to get comfortable on the hard wooden bench, his eye was immediately drawn to the action up front. Payton stood before the witness stand, which meant that she was in the middle of either a direct or cross-examination. He sat back to enjoy the show, figuring this was a great opportunity to observe the enemy in her nor—

Holy fuck—would somebody please tell him why a

massive photo of a *penis* was sitting front and center in the courtroom?

J.D. glanced around warily. What the hell kind of law did Payton practice around here? Everyone else in the courtroom, however, seemed wholly unfazed by the exhibition.

His interest now really piqued by this spectacle of a so-called trial, he turned his attention back to Payton. Remembering why he was there, he sat up to get a better look. He watched as Payton walked around to the other side of the podium, and—wait—

Shit. She was wearing the shoes.

J.D.'s eyes narrowed in on the left shoe—the heel he had made a few, shall we say, "special modifications" to. The heel appeared to be holding together, although it was anyone's guess how long that would last. With every step Payton took, he held his breath, expecting to see her stumble. He would have to pull her aside at the next break and warn her. He only hoped the glue he had applied would hold together until then.

Having no choice but to sit idly by in the galley and wait, J.D. distracted himself by focusing on Payton's interrogation of the witness. He could tell within seconds from the way she leadingly questioned the woman on the stand that this was not a friendly party.

"I'm not sure I understand your position, Ms. Kemple," Payton was saying. "Maybe you can help me understand what it is you believe the company did wrong."

J.D. watched as Payton positioned herself between the jury and the witness, a trial lawyer's trick to get the jurors' attention during cross-examination.

"Earlier we established that you reported the incident involving your former manager on June fourteenth of last year, correct?" Payton asked.

"That's correct," Ms. Kemple answered.

"And the director of Human Resources responded to your complaint that very same day, didn't she?"

"Yes."

"As part of that response, the company immediately fired your former manager, also that same day, didn't they?"

The witness nodded. "That's correct."

"And, in fact, yesterday at trial was the first time you had seen him since the incident in his car, correct?"

Again the witness nodded. "Yes."

"So it's fair to say then, Ms. Kemple, that you never again had any problems with your former manager after that one incident?" Payton asked.

The witness appeared more reluctant to answer this question. "I guess that's fair to say," she finally agreed.

Appearing satisfied with this answer, Payton walked over to the defense attorney's table. Having been drawn into the testimony, J.D. noticed for the first time that a junior associate from their firm—what the hell was his name, Brandon, Brendan, something like that—sat at the table. Perhaps, J.D. mused, he could slip Brandon/Brendan a note to give to Payton.

J.D.'s eyes were drawn back to Payton as she casually leaned against the table facing the witness.

"Ms. Kemple, am I also correct that, after your manager was fired, the director of Human Resources came out to your office and conducted a full-day sexual harassment refresher seminar that was mandatory for all employees?"

The witness tried to hedge here. "I'm not sure it was a *full* day . . ."

"Well, how long was the seminar?" Payton asked.

Ms. Kemple thought for a moment. "I guess it was about seven or eight hours."

"Wouldn't you describe seven or eight hours as a full day?"

"I suppose so."

With this admission, Payton held up her hands. "So? Why are we here, Ms. Kemple?"

The witness stared at her, confused. "Excuse me?"

"To be blunt, you've sued the company for two million dollars. What exactly is it that you think they did wrong in handling your complaint?"

J.D. watched Payton as she continued her cross-examination. Because they had worked in the same group for the last eight years, he had heard plenty about her numerous trial victories. But this was the first chance he'd gotten to observe her firsthand.

She was good. Right away, J.D. saw how relaxed and comfortable she was in the courtroom. Yet always professional. It was obvious that the jury liked her, and more important, they trusted her—he could tell from the way they listened attentively, how some of them even nodded along with her questions.

"Well, I think there's a few things the company could've done differently . . ." the witness was saying in a defensive tone.

"Like what?" Payton asked. "You don't disagree that the company handled the matter promptly, do you?"

As Payton asked this question, she folded her arms across her chest and casually leaned back against the table—on one foot, her *left* foot—for support.

J.D. drew in his breath. Oh, shit.

"I suppose they handled the matter promptly enough," the witness conceded.

"And you would have to agree that they handled the matter effectively, wouldn't you, seeing how you never again saw your ex-manager, let alone had a problem with him?"

Still leaning against the table, Payton crossed her right ankle over her left, so that all her weight now bore down on her left heel.

J.D. cringed. Crap, crap, this was going to be *bad*. He

couldn't watch. But yet he had to. Should he do something? Maybe he could—

But right then, Payton eased onto the table—taking the weight off her shoe—as the witness answered.

"Yes, I suppose you could say that the way the company chose to respond to my manager's harassment was effective enough."

J.D. exhaled in relief. Close call. But he had better get that note to Brandon/Brendan now, while he still had the chance. He glanced over. A few other latecomers had sat down at the end of his row. He would have to sneak past them to get out.

Meanwhile Payton, sitting on the table, gracefully crossed one leg over the other, continuing her cross-examination.

"And when the director of Human Resources interviewed you a week after the incident, didn't you, in fact, tell her that you were *pleased* with the company's response to your complaint?" she asked.

"No, I don't think that's what I said," Ms. Kemple quickly replied.

Payton seemed surprised by this answer, but remained unflustered. "Really? Do you remember when we spoke earlier at your deposition, Ms. Kemple, where you said . . ."

J.D. watched as Payton searched through the files on her table and quickly found the deposition transcript she was looking for. Payton grabbed the transcript—

"Here, Ms. Kemple, let me read to you a portion of your—"

—and before J.D. realized what was happening, Payton did sort of a half leap off the table to approach the witness stand and when she came down on her feet there was a loud *crack!* that sounded throughout the courtroom and holy shit suddenly Payton stumbled wildly off balance, her arms flailing, and she—

—dove headfirst straight into the jury box.

The entire courtroom gasped as J.D. flew out of his seat in horror.

Oh, my god!

Everyone was on their feet, stunned, watching as Payton quickly scrambled to pull herself to a stand, grappling, climbing past the jurors who sat in their box, mouths agape, and she managed to get to her feet, a little flustered but covering as she smoothed her skirt and—

"Sorry about that." Payton smiled calmly at the jurors, regaining her cool. "Now, where was I . . ."

She looked for the deposition transcript she had dropped, she turned around and—

—the entire audience in the galley cried out in shock.

Unbeknownst to Payton, when she had fallen her skirt—those damn slim-fit skirts she liked so much—had torn at the seam and now gaped open, and sweet Jesus, she was wearing a thong and two tiny white butt cheeks peeked out from between the folds of her skirt—

J.D.'s jaw nearly hit the floor.

Oh god, it was horrible, *horrible*—well, actually it wasn't all that horrible for him, she had a *really* great ass—but for Payton, this was a train wreck, a disaster—

Up front, Payton heard the ruckus coming from the audience behind her, so she turned around—

—and the peeky cheeks now faced the judge and jury. The jurors' mouths dropped open, and a few murmured something incoherent, and they all gaped as Payton hobbled about the courtroom on uneven shoes, confused as to the source of the commotion.

At the defense table, Brandon/Brendan timidly whispered something to Payton; J.D. couldn't hear it and apparently neither could Payton because she bent over toward Brandon/Brendan to hear better, exposed white buns up in the air for all to see, and the courtroom erupted in complete pandemonium and J.D. started to climb past the people in his row—he somehow had to put a stop to this—

But Payton finally heard Brandon/Brendan.

She stood up, her hand flew to her skirt, and she felt the rip in the seam. She instantly reacted; she unbuttoned her jacket and quickly tied it around her waist—no more peeky-cheeks—and J.D. heard a few groans of disappointment as the judge finally got things under control, banging his gavel and calling for order in the courtroom.

And as quickly as the chaos had erupted, things quieted back down. As people took their seats, the clamor settling, J.D. sat down, too, hiding, thinking now definitely was *not* the time to be seen by Payton.

As a silence took hold of the courtroom, all eyes were on Payton. Everyone waited to see what she would do, how she would react.

She paused for a moment. Then she turned and faced the jury.

"Raise your hand if you had no idea you'd see so much nudity in one week of jury duty."

Twelve hands flew straight into the air.

And unbelievably, Payton laughed.

The jurors joined in with her. Then the judge raised his hand, too. With that, the entire courtroom laughed and people began to clap.

Payton held her hand up, acknowledging. "Thank you, thank you. I'm here all week."

And it was in that moment, as J.D. sat in the galley with people laughing and applauding all around him, as he watched Payton smiling, embarrassed but undefeated, that it happened.

Something changed.

He didn't know anyone who would've handled such a ridiculous situation nearly so well. Maybe he hadn't noticed it before, but she was actually kind of . . . funny. Or maybe he had already known that, he suddenly wasn't sure. But what he did know was that he had flipped out over a friggin' coffee stain on his suit, and yet here Payton had done a full face-plant right into the laps of twelve jurors and then treated them to a free peep show, but nevertheless managed to remain calm and collected.

And suddenly J.D. found himself looking at Payton with quite a bit of admiration.

He grinned and joined in with the others who cheered her on, and he momentarily forgot the role he had played in the whole debacle until, right then, she glanced down at her shoe.

Uh-oh.

J.D. watched as Payton picked up the shoe and presumably noticed the clean, precise way the heel had broken, the remnants of the glue he had applied. She ran her finger over the broken heel, examining it, and in that moment J.D. knew that she knew.

A random thought occurred to him right then, about how they say that criminals always return to the scene of the crime—wasn't that how Bundy or Berkowitz or one of those guys got caught—and actually, it was kind of funny that he was thinking about murder right then because when Payton looked up from the broken shoe and glanced across the courtroom and saw J.D. sitting there, murder is exactly what was in her eyes.

When Payton met his gaze, J.D. thought he had never seen her dark blue eyes look so cold. And he knew one thing for certain.

He was toast.

PAYTON STORMED OUT the courthouse doors—suit jacket still tied around her waist—with J.D. following closely on her heels.

"Come on, Payton—it's not like I meant for that to happen!" he called after her. "Honestly, who could've planned *that*?"

A part of her wished she never had to come back to

court. Better yet, a part of her wished the earth would just open up and swallow her, she was that mortified.

The judge had called a one-hour recess so that—as he had delicately put it—"anyone who wished to adjust his or her attire could do so." Payton now was in a race to get back to the office, change into her spare suit, then get to the nearest department store to buy a new pair of shoes. On top of everything else, the bastard—no other name was necessary, from now on the man formerly known as J.D. would simply be called The Bastard, The Prick, or The Shithead—had ruined her best pair of shoes. But that was hardly her biggest concern.

Her ass had been hanging out in open court.

Her *ass* had been hanging out in *open court*.

Clomping along the sidewalk unevenly in her broken heel, stomping past innocent pedestrians who were having a lovely, normal day, people who presumably had *not* had their asses hanging out in open court, Payton grumbled out loud to herself about the worst part of it all.

"I just had to wear a thong today, didn't I?" she hissed angrily. She could've smacked herself in the head for that decision.

The Shithead was suddenly at her side. He grinned. "Well, point of fact, I think that women should wear thongs every d . . ." he trailed off, seeing her look. "But I can see you're not in a place to discuss that right now."

Payton couldn't take it a moment longer. She advanced on J.D. "Oh, you think this is *funny*? Please—allow me to disabuse you of that notion."

"Payton—"

"*Don't*. Don't 'Payton' me, don't waste your breath with excuses or explanations—*I don't care*."

She stared J.D. right in the eyes. "If this is how you want to play the game, Jameson, that's fine with me. The gloves are now off. I am about to become the bitch you've always thought I was."

Payton saw that her comment took J.D. aback, that it
wiped his grin—which she interpreted as a smirk—right
off his face. And she saw something momentarily flash in
his eyes, maybe it was anger, maybe it was something
else—right now she didn't care either way. Right now, as
she stood on that sidewalk, facing J.D. in her torn skirt and
broken heel and her naked butt barely covered by the jacket
tied around her waist, all she cared about was at least having the dignity of getting in the last word.

So, seeing that she had momentarily silenced him, Payton
took advantage of the opportunity and turned and walked
away.

Thirteen

"IT COULDN'T HAVE been *that* bad."

Curled up on her couch, Payton gave Chase a look over the carton of pad thai she held. She swallowed, then gestured with her chopsticks for emphasis.

"Oh, no, trust me, it was *that* bad."

Chase had called her earlier, while she was still at the office. Although the rest of her day in court had thankfully passed by uneventfully—after the break she had even managed to get back on track with her cross-examination of the plaintiff—Payton still had been so embarrassed that she told Chase only, in what had to be the understatement of the year, that she'd had "kind of a bad day in court."

An hour later, Chase had surprised her at home with a bag of Asian takeout. To cheer her up, he said. Not sure which one she preferred, he'd brought both tofu pad thai and vegetable fried rice. Touched by the gesture, Payton figured she could at least give him the condensed version of what had happened that morning. She appreciated it when he politely covered his laugh as a cough and blamed the spiciness of the food.

"But you recovered well—that's what the jury will remember," Chase told her. Stretched out comfortably on the couch across from her, he set his carton down on the coffee table and leaned in.

"I'm actually kind of sad I wasn't there—I think I would've liked the view," he said with a boyish grin. Then he leaned over and kissed her.

As Payton had described to Laney the other day, she found being with Chase to be . . . calming. It was a nice change of pace for her—certain situations at work, and certain unnamed someones in particular, had a tendency to get her worked up. But with Chase, there was no fuss. At a time when things in Payton's life seemed uncertain and more than a bit out of control, being with Chase was easy. *He* was easy.

Not that way.

She didn't know that.

Yet.

After they kissed for a moment or two, Chase pulled back and gave Payton a serious look. "There's something I've been meaning to talk to you about. I think maybe it's time we take our relationship to the next level."

Payton raised an eyebrow. Oh, really? "The next level being . . . ?"

"A weekend date."

"Ah, a weekend date." Payton shook her head teasingly. "I don't know, that's a big step. Did you have any particular weekend in mind?"

"Actually, I was thinking about this one," Chase said.

"Wow. I don't know. This weekend, let me see . . ." Payton pretended to mull this over. "There's some laundry I've been meaning to get to, but I suppose if I rearrange my schedule . . ."

With a wink, she smiled. "Okay."

Chase pretended to sigh with relief. "To think I nearly lost out to laundry. My ego never would've recovered."

"Hey, this isn't everyday laundry we're talking about," Payton said. "I was going to do *sheets*. Maybe even a towel or two. If that's not your idea of a Friday night party, I don't know what is."

Chase laughed. "Well, now that I know that I rank above sheets, I feel so much better."

Payton smiled, then fell more serious as she studied him. There was something she felt she needed to say.

"You do know that it's just all this stuff I have going on at work, right? I'm really busy with this trial, and they're going to name the new partners at the end of the month." She had told Chase earlier that there was stiff competition in her bid to make partner, although she hadn't gone into specifics.

Chase nodded and took Payton's hand, lacing his fingers through hers.

"I'm just teasing you. I know how busy you are right now."

Payton peered into his warm brown eyes. Yes, that's all it was, she told herself, she was busy with work. Nothing else.

Before any contrary thought could creep into her mind, she reached up and gently pulled Chase in to kiss him.

AN HOUR OR so later, they said good night. After briefly discussing their plans for Friday, Payton shut the door behind him. She leaned against the door, reflecting.

That Chase. Such a good guy. How she so looked forward to their next date.

Payton sighed peacefully.

Then she eagerly sprang away from the door.

Back to the business at hand. She had some serious plotting and scheming to do. At least eight hours had gone by and she hadn't yet come up with any suitable way to strike back at the evil that was J.D. She needed a plan. Fast.

He had wanted to make her look stupid. Frankly, he had succeeded in that. But the next move was hers.

Now what could she possibly do that would top naked-butt-cheek courtroom pratfalls . . . ?

Payton bustled around her apartment, cleaning up after her dinner with Chase, musing over this. She needed to come up with something final. The kill shot. The checkmate. The move that would lock up the partnership spot once and for all. Then she would be done with J. D. Jameson forever. No more having to prove herself; no more of those pesky jitters she felt whenever she saw him at work—something like butterflies in her stomach, it was actually quite annoying; no more stress; no more fights in the library; and definitely no more sexy I'm-gonna-kiss-you-now-woman blue-eyed heated gazes.

She had no idea why she just thought that.

Sleep deprivation, undoubtedly. Like the high-altitude sickness, it struck suddenly and at the oddest times.

Payton sped through her nighttime routine and crawled into bed. When the lights were off, she did *not* think about J.D.

Except to plot her schemes of revenge, of course.

Fourteen

IF, AS LEX Kendall liked to say, all women were sisters under the same moon, then Lady Justice was no exception. She was kind to Payton indeed.

It took only two days before she stumbled upon her big chance.

The best part of it was that Payton didn't even have to do anything. The opportunity just happened upon her. She took it as a sign that the Fates—also women, she noted— were on her side.

She got back to the office early that afternoon. One of the plaintiff's witnesses had a family emergency and needed to be rescheduled to testify the following day. With no other witnesses present in court or available on such short notice, the judge had recessed the trial until the following morning.

Payton had settled down at her desk and begun reviewing her email, finding over twenty messages marked urgent (some people were far too liberal in their use of that little red exclamation point), when she noticed Irma over at J.D.'s secretary's desk. The two women had their heads bowed and were whispering intently.

Ignoring them at first, Payton continued on with her email. Of course she found no actual emergencies, just everyday, run-of-the-mill client panic attacks. But a few minutes later, after seeing the secretaries still deep in their huddle, she became intrigued. Especially after Kathy, J.D.'s secretary, hurried off from her desk looking frantic.

Payton called out to Irma as she passed by her office.

"Psst! Psst! Irma!"

When Irma glanced over, Payton gestured for her to step into her office.

"What's going on?" she asked as soon as Irma shut the door. "I saw you over at Kathy's desk. She looks like she's freaking out about something."

Irma peeked out the glass window of the office, then turned back to Payton. "I'm not supposed to say anything, but J.D.'s in trouble."

Ooh . . . this was *good*. Payton resisted the urge to rub her hands together gleefully.

"What kind of trouble? Tell me," she said, eager for the details.

"Well, apparently," Irma began, "he got called into court for some sort of emergency motion—what did Kathy say it was—a contempt motion? Contested motion? I can't remember which—"

Payton waved impatiently, moving Irma along. "Either way. An emergency motion. And?"

"*And*"—Irma threw Payton a look, she was getting there—"the judge won't let him leave. He wants to hear oral argument and have a hearing on the motion right now. But the problem is, J.D. has a deposition scheduled for this afternoon that was supposed to start, like, fifteen minutes ago. The other lawyer and his client are upstairs and threatening to leave if the dep doesn't start immediately. Kathy went to try to stall them."

Payton and Irma suddenly spotted Kathy hurrying back to her desk. She did not look happy.

"I better go out there and see if there's anything I can do to help," Irma said.

She headed back out to Kathy's desk. Payton watched through the glass as J.D.'s secretary held up her hands, gesturing anxiously, then ran off again.

Payton called out to Irma once more.

"Psst! Irma! *Psst!*"

Irma walked back into Payton's office. "What is with you today? You're awfully pesty."

Payton ignored this. "What did Kathy say? It didn't look good. Is it bad? How bad? Tell me."

"You know, you could just talk to Kathy yourself," Irma told her.

"I'm trying to be covert. Don't ask. Just tell me what's happening with J.D."

"Kathy says he's freaking out. I guess he called the other lawyer from the courthouse and tried to explain his situation, but apparently the guy's being a jerk about it. And when Kathy went upstairs to talk to him and his client, the lawyer said he had flown into town from New York especially for this deposition and if it didn't start immediately, he was going to file a motion for sanctions, demanding he be reimbursed for his plane fare, hotel, and attorney's fees."

Payton rolled her eyes. Some lawyers could be such assholes. Luckily for her, this particular asshole was somebody else's problem.

"Hmm . . . that really is quite a predicament," she said most sympathetically. "But I'm sure J.D. will work it out somehow. Who's the partner on the case? I guess he'll have to step in and take the dep."

"Actually, it's Ben Gould's case. But he's out of town," Irma said.

"What a shame. Who's the client?"

"KPLM Consulting."

"Ouch."

Having gone to all the firm meetings—the diligent associate she was—Payton knew that KPLM was the firm's third-largest client. Ben would not be pleased to hear of any screwups involving their matters.

"I guess J.D.'s pretty desperate," Irma told her. "He asked Kathy to see if any of the other upper-level associates could fill in for him and take the deposition."

Payton nodded. Then she spun around in her chair and went back to the very important task of sorting through her email. "Well, I hope that works out for him."

She felt Irma's eyes on her.

"I guess that means you're *not* available to help out?" Irma asked.

"Boy, wow—I really wish I could. But with this trial and everything . . ." Payton gestured dramatically to the pile of files on her desk, none of which actually had anything to do with her trial. "I just don't see how I could squeeze it in." She snapped her fingers. Damn.

Irma nodded. If she was suspicious, she didn't let on. "Okay, I'll let Kathy know. Although I wasn't supposed to ask you, anyway. J.D. told her to ask anyone but you. I guess he probably already knew you were too busy."

No, he doesn't want me to know he's royally screwed, Payton thought with satisfaction. But she bit her tongue as Irma left the office.

Once alone, Payton had a moment to assess the fortuity of this most delectable and unexpected turn of events.

She had just won.

Not appearing for a deposition, risking sanctions and attorney's fees against one of the firm's biggest clients—these were not exactly things that partners turned the other cheek to. It may not have been J.D.'s fault, but, well, them's the breaks. Associates seeking to be partner were expected to magically prevent this stuff from happening and if they didn't . . .

Payton knew exactly what would happen. If there was any fallout resulting from today's mishap, Ben would sell out J.D. in a heartbeat. Partner CYA at its best.

And if it truly was that tight of a race between her and J.D., Payton had to think this would be enough to inch her ahead. Coffee-stained suits, exposed thong-buns—these things were mere pittances in comparison to pissing off the firm's third-largest client.

And she never even had to lift a finger to make it all happen.

Outside her office, Payton heard a panicked Kathy ask Irma for help.

"I've tried all the seventh years, and none of them can take the deposition," she heard Kathy say. "Can you call the sixth and fifth years while I run upstairs and ask the attorney to wait just five more minutes? If you find someone, give them the deposition notice—it's on my desk."

Payton sighed.

Pity.

She turned her attention back to the imaginary tasks she was so diligently working on.

Poor J.D. She could just picture him, stuck at the court-house, scrambling, worrying, wondering what was the luck in having something like this happen now.

Good. He deserved it.

This was all his own doing, really. He had obviously taken on too many cases in these last couple of weeks before the partnership decision, trying to show her up. So the mess he was in certainly wasn't *her* problem. Besides, he didn't want her help, anyway. *Ask anyone but Payton,* he had said.

Fine. Great. That officially released her of any obligation to get involved.

Payton sighed again.

Pity.

For some reason, the sentiment felt less and less victorious with every moment that passed.

Payton sat at her desk.

And sat some more. Drumming her fingers.

Dum-de-dum-de-dum.

Oh, fuck it. Without a clue why, she got up and strode out of her office.

PAYTON KNOCKED ON Tyler's door.

When he looked up from his desk and saw her standing there, Tyler looked more than a little surprised. Payton understood this. She could probably count on one hand the number of times she and Tyler had spoken. As J.D.'s best friend, he was de facto off-limits.

Taken aback though he was, Tyler smiled good-naturedly.

"Payton. Hi. Can I help you with something?"

Hmm. He actually seemed pleasant enough, Payton thought. Shame he had such poor taste in friends.

She leaned against the door. Totally blasé. "I just thought you might want to know that J.D. is in trouble. He's stuck at the courthouse and can't make it back for some deposition he's supposed to be taking right now."

She nonchalantly examined the tips of her fingernails. "Not that it's any of my concern, but the deposition is for some important case he has with KPLM Consulting. I guess it's a pretty important matter."

She sighed unworriedly, picking at a cuticle. "He'll probably get fired if he doesn't find someone to take the dep in the next couple of minutes. Not that I care. I just so happened to catch a glance at the deposition notice on Kathy's desk; it's a 30(b)(6) deposition. Whatever."

Not surprisingly, as J.D.'s best friend, Tyler was extremely flustered by this unexpected news.

"Um . . . okay. Wow. Let me think for a second." He got up from his desk, walked around it, then went back. "I guess I should call Kathy. No, J.D." He looked uncertainly over at Payton. "I should call J.D., right? See what he wants me to do?"

"I don't think there's time for that," Payton told him. "Kathy said the attorney's pitching a fit and ready to leave any minute."

"Okay—I'll stall them," Tyler decided.

Payton sighed in frustration. Did she have to spell it out for him?

"Tyler. You have to take this deposition. Now."

He stared at her blankly for a moment, then nodded. "Of course, right. Sure. You said it was a 30(b)(6) deposition?"

"Yes."

Tyler nodded again, then hurried over and pulled his copy of the Federal Rules of Civil Procedure off his shelf. "Um, 30(b)(6) . . . let's see . . ." He flipped through the pages. "Okay—here it is."

Payton stared at him, appalled. "Good god, boy—have you never taken a 30(b)(6) deposition?"

Tyler paused his skimming to peer up at her. "Wow, you just sounded *exactly* like J.D. right then."

Payton scowled. As if.

Seeing her expression, Tyler answered quickly. "I think I may have sat in on a 30(b)(6) dep when I was a summer associate." He looked at her questioningly. "Is that the one where you designate someone to testify as an agent of the corporation?"

Payton rolled her eyes. Were they teaching these kids *nothing* nowadays?

"Tyler—this is kind of a big deal," she said. "These

30(b)(6) depositions can be tricky. The witnesses are usually very well prepared, since everything they say can be held against the company."

Tyler looked her over. "So you've done this before?"

Payton snorted. Was the Pope German? "Uh . . . yes."

"So, you could take this dep?"

"Like a champ. *But.*" She gave Tyler a pointed look. He stared back at her with those little I'm-just-a-sixth-year-associate lost eyes.

Payton spoke cautiously. "You are aware of the situation between J.D. and myself, are you not?"

"I am aware of it, yes."

So he knew what he was asking of her, Payton thought. She continued to stare at Tyler.

He never blinked once.

After a moment, Payton spoke.

"He wouldn't do it for me."

Tyler cocked his head, interested. "Is that what matters to you?"

Payton flung her hair back, deciding to ignore that question. "Fine," she told Tyler through gritted teeth. "I'll do it."

She held up a finger. "But *you* are going to help me. Go upstairs and tell the lawyer and his client that we apologize for the delay, but that everything has been straightened out and the deposition will begin in five minutes. Introduce yourself, and in turn, make sure you get the lawyer's name. Then come back here and run a quick search in Martindale-Hubbell and on LexisNexis—find any noteworthy cases he's handled, major clients, et cetera. I won't have time to review everything before the deposition starts, but I'll call you during our first break and you can give me the highlights. Okay?"

Tyler nodded affirmatively. "Got it."

With that, Payton left his office and headed down the hall to talk to J.D.'s secretary.

"Kathy—I'll need whatever files J.D. has for this deposition," she said as soon as she got to his secretary's desk. "Do you know if he prepares outlines for his deps? If you can't find a copy in the files, run a search on his computer."

Kathy flew out of her chair, extremely relieved. "Does this mean you can cover the deposition? Oh, thank goodness, Payton. I'll get you that stuff right away. Yes, J.D. does prepare outlines for his deps, and I know right where I can find it . . ."

As Kathy hurried off, Payton headed to her own office. Irma glanced up curiously as she passed by.

"Change of heart?" she asked. "What happened to Tyler?"

"Never send a boy to do a woman's job, Irma."

Payton winked at her secretary, then disappeared into her office to get her game face on.

ALL THINGS CONSIDERED, the deposition went pretty damn well. Payton attributed this to the fact that she had seriously mad skills as a lawyer.

And maybe just the teensiest bit to the fact that J.D. had prepared a very thorough deposition outline that set forth virtually every question she needed to ask.

Despite the extremely late notice, Payton found it not difficult at all to step in—along with the outline, J.D. had prepared his exhibits in advance and had organized them sequentially. Sure, some minor deviations from the outline were sporadically necessary to clarify something the witness said. But other than that, she found J.D.'s preparation and strategy to be very much in line with what hers would have been had it been her own case. She even managed—despite the delay in starting—to finish the deposition by four thirty, something J.D. apparently had promised the lawyer so that he and the witness could make their six o'clock flight back to New York.

"Thank you for being so accommodating, Ms. Kendall," the lawyer said to Payton after she had concluded the deposition. He had become far more friendly once the deposition had begun and the complimentary popcorn and cookies had arrived.

"No problem, Mr. Werner," Payton said, shaking his hand in farewell. "J.D. will be in touch with you to discuss the schedule for the remaining depositions. Once again, I know he's very sorry for all the confusion this afternoon. Unfortunately, Judge Pearson didn't leave him much choice."

Payton and Werner shared a sympathetic chuckle. It never failed: lawyers could always at least find common ground in griping about the oft-orneriness of judges.

After the lawyer and his client left, Payton began to pack up J.D.'s files, being careful to keep them organized in the way she had found them. She asked the court reporter to email her a copy of the real-time transcript, figuring she could forward that to J.D. right away.

When she finished, Payton took a seat and proudly propped her feet up on the chair across from her. Not a bad bit of lawyering she had pulled off today, if she did say so herself.

She spotted the tray of cookies left over from the deposition. What the hell? She certainly had earned a treat. She checked out the selection and picked out a double chocolate chip. She grabbed the cookie and was just about to bite in when—

"What have you done?"

At the sound of the voice, Payton froze, mouth open. Cookie midair.

She turned and saw J.D. standing in the doorway.

"How bad is it?" he asked in a gravely serious tone.

Payton took a bite of the cookie. She chewed deliberately, taking her time, then cocked her head. "Actually, it's quite tasty."

J.D. stepped into the room. It was then that Payton noticed how frazzled he looked. Which was particularly striking, because J. D. Jameson never looked frazzled. His hair was uncharacteristically mussed and he seemed out of breath, as if he had run over right after finishing his court hearing.

Payton sympathized. She knew how tough his day must've been—she'd had a few of those days herself. For a moment, she almost felt bad for J.D.

Too bad the moment didn't last.

"Ah, there's that quintessential Kendall sarcasm," J.D. said. "All right—lay it on me. What did you do? Make obscene statements on the record? Feign a stutter? Ask the witness the same question five hundred times?"

"No," Payton told him. Although she made a mental note for future reference—those were not half-bad ideas.

"No, of course not." J.D. scowled. "You would never do anything that would harm your own reputation. Whatever you did to undermine me would have to be much more subtle."

He looked around the room. His voice had an edge as he fired questions at her. "Where are Werner and the witness? They've left? You finished that quickly, huh? Well, forget it—I'm bringing them back here. I want to reopen this deposition and fix whatever mess you made."

Payton stood up and straightened her jacket.

"Sorry, J.D., I'm afraid you're stuck with my mess. Rule 30(c) of the Federal Rules of Civil Procedure: examination of the witness shall proceed as if at trial. That means only *one* attorney can question the witness. Didn't they teach you that at Har-vard?" she drawled sarcastically.

"Yes, they taught me that at Har-vard," J.D. said dryly. He folded his arms across his chest and peered down at her. "I want to see the transcript. Immediately."

Payton glared at him. So this was the thanks she got for helping him. She didn't know why she was surprised.

"No problem," she said. She grabbed her briefcase and pulled out her laptop computer. As J.D. stood there, glowering down at her, arms folded across his chest, Payton opened up her email and found the real-time transcript the court reporter had just sent her. She quickly forwarded it to J.D.

"There," she said. She snapped her laptop shut and threw it back into her briefcase. She stood again to face J.D. "Was that immediate enough for you?"

His eyes flickered, and for a second, he seemed to pause.

"Yes," he said tersely.

"Good." Payton slung her briefcase over her shoulder and headed toward the door. "Your files are all there—I put them back in the same order you had them. And Werner wants you to call him tomorrow to talk about the remaining depositions you need to schedule. Enjoy your transcript, J.D."

With that parting thought, she walked out of the conference room. Furious. With herself, mostly.

For ever having thought that their conversation would've been anything different.

Fifteen

J.D. RANG THE buzzer a second time.

When she still didn't answer, he rechecked the address he had pulled up on his BlackBerry. According to the firm directory, he was at the right place.

The upstairs lights of the two-flat were on, so presumably somebody was home. A thought occurred to J.D. then, the same one he'd had after the dinner with Jasper and the Gibson's team: *maybe she doesn't live alone.* The buzzer and mailbox provided no clues to this.

Earlier, after Payton had stormed out of the conference room, J.D. had immediately headed down to his office and pulled up the deposition transcript she had emailed him. He had feverishly dove in, expecting the worst. As his reading progressed, he continued, tensely waiting to find the twist, the screw she put to him, something. Anything.

But.

What he had discovered instead was . . . nothing. No tricks. Unless one counted the trick Payton had pulled off in managing to take a pretty damn good 30(b)(6) deposition on about thirty seconds' notice. Sure there were a few minor things, a few lines of questioning with which J.D. might have taken a slightly different approach, or maybe not—but nevertheless, all he could think was—

Wow.

And just when he thought he couldn't feel more like a jackass, Tyler called and filled him in on everything.

And thus, J.D. found himself here, on Payton's doorstep.

Standing aimlessly on her front stoop with nothing else to do, he looked around, checking out the neighborhood. There were several row houses on the block, including the one that presumably belonged to her. The tree-lined street had a quaint yet urban feel to it.

He liked it. Not as much as his downtown high-rise condo with a view of the lake, of course, but he found it an acceptable place to leave the Bentley parked on the street. And for J.D., that was saying *a lot*.

He pushed the button on the intercom again. Third time's the charm, they always say, which was good, because given the circumstances, charm was something he definitely need—

"Hello?"

The voice—Payton's—came crackling loudly through the intercom, momentarily surprising him. She sounded annoyed. And he hadn't even spoken yet.

J.D. cleared his throat and pushed the button on the intercom.

"Uh, Payton, hi. It's J.D."

Dead silence.

Then another crackle.

"Sorry. Not interested."

Cute. But J.D. persisted. Again with the button.

"I want to talk to you."

Crackle.

"Ever hear of a telephone, asshole?"

Okay, he probably deserved that.

Button.

"Listen, I've been standing out here for fifteen minutes. What took you so long to answer?"

Crackle.

(Annoyed sigh.) "I was about to get in the shower."

J.D. raised an eyebrow. The shower? Hmm . . . he liked the sound of that. Wait a second—no, he didn't.

Bad J.D.

Button.

"I read the deposition transcript."

Crackle.

"Good for you."

She certainly wasn't making this easy. But he had expected that.

Buzzer.

"Payton," J.D. said in an earnest tone, "I would like to say this in person. Please."

Silence. He could practically hear her debating.

Then the buzzer rang, unlocking the front door. J.D. dove to beat the buzzer before she changed her mind, and let himself in.

PAYTON'S EYES QUICKLY scanned her front room and kitchen, making sure they were presentable. Not that it mattered, because (a) it was The Shithead and (b) he wasn't staying. Her apartment was her sanctuary, which meant 100 percent J.D.-free.

She opened her front door, thinking she'd catch him on the stairs and cut him off at the pass. But instead, she found him already standing there. The quick way she threw open the door caught him off guard.

With one hand on the door frame and the other on her hip, Payton glared at him. "Whatever you have to say, say it quickly. I've had a long day."

Recovering from his momentary surprise, J.D. looked her over. "That's a little abrupt. Can I come in?"

"No."

"Great. Thanks."

He brushed by Payton and stepped into her apartment.

Payton huffed. Oh. Well. Apparently she had no choice in the matter. She shut the door behind him and watched as he looked around curiously.

"So this is where you live," he said as if fascinated, a man who'd snuck into the enemy's camp. "Nice space. Looks like you get a lot of light." He glanced over. "Just you?"

Payton nodded. "Yes. Look, whatever you—"

"Can I have something to drink?" he interrupted her. "A glass of water would be fine. I came here straight from work."

At first, Payton said nothing. She simply stared at him, wondering what the hell he was up to.

"I'm a bit parched," he added.

She thought she saw the faintest trace of a smile on his lips. Was he trying to be cute? Or perhaps he was just stalling.

"Fine." She sighed. Reluctantly, she turned to head into the kitchen.

"Perrier, if you have it."

Payton threw an evil eye over her shoulder.

J.D. grinned. "Just kidding."

Definitely trying to be cute.

Whatever.

Ignoring him, Payton went and got his glass of water. It was weird, him being there in her apartment. It felt . . . personal. She felt oddly jumpy. Skittish.

After unenthusiastically filling a glass with tepidly warm tap water, she went back out into the front room. The room was divided by a wall of built-in bookshelves—one of the few things from the original design she hadn't changed after buying the place—and she found J.D. there, looking at her collection of books.

As he leaned over to check out the lower shelf, Payton noticed for the first time that he wasn't wearing a suit jacket. The sleeves of his shirt were rolled up around his forearms, his tie loosened, and his hair had a casual, raked-through look.

This is what he looks like when he comes home from work, Payton thought. She caught herself wondering if there was someone he came home *to.*

Brushing that aside, Payton walked over and unceremoniously shoved the glass of water at him. "Here."

J.D.'s hand brushed against her as he took it. "Thank you."

There was something about the *way* he looked at her, Payton noticed. For years, his expressions had fluctuated somewhere along the smug/haughty you-have-no-idea-what-you're-talking-about-silly-Clintonite to the more frustrated I-would-strangle-you-dead-except-I-don't-have-time-to-pick-up-your-workload spectrum. But lately it was different, and she found it very hard to read him.

"Why are you here?" she asked bluntly.

After skeptically eyeing the cloudy glass of Eau du Lac Michigan she had poured him, J.D. took a sip, then paused as if still figuring out the answer to that himself.

"I have questions," he finally said.

"Questions?" Payton asked, surprised. Whatever she had been expecting him to say, it wasn't that.

"About the deposition," he explained.

"Oh. Well, you read the transcript. Was there something you didn't understand?"

"Yes." J.D. set his glass down on the nearby end table. He stood up and peered down at her, reminding her just how tall he really was. "Why did you do it?"

Payton cocked her head. "You didn't really think I would screw up a deposition, did you? Aside from my *reputation*"—

she emphasized this in reference to his earlier insult—"I would never do that to a client."

J.D. waved this off. "No, I get that part. But I talked to Tyler. He said that you came to *him* about the deposition. You had me in a corner—if you'd done nothing, I would've been screwed. You know how Ben works: there's no room for error when it comes to his clients." He paused, coming around to his original question. "So? Why did you help me?"

She held up a hand. "Easy there, buddy. I didn't do it to help you."

"Okay, fine. Why then?"

Payton, herself, had thought long and hard about this very question after she had gotten home that evening. So she told J.D. the only logical answer she'd come up with.

"I decided that I don't want to win by default. If the Partnership Committee chooses me—*when* they choose me, I should say—I want to know that it's because I earned it, not because some stupid mix-up edged you out at the last minute."

J.D. didn't say anything at first. Then he nodded. "Fair enough." He hesitated with the next part. "Well, regardless of your motives, the real reason I came here tonight is because I . . ." He took a breath, as if needing to steel himself. "I wanted to thank you. And to apologize. When I found you in the conference room after the deposition, you had this satisfied expression on your face and, well, I guess I assumed the worst."

He paused.

"Is that it?" Payton asked, not entirely mollified by this apology.

"Oh—I was just waiting for you to say something sarcastic about assholes and assumptions."

Payton gave him a level stare. "As if I would be that cliché."

She noticed he was watching her. Again. "*What?*"

J.D. grinned. "Now I'm waiting for you to do the thing with your hair. The little flip."

Payton glared. *Note to self: invest in hair clips.*

"You know, as apologies go, this one could use a ton of improvement," she told him. "Is there more?"

"Not really." He shrugged matter-of-factly. "Well, except that I was thinking . . . *I* don't want to win by default, either. So maybe we could call a truce."

"A truce?" Payton asked. "That's very magnanimous of you, considering the next play is mine. What do I get out of this?"

J.D. took a step closer to her. "Hmm. How about the satisfaction of being the better person?"

Payton paused, highly intrigued by this. "You would admit to that?"

J.D.'s eyes shone with amusement. He took another step closer. "In this context, Ms. Kendall, yes."

Payton considered the terms of his proposal. Higher stakes for her there could not be.

"All right," she agreed. "A truce."

She had to tilt her head back to meet J.D.'s gaze, they were suddenly standing that close. *Uh-oh*, she thought, *this is how it all started last time.* She felt that familiar rush and thought about stepping back, but heaven help her if she ever gave an inch to J. D. Jameson.

"I suppose now I owe you." J.D.'s voice had turned softer.

Payton shook her head. "No, you really don't."

He nodded yes. "I read the transcript."

"You said that already."

"You were amazing, Payton," he murmured, his voice husky.

Well.

Goddamn if that wasn't just about the sexiest thing she had ever heard.

J.D. gazed down at her with a coy expression, as if interested to see what she was going to do next. And from his look Payton realized that somewhere in the middle of all this, the game between the two of them had changed.

It had all started with that stupid fight in the library. Or had it begun before that . . . ? Standing there, looking up into J.D.'s fantastically blue eyes, Payton suddenly wasn't so sure.

Hmm. He had really long eyelashes for a guy—she had never noticed that before. Almost blondish, like the warm streaks of gold in his brown hair. And speaking of his hair, she kind of liked the way it was slightly mussed that night. Something about it made her want to grab him by that designer tie of his and get him really mussed spending hours doing something she suspected would be far more amazing than this afternoon's deposition.

Wow—she really needed to get laid.

Not by J.D. He was far too type A for her tastes. She'd bet he'd be all controlling and dominating in bed. Although that could have potential . . .

And now she was blushing.

Seeing she wasn't backing away from him, J.D. raised an eyebrow. Payton saw the corners of his mouth tilt up in a smile, and if she didn't know better, she'd swear that he was daring her to make a move. *Wanted* her to make a move, even. And she wouldn't have to do much—if she tilted her head a mere inch, they'd be kissing.

Hmm.

She wondered if J.D. had polo ponies on his condoms.

"You have to go," Payton blurted out emphatically.

J.D. cocked his head but didn't move, so to hurry him along Payton put her hand on his chest, pushing him to the door—wow, he had a *really* firm chest for someone so fancy—

"Now—you have to go *now*," she said as she opened up the front door and literally shoved him out into the hall-way.

J.D. protested. "Hey! Wait a second, there's something else—"

Payton tried to shut the door, but J.D. blocked it with his arm.

"Jesus, woman, will you just let me speak?!"

"No. You've said what you came here to say. Apology accepted, no more sabotage, et cetera, et cetera. And by the way, I can't believe you actually just called me 'woman.' That's almost as bad as 'cupcake.' "

"I bet there are a lot of women who think it's endearing to be called 'cupcake.' "

"If there are, they sure don't live in this apartment."

J.D. looked ready to tear his hair out. "You know what? Forget it. I changed my mind, I don't have anything else to say. And seriously, *woman*—I think you might actually be crazy. Or maybe that's just the effect you have on me!" He finished his speech in a shout, then turned and stormed off down the stairs.

Payton half shut, half slammed the door behind him—good, she didn't want to hear anything else he had to say anyway and now at least he was out of her apartment, and by the way, he really needed to come up with some snappier comebacks and—

An impatient knock at her door. Then again, louder.

What, did he just think of a better line? Payton threw open the door and—

J.D. immediately held up his hand.

"Don't. Say. Anything."

Payton opened her mouth.

J.D. pointed and shook his head with a firm stare. "No."

Payton rolled her eyes. But she didn't speak.

"What I wanted to tell you," he began deliberately, "was that you were wrong."

Now there was a friggin' surprise. Payton glared.

J.D. continued, more calm now, his voice steadier. "I mean, about what you told Tyler."

His eyes met hers and held them.

"I would've done it for you in a heartbeat."

Payton felt it.

The ice around her heart, she felt part of it crack off and melt right then. And for the first time in eight years she had no idea what to say to J. D. Jameson.

He gave her a slight nod. "I just wanted to set the record straight on that."

With that, J.D. turned and left, for real this time, and Payton slowly shut the door behind him. She resisted the urge to look out the front window and watch as he left her apartment building. Instead, she busied herself by picking up the empty glass he had left behind. She washed the glass in the kitchen sink and put it away, eager to get rid of the remnants of his visit.

She knew that something had changed that evening and, frankly, she wanted to ignore that fact—or at least try to— and get things back to the way they were. A truce was one thing, but—heaven forbid—she really hoped this didn't mean J.D. was going to start being *nice* to her or anything. Suddenly being on friendly terms with him could make things complicated. And she certainly didn't need any complications at work right now.

I would've done it for you in a heartbeat.

Payton's thoughts lingered over those words. And despite herself, she smiled.

Not that it mattered.

Really.

Sixteen

"FOR EIGHTY DOLLARS per person for brunch, there better be diamonds stashed in that omelet."

It was the fifth comment that morning about the stupid omelet. Payton knew she just should've gone with the Belgian waffles. But resolved to have a pleasant brunch, she ignored the remark and gestured to her mother's plate.

"How's the fresh fruit and granola?" In NoMI restaurant's entire 100-plus-item buffet, they were the only two things her mother had deemed acceptable to eat.

Lex Kendall was in typical form that morning. And not about to be sidetracked so easily.

"You're trying to change the subject," she said.

"Yes, I am." Payton took a sip of her mimosa. At this rate, she was likely to need a second one, so she raised a finger to the waiter. Service, please. Quickly.

Sitting across the pristine white-linen-covered table, Lex shook her head in frustration. Her long brown hair fell over the sleeves of her floral peasant blouse in kinky, unstylized waves. In her faded jeans and animal-cruelty-free clogs, she was a bit underdressed for brunch at the Park Hyatt hotel's premiere restaurant. Not that Payton ever would've dared to tell her that.

"Come on, Sis," Lex urged, "you know that the poultry industry is more concerned with financial shortcuts than providing humane conditions for the birds they carelessly mistreat. I don't see how you can ignore that."

Payton resisted the urge to rise to the bait. She knew she'd been pushing it, bringing her mother here. But there were only so many vegetarian restaurants in the city, many of which she had already taken her mother to on prior visits, and she had wanted to try something different, something more upscale. She knew Laney was right—if she made partner, being around money was something she'd better get used to, because she certainly would have enough of it. Last year the most junior partner at her firm earned 1.1 million dollars. And while Payton certainly was never one to throw money around—frankly, she'd never had any *to* throw around before starting with the firm—on that salary she could afford to treat her mother to a decent brunch.

With this thought in mind, instead of arguing with her mother, Payton smiled amiably. "Maybe—since we have so little remaining time together this weekend—we could save the debate over the virtues of a vegan diet for another time. Let's just have a pleasant meal, shall we, Mom?" She gestured with her glass to the restaurant. "When I asked around at the firm, people said this was the best brunch in the city on Father's Day."

While it might seem odd to some people, the fact that she celebrated Father's Day with her mother gave Payton little pause anymore. It was something the two of them did every year, alone, even continuing the tradition after Lex and her husband had moved out to San Francisco when Payton started college.

Payton had virtually no memory of her father—he and her mother had split up shortly after she was born and he had come to visit her sporadically for only a couple of years after that. And while her father's lack of interest in maintaining a relationship was something that had upset her earlier in life, at thirty-two years old she was pretty much over it. Her mother rarely spoke about Shane—as even Payton referred to him—and as a result she felt wholly disconnected from him. She didn't even share a last name with her father, since he and her mother had never married.

Apparently, however, they had one thing in common: she had her father's eyes. At least that's what her mother used to tell her, in sort of a wistful way, when she was younger.

In response to Payton's comment about the restaurant, Lex looked around with a critical eye. Per Payton's request, they had a table by the window overlooking Michigan Avenue. As one of the few parties of two that morning, it had been an easy request to accommodate.

"Sure, it's a nice place. If you're into the whole brunch scene." She turned her scrutinizing eye to Payton. "*You* fit in here."

Payton sighed. "Mom—"

Lex held up her hand. "It's not an accusation, Sis. I'm just having one of those 'mom' moments where I wonder what happened to the little girl who used to dress up in my old clothes as a gypsy for Halloween." She smiled fondly. "Do you remember that? You did it five years in a row."

Payton didn't have the heart to tell her mother that the reason she had dressed up as a "gypsy" was because she had known even as a little girl that they couldn't afford to waste money on store-bought costumes.

"Now you look like you should be on a runway in Paris or something," Lex continued, gesturing to Payton's outfit.

Payton laughed. Hardly.

"They're just work clothes," she said. She wore tailored black pants, heels, and a V-neck sweater. It was unseasonably cool for June that day, even by Chicago standards.

"Well, normally I would point out that your 'just work

clothes' could probably feed ten of my girls for a week," Lex said, referring to the women who temporarily lived at the crisis shelter at which she worked in San Francisco. "But since we have so little time together—and in the spirit of having a pleasant meal, of course—I will bite my tongue and say only that you look very stylish. Very fancy, big-time lawyer-y." With that, Lex tipped her mimosa to Payton and took a sip. Cheers.

If Payton had ever wondered how she'd gotten to be so sarcastic, well, consider that question answered.

Lex looked up from her drink at Payton's silence. "What?"

"Sorry. Now I'm having one of those 'daughter' moments, wondering when, exactly, I turned into my mother."

Lex smiled. "Aw, Sis, that's the nicest thing you've ever said to me. Because of that, I won't point out that a cow had to die in order to make your purse."

Payton glanced up at the ceiling. The woman went through eighteen hours of labor to give her life, she reminded herself. Drug-free.

"Let's talk about something else," she told her mother. She inquired about Steven and his daughters, who were around the same age as Payton and lived in Los Angeles with their husbands. Her mother talked about her work at the shelter, the circumstances that had brought in some of her newer residents, and then—in a rare expression of interest—actually asked Payton a question or two about how things were going with the firm. Payton answered in generalities, seeing no reason to go into the whole partnership issue since there wasn't any news yet on that front. Instead, she talked about her cases, even getting a laugh out of her mother when she told her about the six-foot penis photo that was Exhibit A of her current trial.

"A six-foot penis, huh? That puts to shame any I've ever seen." Lex threw Payton a sneaky look. "Although, did I ever tell you about this guy I met at Woodstock—"

Payton cut her off with a hand. "No. And you never will." Her mother's "free-spirit" open-door discussion policy was something she could do just fine without when sex was the topic at hand.

Lex sat back, disappointed in being unable to tell her story. "Wow—when did you get to be such a prude?"

With a shock, Payton realized what had just happened.

She had become Laney.

"I don't think it makes me a prude just because I don't want to hear about my mother's back-in-the-day free-love sexual antics," she retorted.

"Fine, we'll talk about you instead," Lex threw right back at her. "Are you seeing anyone these days?"

Payton had debated all weekend whether to tell her mother about the Perfect Chase. He was out of town, visiting his parents in Boston, and when he got back in that evening, he had plans with his friends, so whether to introduce him to her mother had not been an issue.

It was strange, because for once she was dating someone with whom even her mother would have trouble finding fault, yet still she hesitated to bring him up. Perhaps she just didn't want to jinx things.

"Actually, I just started seeing someone a few weeks ago," Payton told her mother. "You'd love him." And as she went on, describing Chase, it struck her once again what a great guy he really was. And she—being the logical, pragmatic person *she* was—knew that he was one of those men that no woman should let get away, even if the timing wasn't the greatest. Even if she was presently sidetracked with other things.

Meaning work, of course.

ON THEIR WAY out of the restaurant, Payton and her mother stopped at the coat check. The unseasonably cool weather had provided the perfect opportunity for Lex to go

off on another of her diatribes about the politics and eco-
nomics of global climate change. Payton nodded along
distractedly—yes, yes, suppressed scientific reports; certainly, the government had undermined efforts; of course,
hidden agendas over oil; indeed, the planet was headed
toward imminent catastrophe—as she collected their jackets and tipped the attendant with one hand. In her other
hand she held the daintily wrapped but sizable box of food
her mother had insisted they take for the "unhoused" people (her mother refused to say "homeless") that they had
passed on their way into the hotel.

Payton struggled with the cumbersome box as she tried
to find the other sleeve to her jacket. She reached back, grop-
ing, still feigning interest in her mother's lecture, when—

—someone held up her jacket and gently settled it across
her shoulders.

Grateful for the assistance, Payton turned around—

—and unexpectedly found herself staring at J.D.

She blushed. No clue why. "Oh. Hello."

"Hello," he smiled.

"It's you."

"It's me."

Payton suddenly felt the need to appear casual. "So
we're here for the brunch," she said breezily. "They said it
was the best in the city for Father's Day."

"You're here with your family, then?" J.D. asked. He
appeared curious about this.

Before Payton could respond, she heard a not-so-subtle
cough behind her. Shit!—her *mother*. She had completely
forgotten about her.

Normally, Payton liked to give people a preparatory
speech before they met her mother—topics of conversation
to avoid, what not to wear, and if a meal was involved, what
not to eat. Men introduced to her mother needed additional
coaching, at least several days' worth of Lex Kendall 101.
Despite all this, very few people—even normal, perfectly

harmless people—managed to come through an encounter with her mother unscathed.

From behind Payton came a second, more pointed cough.

J.D. and her mother could *not* meet.

And if they did, she absolutely did not want to be anywhere in the vicinity. Payton eyed the door. Was it too late to make a run for it?

J.D. pointed. "Um, Payton? I think someone's trying to get your attention."

Oh, bloody hell. Payton turned around and saw her mother's fierce gaze—nobody put Lex Kendall in a corner— and reluctantly made the introduction.

"J.D., I'd like you to meet my mother, Lex Kendall. Mom, this is J. D. Jameson. He works with me at the firm."

Payton watched as J.D. politely shook her mother's hand. It felt strange, the two of them meeting. She quickly tried to think—was there any safe topic, anything they had in common? She came up with zilch. Nada.

Lex carefully looked J.D. over, suspicious from the outset. Payton knew she was making mental note of the expensive cut of his pants, the fine quality of his dark gray shirt, and the way he wore his jacket, without a tie, in an effortlessly stylish look.

"It's a pleasure to meet you, Mrs. Kendall," J.D. said.

Payton winced. Already a screwup, and on the basics at that. Having kept her own name, even after marrying Steven, Lex Kendall was no "Mrs."

J.D. smiled at her mother, obviously unaware of the shaky ground on which he stood. "I hope you and Mr. Kendall had a nice brunch."

Oh . . . no. Payton saw her mother's eyes flash.

"Well—*J.D.*, is it?" Lex led in with what could only be described as a "tone." "Putting aside your blatant patriarchal biases in assuming the necessary presence of a male familial figurehead, yes, I had a nice brunch, thanks."

Payton rolled her eyes in exasperation. "He was just being polite, Mom." She glanced over apologetically at J.D., expecting to find him annoyed, irritated, offended, or some combination thereof.

But instead, he seemed amused. "My mistake, *Ms.* Kendall," J.D. corrected himself. "And thank you." He looked over at Payton, his eyes dancing. "Suddenly, everything has become much clearer."

Payton shot him a look. Very funny.

She was about to say something to extricate her and her mother as quickly as possible, before this encounter that teetered on the brink of disaster got any worse, when a voice, a woman's, came from behind J.D.

"If you don't intend to introduce us to your friend, J.D., perhaps your father and I should go ahead and be seated at the table."

Payton turned to J.D., her eyes wide. Now *this* was interesting. "You have parents," she said.

"Yes, shockingly, even I have parents."

Payton laughed. She had forgotten that J.D. could actually be kind of funny every once in a while. If you liked that whole dry-humor kind of thing.

"No, I meant here, with you." Curious, Payton peered over and saw a distinguished-looking couple in their early sixties heading in their direction.

J.D. made the introductions. "Payton, these are my parents, Preston and Evelyn Jameson." He gestured to Payton and her mother. "Mom, Dad, this is Payton Kendall and her mother, Lex Kendall. Payton is a coworker of mine; she works in the same group as me."

With a formal air, J.D.'s father stepped forward to shake Payton's hand. He was tall, like his son, had salt-and-pepper hair, and looked very dignified in his gray tweed sport coat and wire-rimmed glasses.

"So you're a lawyer as well, Ms. Kendall?" he inquired.

"Yes, Judge," she said, shaking his hand. "It's a pleasure to meet you." As a member of the legal profession, it was indeed an honor for her to meet the Honorable Preston D. Jameson of the Seventh Circuit Court of Appeals.

Judge Jameson gave her a slight nod, as if to acknowledge her acknowledgment of his judicial status. He had a stern demeanor, Payton noticed, which struck her as being very unlike his son. There were lots of words she could use to describe J.D.—no comment on whether any of them would be particularly complimentary—but "stern" would not be among them.

Payton turned next to Evelyn Jameson, and the first thing she noticed was a pair of brilliant blue eyes. J.D.'s eyes.

The startling familiarity of those eyes was immediately overshadowed, however, by the second thing Payton noticed about J.D.'s mother: the beige suede car coat she was wearing that had—oh, lord—a sable *fur* collar.

Payton shook her hand. "It's nice to meet you, Mrs. Jameson. Could you excuse me for one second?"

She spun around to her mother and whispered quietly. "If you let the coat slide, I'll give up dairy for a week."

Lex gave her a look that was 100 percent pure motherly reassurance. "Of course, Sis, if it's that important to you. Make it a month."

Quintessential Lex Kendall.

"Fine," Payton hissed softly. "Just be polite."

Lex snickered, stealing a glance at the Jamesons. "Don't worry, I know how to deal with people like this. They look exactly like your father's parents, the first time I met them."

Payton blinked, shocked. Her father had *money*? This was the first she had heard of any such thing.

But she tabled that discussion and held her breath as she watched her mother introduce herself to J.D.'s parents. Lex was pleasant enough but—it never failed—still Lex.

"Nice coat," she told J.D.'s mother. "I have two just like it at home."

Evelyn smiled politely. "Oh, I don't think so," she replied, somehow managing to sound both condescending and genteel. "This is a Christian Lacroix, you know."

Payton stifled a laugh. Ah, J.D. was right. Suddenly things had become much clearer. She heard a voice, low in her ear.

"You don't have to say it out loud; I already know what you're thinking."

She looked over her shoulder to see J.D. standing next her. "You think you know me so well."

"I do," he said, still speaking so that their parents couldn't hear.

"Then what am I thinking now?" Payton asked coyly. Wait—was she *flirting*? No. Yes. To be determined.

"You're thinking that out of all the brunches in the city, you had to pick the same one as me," J.D. said.

Payton couldn't help but smile at that. She had a view of their parents, and she watched as her mother—undoubtedly on yet another diatribe—took off one of her animal-cruelty-free clogs and held it up to Evelyn Jameson. J.D.'s mother looked pained.

"Close. I was thinking that if I knew we were going to pick the same brunch, I would've had that third mimosa before our parents met."

J.D. turned in the direction of their parents and eyed the scene with amusement. "There's always the bar off the lobby."

Payton laughed.

J.D. studied her for a moment. "Actually . . . I was thinking I might have to sneak off to the bar myself."

Now it was Payton's turn to study him. Was that an invitation? Hard to tell. "That does sound tempting," she said, figuring that answer worked either way.

"Tempting," J.D. repeated.

Then his gaze fell to her lips.

Payton suddenly felt a hand on her shoulder, interrupting them. She glanced over and saw her mother's pointed look.

"We don't want the food to get cold, Sis." Lex gestured to the box of food for the unhoused people.

Payton nodded. "Yes." She glanced up at J.D. "We should get going."

J.D. nodded. "Of course. I'll see you tomorrow, then."

Payton murmured a quick good-bye to J.D.'s parents, then left the restaurant with her mother. When they got outside, she handed the ticket to the valet.

She and her mother waited in front of the hotel, neither of them saying a word. Finally, Lex broke the ice.

"Do you want to tell me what that was all about?"

"He's just a coworker, Mom."

More silence.

"Why have you never mentioned that my father had money?" Payton asked.

Lex shrugged. "I don't know. I didn't think it was relevant, I guess."

Payton didn't buy her mother's nonchalance. "Did that have anything to do with why you two never married?"

For a moment she didn't think her mother was going to answer.

"When his parents found out I was pregnant, they told him to choose me or his inheritance," Lex said. "He didn't choose me. He didn't choose *us*."

"You don't think that's something I might've wanted to know?" Payton couldn't believe she was first finding out about this after all these years. It explained so much.

Her mother turned to her. "Listen, Payton—I know you tune out a lot of what I say, but trust me on this: stay away from him."

At first Payton thought her mother meant she should stay away from Shane, her father, but then realized she was referring to J.D.

"I don't even like him, Mom." Most of the time.

Lex studied her shrewdly. "That's not how it looked to me."

"I didn't realize you could see us through all those witty barbs you were flinging at J.D.'s mother."

"I saw enough."

Payton cocked her head, conceding. "The part where he helped me out with my jacket wasn't half bad."

"Chivalrous crap."

"Don't hold back, Mom. Tell me what you really think."

Her mother eyed her warily. "I think you've gone soft, that's what I think," she grumbled.

Payton thought about this. Maybe she had.

Her mother, of all people, had once fallen in love with a high-society rich man. At this point, anything was possible.

Even being civil to J.D.

Maybe.

Seventeen

"SO WAIT—WHERE was this great moment between you and Payton? Did I miss it?"

J.D. shook his head, sighing. Sometimes he really regretted telling Tyler anything.

"I didn't say we had a 'moment.' What I said was, at the restaurant, there was a brief second—"

"—You said a 'brief *moment*,'" Tyler corrected.

Growing agitated, J.D. sat back in the aged leather nail-head armchair, gesturing distractedly.

"Fine, whatever, maybe I used the word 'moment,' but I didn't mean, you know, '*moment*.'" He mockingly emphasized the word, tempted to use finger quotes, but he really hated when people did that.

"What I meant to say was, there was a brief *period of time* at the restaurant when I thought we were . . ." he searched for the right words ". . . getting along." He decided that was the safest way to describe his and Payton's interaction earlier that morning.

He and Tyler were in the cigar bar at Crimson, a private

club for Harvard graduates. It was an unofficial tradition
they had started several years ago: every Father's Day evening, J.D. and his friends met here to unwind. Some people, particularly in his social circle, sought out the comfort
of their therapists to recover from the stress of family holi-
days. J.D., not a believer in the whole my-father-never-played-
catch-with-me psychoanalytical crap, found that a nice,
smooth glass of single-malt Scotch did the trick just as
nicely, and for about one-tenth the cost. (Yes, fine, Payton
had guessed right in her tirade in the library, he liked to
drink Scotch, so sue him.)

Being a private club—although a Harvard degree was
the only membership requirement—the bar was small. It
had been designed to resemble a private library: warm brown
bookshelves lined two walls; the other walls were decorated
with paintings boasting various equestrian scenes. Leather
armchairs, all of which were taken that evening, had been
arranged in intimate groupings throughout the room. J.D.
and Tyler had been lucky to score two chairs in the back
by the fireplace. Their friends Trey and Connor, who had
arrived fifteen minutes later, had not been so lucky and
were now part of the seatless masses that lined the main
bar.

Somewhere around their second drink, J.D. had found
himself mentioning to Tyler that he had run into Payton
and her mother at the Park Hyatt hotel. His friend had been
on his case ever since.

"You thought you and Payton were 'getting along,'"
Tyler repeated.

"Maybe more than that, even."

"That would be a shock," Tyler said. "Do you have any
support for this claim?"

Holding his glass by the stem, J.D. gave the Scotch a
swirl, watching the legs run down the side of the crystal. "I
don't know. I thought I saw something different in her
look."

"Now there's hard evidence if I've ever heard it."

J.D. folded his arms behind his head contentedly. Tyler's quips had no effect on him today. "Ah . . . my droll friend, I guess you just had to be there."

Tyler looked him over. "You're in an awfully good mood for having spent the day with your father. Is there more to this story with Payton than what you're telling me?"

J.D. shook his head matter-of-factly. "Nope."

"Then I want to make sure I understand the scene correctly: there was this alleged nebulous look that took place during these couple of minutes at the Park Hyatt hotel where you two somehow miraculously managed to string a few polite sentences together."

"I think it was a bit more than that," J.D. said.

"Do tell. Because this is really steamy stuff. What happens next?"

J.D. grinned. "That's the interesting part—I don't know."

"Well, I hate to be the one to point this out, but whatever is going on, the fun's about to end. Because you and Payton have all of about, oh"—Tyler checked the date on his watch—"less than two weeks left before the firm makes one of you partner and the other of you . . . well, you know."

"Thanks for the reminder," J.D. said dryly. As if he needed Tyler to mention it. As if he didn't already know that fact himself, as if this hadn't been the very thing he'd been thinking since the moment he'd left Payton's apartment the other night.

It was the worst possible circumstances. She was the only one standing in the way of his making partner. He needed to *crush* her. But that desire had ended the moment he had found out how she'd helped him with the deposition.

He wished they had more time.

Tyler was right—he and Payton were speeding toward the end of their eight-year race and there was nothing he could do to change that. Which meant that if there was anything to be done, he had to do it fast.

So the question was: Was there anything to be done?

A few weeks ago, J.D. never would've believed he'd be having these thoughts. But things had changed. And not just for him, for Payton, too. Unless he was really, really reading her wrong, that is.

So again, *if* he wanted something to happen, the time was now.

For what might've been the first time in his adult life, J.D. didn't know what to do. He cleared his throat. "I need your advice, Tyler."

His friend did not seem particularly surprised by this lead-in. "Lay it on me. But first—shall we?" Tyler pulled a black leather cigar case from the inner pocket of his corduroy jacket and offered one of the cigars, a Padron Millennium 1964 Series, to J.D. It was part of their Father's Day tradition, an homage to the time when they were kids and had discovered J.D.'s father's premium cigar collection in a locked cabinet in the den. It had been a Padron that they had smoked that day, out on the verandah, thinking they were hotshots, not realizing that shortly thereafter both of them were going to be violently ill for the next twenty-four hours for amateurishly inhaling the smoke.

J.D. took one of the cigars out of the case. Tyler pulled out a matchbook, lit his cigar, then he handed the matches to J.D. After lighting his own cigar, J.D. eased back in his chair, puffing and rotating and tasting—not inhaling—the smoke.

After they sat in silence for a few moments, Tyler glanced over. "I can start you off, if you'd like."

"Oh, this should be good—by all means." J.D. gestured for him to proceed.

Tyler raked his hand through his hair to get it mussed just right. He casually leaned back in his chair, then raised one eyebrow in an over-the-top smirk. "Tyler—I've been thinking about a few things—"

J.D. held up his hand, offended. "Hold on. Is that supposed to be *me*?"

"Don't interrupt. It takes me out of character." Tyler went back to his impersonation. This time, instead of the sly eyebrow and smirk, he folded his arms across his chest, held his cigar aloft, and sighed melodramatically.

"Tyler—I've led quite the charmed life, haven't I? I drive the right car, I wear the right clothes, and I'm fantastic—if I do say so myself—at every sport I play, and well, let's be honest here"—he winked ever-so-proudly—"women love me."

J.D. was not amused. "Your life has hardly been any less char—"

"But, Tyler," Tyler went on, talking over J.D., "lately I've begun to suspect that something's missing from my perfect existence, that perhaps there's something more I want, a certain female, perhaps, who, shall we say . . . intrigues me."

Tyler paused here and looked at J.D. expectantly.

"Oh, is that my cue?" J.D. asked sarcastically. "Now am I supposed to be me or you?"

"I could keep going if you like."

"Thanks, I think I can take it from here," J.D. retorted. "You're worse than she is," he grumbled under his breath.

"Admit it, you love it," Tyler said. "You subconsciously feel guilty about your overprivileged upbringing, so you purposely hang around people who castigate you for exactly that as a form of self-flagellation."

Now *that* J.D. laughed at. "I didn't realize you were still TiVo'ing *Dr. Phil.*"

"Ha. Try Psych 101. Your ego is trying to balance the desires of your id while not upsetting the goals of your superego."

J.D. rolled his eyes. "Speaking of superegos, if we could get back to the subject of Payton—"

"Please—you'd just love for your id to be all over that superego."

J.D. paused. He wouldn't have put it that way, but come to think of it . . .

"Help me out here," he said to Tyler. "Give me your honest opinion. Do you think it would be totally crazy if I—"

"*No fucking way!*"

The shout, resonating through the bar, came from behind Tyler. Recognizing the voice as that of their friend Trey, J.D. glanced over and saw him shaking hands with some other guy—whose back was to them—whom Trey was obviously excited to see. Momentarily tabling his conversation with Tyler, J.D. watched as Trey gestured in his direction. The mystery guy turned around.

Surprised to see a face he hadn't seen since law school, J.D. stood up, grinning, as the man walked over.

"Chase Bellamy . . ." J.D. said, extending his hand in greeting. "What are you doing here?"

Chase slapped him on the shoulder. "J. D. Jameson. It's good to see you." He pointed to Trey, explaining. "I ran into Trey the other day when I was coming out of court. He told me about this place and said I should stop by tonight." He looked J.D. over. "I haven't seen you since graduation. You wished me luck and said something sarcastic about saving the world."

J.D. grinned. Say something sarcastic? Who, him? While he and Chase hadn't hung out regularly in law school, he liked the guy well enough. He could sum up Chase Bellamy in one word: harmless. A bit of a liberal do-gooder, and maybe too agreeably passive in J.D.'s mind, but harmless. He remembered a strident debate he and Chase had once gotten into in their Constitutional Law class, over the Second Amendment's right to bear arms. What he recalled most distinctly about that debate was that Chase had given up far too easily.

"So the last I heard, you were in D.C. working on a campaign," J.D. said. "Are you living in Chicago now?"

Chase nodded. "I just moved here a few months ago—I'm doing pro bono work with the Chicago Legal Clinic."

J.D. smiled. Of course he was. He introduced Tyler, who had been in the law school class below them. The three of them quickly fell into talk about work.

"So what about you? Where did you end up?" Chase asked.

"Ripley and Davis," J.D. told him.

A look of recognition crossed Chase's face. J.D. assumed this to be an acknowledgment of the prestige of his firm, until Chase remarked, "Oh, I know someone else who works there. Are you in corporate or litigation?"

"Litigation."

"Then you probably know her—Payton Kendall?"

"Sure, I know Payton." J.D. grinned. Funny. Small world. "How do *you* know her?" he asked. Strange, he hadn't meant for his tone to sound so proprietary.

Now Chase grinned. "Actually . . . we're dating."

J.D. probably would've been less stunned if Chase had hauled off and punched him straight in the gut. He cocked his head. "Wait—Payton *Kendall*?" As if there were just too many Paytons floating around the litigation group to keep track of.

"Yes, Payton Kendall." Chase looked him over curiously. "You seem a bit surprised."

It didn't matter, J.D. told himself. Really. He was fine with it.

He shook off Chase's question. "No, not at all. Why would I be surprised? You and Payton have a lot in common. Good. Yes. That's great. Tyler, did you hear that? Chase here is dating Payton Kendall. You know Payton, don't you?"

Tyler gave J.D. a look that said he quickly needed to shut up.

Too late. Chase seemed to suspect something. "Wait a second . . . I just realized what's going on here. You're the competition."

"The competition?" J.D. asked loudly. "Why, whatever do you mean?" Christ, now he sounded like he was doing bad dinner theater. He needed to pull his shit together.

"Payton didn't mention any names, but she told me there was stiff competition in her bid to make partner," Chase said.

J.D. blinked. Oh . . . competition for the *partnership*. Of course.

"You're in the same class as her," Chase continued. "It's you she's talking about, isn't it?"

A few weeks ago, J.D. would've been pleased to hear Payton describe him as "stiff competition." But now he had thought things were different.

But why was Chase asking him about this, anyway? This was *his* personal business with Payton. No one else's.

"Payton and I are both up for partner this year, yes," was all J.D. said.

But then he wondered just how much Chase knew about recent events. He could only imagine how Payton might have described certain situations—in particular, certain situations involving, say, a shoe and perhaps a couple of peeky-cheeks—to outside third parties. And if Chase did know about said certain situations, well . . .

J.D. did a quick assessment. Chase appeared to be about five-ten, maybe one-sixty, one-sixty-five pounds. No problem. If the little tree-hugger started swinging, coming in at a lean six-two, J.D. was quite certain he could hold his own.

But Chase, being Chase, merely grinned good-naturedly. "Well, Jameson, I'd love to wish you luck in making partner, but I guess I have a conflict of interest." With that, he stuck out his hand. "It was good seeing you, J.D."

Harmless, easygoing Chase Bellamy. He really was the kind of guy no one could find fault with. The kind of guy who never got angry or annoyed. The kind of guy who preferred to amiably let things roll off his back rather than stick it out and fight. The kind of guy that Payton liked, apparently.

And J.D. knew that he was not that kind of guy.

Furthermore, he would never be that kind of guy. Frankly, he didn't *want* to be that kind of guy. He just wasn't wired that way.

So with that in mind, he shook Chase's hand firmly.

"It was good seeing you, too, Chase," J.D. said. "And good luck. With everything." He even managed a polite smile.

After all, while he might not be the kind of guy Chase was, he could at least still be a gentleman.

J.D. AND TYLER waited outside the bar, trying to catch a cab. In addition to being unseasonably cool that evening, it had begun to rain, and finding an available taxi was proving to be a challenge.

Tyler hadn't brought up the subject of Payton since their conversation with Chase and for that, J.D. was grateful. He wasn't sure he wanted to talk about her right then. He needed to sort through his thoughts, to process this new development that she was dating someone, and figure out exactly what that meant. *If* it meant anything.

An open cab finally pulled around the corner, and J.D. and Tyler agreed to share it. As the cab pulled away from the curb, J.D. glanced out the window and saw everyone running in the rain with their collars turned up and purses over their heads. The weatherman had predicted a cool and clear evening, so now people were scrambling.

"In answer to your earlier question, no, I don't think it would be completely crazy."

J.D. glanced over at Tyler. All joking aside, they had been best friends since grade school and normally he put more weight in Tyler's opinions than pretty much anyone else's. But things had changed in the past couple of hours.

"It's not that simple anymore," he said. "Actually, it wasn't simple before, and now it's even less so."

"Why? Because of Chase?" Tyler asked.

"In part because of Chase. It certainly suggests I misinterpreted things."

"You don't know jack-shit about their relationship. Who knows how long they've been dating? Or whether she's even into him? Chase might be nice, but I don't see Payton with him for the long haul."

"It's also quite possible she still detests me."

Tyler dismissed this with a wave. "You're going to let a thing like that stop you?"

"I was thinking intense despisement might be an obstacle in pursuing her, yes."

"No, see, that's what makes it all the more interesting," Tyler said. He adopted a grandly dramatic tone. " 'Does our fair Ms. Kendall truly loathe the arrogant Mr. Jameson as she so ardently proclaims, or is it all just a charade to cover more amorous feelings for a man she reluctantly admires?' "

Up front, the cabdriver snorted loudly. He appeared to be enjoying the show.

"Psych 101 again?" J.D. asked.

Tyler shook his head. "Lit 305: Eighteenth-Century Women's Fiction." He caught J.D.'s look and quickly defended himself. "What? I took it because of the girls in the class. Anyway, I see a bit of a *P and P* dynamic going on between you and Payton."

J.D. didn't think he wanted to know. Really. But he asked anyway. "*P and P?*"

Tyler shot him a look, appalled. "Uh, hello—*Pride and Prejudice?*" His tone said only a cretin wouldn't know this.

"Oh right, *P and P*," J.D. said. "You know, Tyler, you might want to pick up your balls—I think they just fell right off when you said that."

Up front, the cabdriver let out a good snicker.

Tyler shook his head. "Laugh if you want, but let me tell you something: women go crazy for that book. And even crazier for men who have read it. If I plan to bring a girl back to my place, I might just so happen to leave a copy of it sitting out on my coffee table and, let's just say, hijinks frequently ensue. And you know what? It's not a bad bit of storytelling. I like to put on a nice pot of Earl Grey tea, maybe a slice of almond biscotti, and—yeah, that's fine, keep right on laughing, buddy, but I bet I've gotten laid more recently than you."

"Hey—not that I'm not thoroughly amused at the thought of your little tea cozy and you wrapped up in a blanket reading your book—"

"I didn't say there was a blanket." Tyler paused. "Fine. Sometimes there may be a blanket."

"—but my question is, were you going anywhere with this, or is it just some sort of weird sharing moment?"

Tyler had to think. "Where *was* I going with this . . . ?" He snapped his fingers. "Oh, yeah—*Pride and Prejudice*. Women and the whole Darcy complex. For Payton, that's you."

"I thought Darcy was the asshole."

Tyler smiled fondly. "You know, he really kind of is."

"Great pep talk, Tyler. Thanks."

"But he doesn't *stay* the asshole," Tyler said. "See, you just don't understand women the way I do, J.D. They want it all: a career, apple martinis, financial independence, great shoes; but at the same time—and *this* they'll never admit— they are drawn to patriarchal men who are dominant and controlling. That's the essence of the Darcy complex. He may be an asshole, but he's an asshole that gets the girl in the end."

J.D. rolled his eyes. This entire conversation was just so ridiculous.

But still.

"And how does he accomplish that?" he asked.

"Oh, it gets a little complicated," Tyler said. "See, Lizzie has this troublesome younger sister who runs off with the guy she originally *thought* she liked—wait, back up—to really understand, I should start with the visit to Pemberley, because it actually starts with the aunt and uncle, see—her uncle loves to fish and Darcy asks—"

J.D. held up his hand, very, very sorry he asked. "The short version please. We're already at your stop."

Tyler looked out the window and saw that the cab had indeed pulled up in front of his building. He turned back to J.D. "Okay. The short version, the very short version: he gets the girl by being nice to her."

J.D. waited. "That's it? He's *nice* to her? That's so . . . lame."

"Look, if you want to win Payton over—"

J.D. stopped him right there. "Hey, we're only speaking in hypotheticals, okay? I haven't decided that I want to win anyone over."

"Oh. Then my advice is that you should start there. Figure out what you want." With that, Tyler got out of the cab and darted through the rain into his building.

Great. Thanks for the help. J.D. gave the cabdriver his address. He stared out the window as the taxi made its way the six blocks to his building. When they arrived, J.D. reached through the divider and handed the cabdriver a twenty and told him to keep the change.

The driver turned around. "Hey—your friend back there was giving you some pretty strange advice." Around fortyish and wearing a ragged flannel shirt and a Sox cap that had seen far better days, the guy had one of the thickest Chicago accents J.D. had ever heard. "He seemed a little off the wall, if you know what I mean. I don't think I'd listen to him if I were you."

J.D. grinned. "I'll take that under advisement." He opened the door to the cab and stepped out.

"Because everybody knows that Darcy doesn't win Lizzie over just by being nice."

J.D. stopped. He looked back over his shoulder.

The driver rested his arm on the divider. His rolled-up sleeve revealed a tattoo of a black scorpion that covered his entire forearm. "See, it's all about the Grand Gesture. That's how you get the girl."

"Thank you," J.D. managed to say.

The driver shrugged. "No prob-lem. Frankly, it sounded like you could use all the help you can get."

He put the cab into gear.

"And listen—tell your friend to try English Breakfast next time. It's a little more robust. Earl Grey is really more of a *Sense and Sensibility* kind of tea."

AT HOME LATER that night, after J.D. had done the final checks for the evening of his email and work voice mail and cell phone voice mail and home voice mail and was satisfied that there were no work matters that required his immediate attention, he thought about Tyler's advice. *Figure out what you want.* And it was then that J.D. realized.

He didn't know.

As he had told Tyler, things weren't that simple. Chase *did* complicate things. Of course he did. Maybe Payton really liked him. J.D. could see the two of them together—with all they had in common, they just seemed to make sense.

Tyler had been dismissive of this, and maybe to him Chase and every other obstacle just made the whole Payton issue a better intrigue, but then again, Tyler wasn't up for partner that year. Tyler also wasn't competing with Payton for only one partnership spot. And Tyler certainly didn't have the history he had with Payton. *Eight years* of history.

It was a long time. It struck J.D. then, that he had become so swept up in beating Payton that he hadn't directed his anger where he should have: at the firm. *They* were the ones who had put him and Payton in this position. Making partner was never a guarantee, but after all his hard work he deserved better. She deserved better.

But what bothered J.D. most was not the unfairness of the firm's decision. Rather, it was the fact that when he looked back on the past eight years, he wasn't necessarily proud of his own behavior. He had regrets, and there were things he wished he could go back and do differently. There was that one thing in particular that even Tyler didn't know about . . .

Figure out what you want.

J.D. knew that he wanted to scrap the past. To start over. For the next fourteen days at least, he wanted to do things right. If he couldn't change the fact that things had to come to an end with Payton, he could at least change the *way* they ended.

It wasn't much, J.D. realized, and it certainly didn't answer all the lingering questions.

But it was a start.

EARLY THE NEXT morning, Payton rushed around her office, packing up her trial briefcase. Yes, *now* she wished she had packed it the night before, but her mother had taken a late flight out and Payton hadn't seen the need to make a special trip into the office at midnight. A good trial attorney should be prepared for anything, she knew, and that's why she always built in extra time, particularly since she took the "L" to work. Ah, those little tricksters at the

Chicago Transit Authority, she could always count on them to keep things spicy. Because, really, who didn't want to spend an extra fifty-five minutes in the packed, hot, smelly car of a train that inexplicably moved only three miles an hour the entire trip downtown? That was *fun stuff*.

Payton grabbed the case files she had reviewed over the weekend and stuffed them into the large, boxy trial briefcase that weighed nearly a ton. She hoped Brandon would show up soon so she could pawn the thing off onto him—after all, wasn't that what junior associates, and men, were for?

Payton heard a knock on her door and looked up. Instead of Brandon, she saw J.D. standing in the doorway. He was armed with a Starbucks cup.

Blimey.

"I noticed that you seem to be running late," he said. "I didn't think you'd have time to grab this on your way to court. Grande sugar-free vanilla latte, right?" he asked, gesturing to the coffee. "I've heard you say it to Irma a few times," he added quickly.

He held the cup out to her.

Payton looked at it, then back at J.D. It was a trap, it had to be. She remained where she stood.

The corners of J.D.'s mouth curled up. "*No*, I don't plan to throw it at you."

Payton smiled. Ha-ha. Throw it at her? As if that had ever crossed her mind.

"That's not what I was thinking," she assured him as she walked over and took the cup. He certainly was taking their truce seriously, she thought. How sweet.

She subtly sniffed the coffee for poison.

J.D. smiled again. "And *no*, I didn't put anything in it."

Payton took a sip of the latte.

J.D. winked. "Nothing that can be detected by its smell, anyway."

Payton stopped, mid-swallow, and held the liquid in her

mouth. He was kidding, of course. Payton smiled and shook a finger to let him know she was in on the joke. *Ah, J.D. you funny guy, you.* She looked around her office. Seriously, why was there never a spittoon around when you needed one?

"I'm kidding, Payton," J.D. said. "You don't have to act so shocked. I'm just trying to be . . ." He hesitated. "Nice?"

Payton swallowed. "Nice?"

J.D. nodded. "Sure. Call this, you know, a *gesture*." He looked around her office. "So how's your trial coming along? From the little I saw the day your shoe, uh . . . and then you . . . well, you were there, you know what happened—it looked like the jury's on your side. What do you think?"

Payton stared at him. "Seriously. What are you doing?"

J.D. blinked innocently at her. "What do you mean, what am I doing?"

"First the coffee, and now you're—what—making idle chitchat? Is that what this is?"

J.D. shrugged. "Sure."

"Another gesture, I suppose?" she asked.

"Exactly—another *gesture*." J.D. smiled. "So now there's been two *gestures*."

Payton carefully looked him over. "Are you sure you're okay?" He was acting so bizarre right then. Maybe he was ill.

"I'm fine," he said. "You were going to tell me about your trial?"

"Well . . . things are going good, I guess. Assuming there aren't any surprises, we should start closing arguments in two days. Thank you for asking."

"Of course."

Payton waited as J.D. continued to linger in her doorway. Was there . . . something else? "I really should get going to court."

"You really should," he agreed.

Still, with the lingering.

Payton gestured to her coffee cup. "Thank you for the Starbucks?" Maybe he was waiting for a tip.

J.D. seemed pleased with this response. "You're welcome." He straightened up. "Well, then. Good luck in court, Payton." With a nod, he turned and left.

Payton shook her head as she watched him leave. Whatever the hell that was, she had no clue.

In eight years—all their fights, coffee-stained suits, peeky-cheeks, and everything else considered—*that* had to be the oddest interaction she'd ever had with J. D. Jameson.

Eighteen

"I THINK WE need to talk."

Six such simple words, but Payton hated hearing them. Everyone hated hearing them.

It was part of a voice mail message Chase had left her, one she'd first heard when she'd got back to the office after finishing up in court. It had been a long day—the judge had dismissed them later than usual; he was trying to make sure the trial ended as scheduled in two days. Payton was wiped out, vaporized, as she was during every trial on the days her witnesses were cross-examined by opposing counsel. She personally found it to be the most exhausting thing a lawyer had to do: protect her own witnesses during cross-examination and pray, pray, pray they didn't say anything stupid.

So, needless to say, when she first heard Chase's message in which, in addition to wanting to "talk," he suggested they meet at some coffee bar called the Fixx, she hesitated and yes, the terrible person she was, Payton thought about not calling him back. But then guilt set in (he's such a nice guy, he's Laney and Nate's friend), followed by rationalization (she would only stay for a half hour, then come back to the office to work), and one short cab ride later, here she was, about to start her third latte of the day, as she smiled apologetically at Chase because, of course, she had been fifteen minutes late.

"I'm sorry," she told him for the second time. She was frazzled with everything going on at work and, P.S., a little wired from all the caffeine.

They grabbed a table near the front of the coffee shop, by the windows. As Payton had quickly learned when she had mistakenly ordered a "grande," the Fixx was one of those indie, we-piss-on-Starbucks kind of coffeehouses that catered to an eclectic mix from the multi-tattooed/ pierced grunge and Goth type to the scarf-and-turtleneck-wearing literati crowd. The kind of place her mother would love.

As she and Chase took their seats, Payton felt overdressed in the tailored suit and heels she had worn for court. She glanced around, wondering when exactly it was she had stopped fitting into places like this.

"You said you wanted to talk?" she prompted Chase, not trying to hurry him along, but . . . okay, fine, she was trying to hurry him along.

Chase nodded. "First, I want to start by saying that I understand now what's going on. With you and J.D., I mean. I ran into him last night and we started talking and, well, I kind of put two and two together."

Payton had no idea what Chase was talking about. Although she had picked up on one thing. "You talked to J. D. Jameson? You know him?"

"We went to law school together."

Of course. Payton knew they had both gone to Harvard; she didn't know why it hadn't clicked that they would have been in the same class. She was interested to hear what J.D. had been like back in law school, particularly since for years she had viewed him pretty much as a one-dimensional character: the Villain, the Archrival, the Enemy. Doing so had made it easier for her to dismiss all the times he'd been such a jerk to her. But now . . . well, things had changed and she found herself wanting to know more about him, more personal things. For starters, she was *very* curious to know what "J.D." stood for.

Payton sensed, however, that now was not the time to ask Chase for the behind-the-scenes tour. "So you ran into J.D. last night, and this two and two you put together is, what, exactly?"

"That he's the one you're competing against to make partner," Chase said. "And now I totally get why you've been so stressed out these days. I wouldn't want to go up against J.D., either."

Payton sat back and crossed her legs defensively. "I'm not afraid to take on J.D. I think I have a pretty decent shot, you know."

Chase was quick to assure her. "Of course you do, that came out wrong," he said apologetically. "What I meant to say is that I know how stressful this must be for you, with the way J.D. is."

"Meaning?"

"Well, honestly, I think he's kind of an asshole. He's full of himself, stubborn, and most of all, extremely competitive. He's one of those I-always-have-to-win, I-always-have-to-be-right types. I hate people like that."

Payton laughed. "Well, then, we *do* need to talk. Because you just described me."

Chase grinned affectionately. "You're not like that."

"Yes, I am, Chase. I'm exactly like that."

Chase tried to dismiss this. "But it's different with you—those qualities are admirable in a woman. That's how you have to act in order to be successful, particularly in the legal profession."

"That's kind of sexist against men, isn't it?" Payton

glanced out the window. Wait—was that a *pig* she just saw go flying by?

Chase shifted uneasily in his chair. "Look—I think we're getting off track here. All I'm trying to say is that, before, maybe, I thought you were getting a little too worked up about making partner, but now I understand why. I'm sure J.D. has taken the stakes up, like, ten notches."

Well, yes. But then again, so had she. And on another note, Payton found it very interesting that Chase had thought she was getting "too worked up" about making partner. Who was he to decide the proper level of importance she should place on the advancement of *her* career?

And frankly, while she was thinking about it, she didn't particularly like the way Chase talked about J.D. Sure, J.D. could definitely come off a little arrogant and perhaps overly confident at times, but he did have his moments. For instance, she begrudgingly had to give him credit for the fact that, after the deposition, he had come to her house to apologize in person. She knew that hadn't been easy for him. And there were other things, little things, like at dinner with the Gibson's reps, when he'd kept her company while the other men went off to smoke cigars. Or the way he'd come looking for her in the library after Ben had given them the news that only one of them would make partner. He only had been trying to be nice, she knew, yet in return she had been rude and defensive.

And then there was the thing he'd said to her the other night as he left her house. *I would've done it for you in a heartbeat.* Payton had gone over those words a hundred times in her head. She needed to be careful when it came to J.D.—she had to protect herself; she didn't want to misread him, couldn't afford to mistakenly attach too much significance to something he'd maybe meant only as a professional courtesy.

Payton realized that Chase was studying her, presumably waiting for her to say something similarly negative about J.D. But oddly, the person she had questionable feelings about as a result of this conversation was Chase. He had been very emphatic in wanting to talk to her, but so far she hadn't heard anything that merited pulling her out of work and away from the hours of research she still had ahead of her that evening.

"I don't mean to be rude, Chase, but I really have to get back to the office," she said. "As a last-ditch effort, the plaintiff moved to strike some of our jury instructions and the judge wants to hear our arguments tomorrow," she explained. "So is this why you asked me to meet you here? To talk about J.D.?"

Chase shook his head. "Actually, I wanted to talk about us. Look—you obviously have a lot going on with work right now, and maybe that's all it is, but I was thinking about you last night, that I wanted to do something nice for you, something to take your mind off of things. But then it hit me, that I wasn't sure you actually *wanted* me to take your mind off of things, that maybe all you want is to be focused on your job—and that's great, Payton, don't get me wrong—but . . ."

He hesitated, his brown eyes full of questions. "Is that really all it is? Because I can wait out these last few days until your firm makes its partnership decisions, but if it's more than that, then . . . maybe it just would be better if I backed off now."

At first, Payton didn't know what to say. She wasn't ready to have this conversation, at least not now, anyway. She took a deep breath.

"I blindsided you with this, didn't I?" Chase asked, grinning sheepishly.

"Yes, you could say that," Payton said, exhaling with a nervous laugh.

Chase reached across the table and took her hand. "Look, we don't need to finish this conversation right now.

I just thought this was something I needed to say. And I hate talking about these things over the phone."

Payton nodded. She probably was a fool to not immediately say, no, of course she didn't want him to back off. But Chase was right: she needed to think before she answered him. Right now, she was confused and—while she hated to admit it—fighting the urge to check her watch. But since he had brought up the subject, she responded as honestly as she could. He deserved that at least.

"This trial is the last thing the firm will judge me on before making its partnership decision," she told him. "I get that you have questions, but it's hard for me to focus on anything else right now. But it will be over in two days. If you could just wait until then, I promise that we'll sit down and really talk."

Chase smiled and said he understood.

Funny, Payton thought. Because she personally had no clue what she was doing.

BACK IN THE office.

Again.

Sometimes, she felt like she never left the place. Probably because she rarely did.

It was nearly seven o'clock, which meant the secretaries were gone and the office was quiet. When Payton got to her office, she saw that Brandon had left three stacks of cases on her desk for her review—the results of his research into each of the three jury instructions the plaintiff had challenged. Unfortunately for Payton, each pile was at least two inches thick, which meant her chances of leaving the office anytime soon were nonexistent to none.

She had just barely begun to tackle the first mound of cases when she heard a knock on her door. She glanced up and saw Laney.

"Hey—why are you still here?" Payton asked. She lowered her voice to a near whisper. "I thought tonight was the big night." Laney—so Payton had learned yesterday in a conversation that included entirely too much information—was ovulating tonight. She had planned to leave early and surprise Nate. Et cetera.

"I'm on my way out," Laney said. "What time are you leaving for the cocktail hour?"

Payton frowned, confused. "The cocktail hour?" She smacked her forehead, suddenly remembering. "Shit—the cocktail hour!"

Every June, the litigation group hosted a cocktail hour to welcome that year's crop of summer associates, and all lawyers in the group were "strongly encouraged" to attend. With everything going on, she had completely forgotten that the party was tonight. She had set a reminder on her computer's daily planner that must've gone off while she was at the Fixx with Chase.

Crap.

With a groan, Payton rubbed her forehead. "I'm not going to be able to go to the cocktail hour tonight." She gestured to the five and a half inches of cases on her desk that she still needed to read. "I've got too much work to do." She sighed. Poor Cinderella. Couldn't go to the ball because she had to read up on evidentiary limitations of the Ellerth/Faragher affirmative defense standards.

"But you need to go," Laney urged her. She nodded subtly in the direction of J.D.'s office. "You know he's going to be working the crowd, schmoozing with Ben and everyone else on the Partnership Committee. You have to be there, too."

Payton suddenly felt very tired of the whole ordeal of competing against J.D. If the Partnership Committee's decision was at all based on who scored more face time at the litigation group cocktail hour, then, frankly, they were a bunch of assholes.

"As much as I really hate to miss out on the opportunity to give a series of peppy, come-work-for-our-firm, of-course-I-never-bill-more-than-two-thousand-hours recruitment speeches to a bunch of summer associates who clearly have no clue that they're about to sign away their *lives*, I'm going to have to pass tonight."

Laney stared at Payton, surprised. "I don't think I've ever heard you bad-mouth the firm before. You're normally so party line." She nodded approvingly. "Good for you. I'll tell you what—I'll stay and help you read through those cases, and maybe you'll be able to catch the end of the cocktail party."

Payton smiled in appreciation. "That's very sweet of you to offer. But don't worry about me—I'm fine. Go home and enjoy your evening with Nate."

Laney hesitated. "Are you sure?"

Payton nodded emphatically. "Yes. Go. It's nice to know at least one person is somehow managing to find the time to have sex while working here."

She caught Laney's look.

"Don't worry, no one's around to hear me anyway."

Nineteen

"WHY DON'T YOU have the kid work on that?"

Hearing the familiar voice, Payton looked up from her reading. She had been facing the window, which she liked to do when working at night. The view of the other skyscrapers towering around her with their twinkling lights was spectacular. And somehow, it made her feel a little less lonely to see other lit offices.

She spun around in her chair and saw J.D. standing in the doorway.

"The 'kid' is in his office, slaving away on the fifteen other things I asked him to do," she told him, assuming he was referring to Brandon. "So unfortunately, I'm stuck here."

J.D. glanced at his watch. "You're not going to the cocktail hour?"

Payton shook her head no. "Why aren't you there?"

"I was on a conference call that ran late. But I'm heading upstairs now."

J.D. paused, then shifted in the doorway.

"You're not going to do the weird lingering thing again, are you?" Payton asked. "Because it's starting to freak me out."

"No, I'm not going to do the weird lingering thing again," J.D. retorted, although Payton thought she detected the faint trace of a smile on his lips.

He stepped into her office and walked over to her desk. "What are you working on, anyway?"

"Just some research related to jury instructions," Payton said, sighing. "The judge wants to hear oral argument first thing tomorrow, before he brings in the jury. I'm pretty comfortable with our position—I just want to make sure there aren't any outlying cases that the plaintiff can cite."

J.D. studied her. "Would you like some help?"

"From you?"

"Yes, Payton. From me."

"But you'll miss out on the cocktail reception. Don't you need to go chat up Ben and the other litigation partners?" she asked.

"Not if you don't," he said.

Good point. Maybe J.D. really was trying to help. He seemed very big on the *gestures* these days, Payton thought. Or maybe he was just that confident in his chances of making partner. Her mind went back and forth, and part of her wanted to tell J.D. that she didn't need his help, that he didn't need to pay her back for the deposition. But the truth was, she could actually use the help, and the second truth was, she kind of wanted J.D. to stay—and not just because she didn't want him to go to the cocktail reception and schmooze without her.

She nodded. "Okay."

J.D. smiled. "Okay."

He took a seat in one of the chairs in front of her desk. "Why don't I start with this pile here?" He pointed to the stack of cases closest to him.

"Sure." Payton began to explain. "I had Brandon pull

all the relevant decisions from both the Seventh Circuit and Northern District of Illinois, plus he found a couple of cases from the Central District, those would obviously only be persuasive authority—"

"I'm not a first year, Payton. Just tell me what the issues are."

"Look, just because I accepted your offer of help doesn't mean this still isn't *my* case."

"I had a feeling I was going to regret this . . ."

"Well, then, you're certainly free to leave at any time . . ."

"And deny you the pleasure of your power trip? I wouldn't dream of it."

Et cetera.

HMM.

He was wearing his hair a bit longer these days.

Payton snuck another look.

J.D. leaned back in his chair, his long legs stretched out in front of him as he read through the next case in his pile. His head tipped slightly downward as he read, and Payton could see that the back of his brown hair just nearly brushed up against the starched blue collar of his shirt. Definitely a good one-eighth inch or so longer than he usually wore it. Not that she paid attention to these things.

She had moved and now sat in the chair next to J.D. It was easier for them to work like this—this way, she didn't have to keep leaning across her desk whenever he wanted to point out something he had come across in one of the cases he was reviewing. And that was her story and she was sticking to it.

The stacks of cases on her desk had been whittled down to nearly nothing. It was a good thing she'd flown through her pile when she and J.D. had first begun working together, because her pace had slowed drastically over the course of the past half hour. Over the last fifteen minutes in particular she had become, some might say, a tad distracted. She'd strangely found herself having thoughts that some might call a bit . . . racy.

It was the stupid tie again, Payton thought. She had been innocently minding her own business, reading, when J.D. had casually reached up to loosen his tie and she had thought, hmm . . . he really should just take the damn thing off, no one else was in the office anyway. Then, hmm . . . speaking of no one else being in the office, she wondered what J.D. would do if—hypothetically speaking—she reached over and loosened the tie for him . . . And then, hell, if she was already going that far—still hypothetically of course—she supposed she should also undo those top buttons of his shirt, they looked a little constricting, too, and, oops, in that case she might as well just throw in the towel and move right on down to the button on his pa—

"So how long have you been seeing Chase?"

The question—from J.D.—abruptly yanked Payton back into reality.

"Hmm? What?" Flustered, she covered by gesturing to the case she held. "Sorry. Reading. The law and all. Damn, that's good stuff." She fanned herself. "I'm sorry, you asked me something?"

J.D. shifted in his chair. "I was just asking how long you've been seeing Chase. He said you two were dating. I ran into him last night," he explained.

"Yes, he mentioned that when I saw him earlier today."

Payton could've sworn she saw J.D.'s eyes flash at this.

"You two are serious, then?" he asked.

Payton hesitated. Did she care what J.D. thought about her and Chase? Surprisingly, she thought she might.

"We've been seeing each other for a few weeks," she said.

Tiptoe, tiptoe.

J.D. nodded. "You two seem to have a lot in common." He waited to see where she would pick up with that.

Tiptoe, tiptoe.

"We would seem to, yes."

Silence. Once again, they were at a standstill.

Then Payton thought, *What the hell*? and decided to go for broke.

"Why are you here, J.D.?"

"I work here, remember? See, right over there is my office and—"

Payton put her hand on top of his. "Don't. Let's just skip over the sarcastic part for once."

J.D. glanced down at her hand, then up to meet her gaze. "What is it you really want to know, Payton?"

She asked him the question she had been asking herself for the past few days. "Why are you being so nice to me *now*?"

J.D. leaned forward in his chair. He gazed directly into her eyes, and Payton suddenly found herself wondering why it had taken him eight years to look at her that way.

"Because you're letting me," he said softly.

And in that moment, Payton knew.

The Perfect Chase was doomed.

And not because of a maraschino cherry. The Perfect Chase had been doomed from the very start and the reason—and, in fact, Payton was beginning to suspect, the reason pretty much all of her relationships over the past eight years had been doomed from the very start—was sitting in the chair right across from her, staring her in the eyes.

Realizing that, Payton had only one thing to say. "Oh . . . *no*," she gasped.

Except she hadn't exactly meant to say it out loud.

J.D. cocked his head. "Interesting response."

Payton couldn't tell if he was amused or angry. She

opened her mouth to explain, but was interrupted by a knock at her door.

Brandon strolled into her office, oblivious to everything. "So I found a couple more cases you might want to take a look at—oh, hey, J.D.—I didn't realize you were here."

Payton and J.D. bolted up from their chairs at the same time.

"Actually, I was just leaving," J.D. said hurriedly. "Payton, I don't think you need my help anymore; the two of you should be able to finish off the rest of those cases. It was good seeing you again, Brendan."

"It's Brandon."

"Of course."

Payton watched as J.D. left her office and strode across the hall to his own.

"I hope I wasn't interrupting anything," Brandon said.

"No, not at all," Payton assured him. That's all she needed right now, to be the target of tawdry office gossip. That kind of stuff could kill a career. "J.D. was just helping me get through some of this research." She took a seat at her desk. "So, what did you find?"

Brandon sat down in one of the chairs in front of her desk. And as he began to explain—as eager junior associates always did—the big break in the trial he believed he had just discovered, Payton paid vigorous attention. In between stolen glances across the hall, that is. She wondered what J.D. was thinking, if this was going to be another one of those moments between them that neither of them acknowledged, or if he was angry even, thinking she meant something by the "oh . . . *no*" that she didn't actually mean, or maybe she did mean it, she didn't know anymore; her mind was a mess of a thousand dangling thoughts and she couldn't seem to grasp any of them except for the fact that she knew she should be focusing on her trial and—

Next to her, on her computer screen, the alert box suddenly popped up, indicating she had just received a new email message. Still nodding as she listened to Brandon, Payton clicked her mouse and saw she had a message from J.D. Nothing in the subject line, so she clicked again and read:

I'd like to drive you home tonight.

Without breaking stride, Payton simultaneously asked Brandon a follow-up question regarding his research and fired off a quick reply to J.D.'s email.

Twenty minutes.

"WELL, AT LEAST now I can say that I've ridden in the infamous Bentley."

As they walked along the sidewalk, approaching her two-flat, Payton saw J.D. grin and check his watch.

"What? What was that?" she asked.

"I've been timing how long it would take you to make a comment about the car. I'm actually surprised you made it the whole ride here without saying anything."

"I'm hardly that predictable," Payton said, starting to fling her hair back over her shoulders, but catching herself.

J.D. noticed and laughed. "Yes, really, you are. In eight years, I don't think I've ever known you to refrain from commenting on anything."

They had reached her front door. Payton turned around to face J.D. "That's not true."

"It's not, huh?" He raised an eyebrow.

Payton looked him over. "I didn't comment on the fact that you parked your car down the street instead of dropping me off out front. Because if I did comment on that, I would've said that you appear to think you're coming inside."

J.D. took a step closer and peered down at her. "And if that thought had occurred to me, would I have been wrong?"

"Hmm . . . no comment." Payton unlocked the front door, and J.D. held it open for her.

"Maybe I'm just making sure you get inside safely," he said as they walked up the stairs to her apartment. "Call me old-fashioned." Then he sprang ahead of Payton, walking backward up the steps and facing her. "Or wait—is it uptight, pony-owning, trickle-down-economics-loving, Scotch-on-the-rocks-drinking, my-wife-better-take-my-last-name sexist jerk? Somehow, I always get those two mixed up."

They had reached the door to Payton's apartment.

"I don't know . . ." she said, "remind me—was that before or after you called me a stubborn, button-pushing, Prius-driving, chip-on-your-shoulder-holding, 'stay-at-home-mom'-is-the-eighth-dirty-word-thinking feminazi?"

She unlocked the door and stepped into her apartment. She tossed her briefcase and purse onto the living room couch.

J.D. followed her inside, shutting the door behind them. He grinned hearing his words thrown back at him. "After, definitely after. That's how it's been since the beginning—you fire the first shot, and *I* merely react."

He said it lightly, teasingly, but Payton caught something in his choice of words.

"What do you mean, that's how it's been since the beginning?"

She saw a momentary flicker in J.D.'s eyes, as if he realized he'd said more than he'd meant to. He waved her question off.

"Never mind. Forget I said that. It's not important."

Payton was curious. But she backed off, sensing that pressing the issue would only lead to an argument. And the two of them had had enough of those to last a lifetime.

"So . . ." she said, trailing off. She leaned against the wall of built-in bookshelves, facing J.D., who stood across the room from her.

"So . . ." he replied. He looked her over, as if waiting for her to do or say something first. Which was fine because, actually, there was something she did want to say. She cleared her throat.

"You know, J.D.—for the record—I actually don't think you're sexist." She saw him cock his head at this sudden admission, so she explained. "I just thought, you know, that was a bad thing for me to say. In a few days we won't be working together anymore and I didn't want that left hanging between us."

J.D. slowly began crossing the room toward her. "In that case, as long as we're clearing up the record, *feminazi* was probably a little harsh."

"A little? You think?"

"A *lot* harsh." J.D. moved closer to her, then closer still. Payton felt her heart begin to race.

"And, actually, I don't think you're uptight," she said, still managing to appear cool and collected on the outside at least. "Obstinate and smug perhaps, but not uptight."

"Thank you," J.D. said, with a nod of acknowledgment. He stood before her now, so that she was trapped between him and the bookshelves.

"Also for the record," Payton said in a lower voice, "I don't drive a Prius."

J.D. gazed down at her, his eyes dark and intense. "For the record, I've never owned a pony."

"That's a shame," Payton told him in a whisper. "I was thinking it must be kind of nice to own a pony." She felt J.D.'s hand at the back of her neck.

"You're going to stop talking now," he said, pulling her to him. "Because I've already waited long enough to do this."

Then his mouth came down on hers, and finally, after eight years, J. D. Jameson kissed her.

Payton's lips parted eagerly, teasing him as her tongue lightly swept over his. J.D.'s hand moved to her waist and pulled her closer as his mouth searched hers, deepening the kiss. She pressed her body instinctively against his and he instantly reacted, pushing her back against the shelves. With his arms on either side of her, holding her there, his lips trailed a path along her neck.

"Tell me you've wanted this," he said huskily in her ear, and Payton thought her entire body might have just melted. She arched back as his mouth made its way to her collarbone.

"Yes," she whispered thickly, about the only thing she was capable of saying right then. J.D. kissed her again, more demanding this time. Suddenly they both were impatient; Payton pushed at his jacket, needing it off, and J.D.'s hands grasped her hips and pulled her with him as they stumbled out of the living room and into the kitchen. They hit the counter, and J.D. shoved the bar stools out of the way and flung her up onto it.

Perched on top of the counter, Payton pulled back to look down at J.D. Her breath was ragged. "I like this—you're not towering over me for once, trying to intimidate me."

"I doubt there's anything that intimidates you," J.D. teased. "Not even being naked in court, apparently."

"I'm beginning to remember why I don't like you," Payton said. But then her breath caught as he pinned her hands behind her back with one of his and stepped between her legs.

J.D.'s eyes sparkled wickedly. "Good—now call me an 'asshole' and give me that look like you want to throw something at me—that's my favorite part."

Payton laughed, but J.D.'s mouth came down on hers and all joking fell by the wayside. She felt his hands move to her shirt, yanking at the buttons as she simultaneously reached up and tugged at his tie, loosening the knot. There was a rush to their movements, as if each of them was afraid the other would change his or her mind, and Payton was just beginning to have vague musings in the back of her mind about how far this might go, and whether her kitchen counter was the best venue for however far this might go, when—

Her phone rang.

"Ignore it," J.D. said, his hands moving to the front hook of her bra, and for once Payton wholeheartedly agreed with him.

The ring—coming from the phone in her living room—was easy enough to ignore, but then the answering machine clicked on and Payton's voice echoed throughout the apartment, sorry, can't answer the phone, blah, blah.

"Ever hear of voice mail?" J.D. asked as his fingers teasingly trailed along the lacy edge of her bra and Payton tried to muster the wits to think of something sassy to say back when a second male voice called out to her.

"Payton—it's Chase."

It was a true marvel of technology, Payton noted, the way the clarity of her answering machine made it seem as though the guy she was dating was standing right there in the kitchen with her and the guy she had straddled between her legs.

"I just wanted to call to say good night and make sure you got home okay," Chase continued on the machine. "I know you have a long evening ahead of you, and with everything we talked about earlier I forgot to wish you good luck with your trial. I know how much you have riding on this, so try to get some sleep. And just remember what I said about J.D. Watch your back—the guy will do anything to win."

Payton heard the beep, signaling the end of Chase's message. J.D. pulled back to see her reaction.

"And here I was worried that he might say something that would make this awkward," she said. "Thank god we dodged that bullet."

J.D. ignored her sarcasm. "He calls you to say good night? How serious are you two?" he demanded to know.

Payton pushed past him, slid down from the counter,

and began buttoning up her shirt. "*That's* the part of his message you have a problem with? That he called me to say good night?"

"Oh, am I supposed to respond to the accusations your *boyfriend* made against me? Fine—here's my response: he's fucking full of shit."

Payton nodded as she smoothed down her skirt. "Perhaps not your most eloquent response, but I'll give you points for directness."

With a confused look, J.D. watched as she pulled herself together. "Wait—what's going on here? You're not actually buying into what Chase said, are you?"

"No." *Not really,* she almost added, but stopped herself.

Should she be suspicious of J.D.? Until Chase had left his message, the possibility hadn't even occurred to Payton that J.D. might have some hidden agenda that night. True, she was due in court very early tomorrow morning, but so what? What was she supposed to think, that this was all some elaborate seduction scheme to get into her apartment, and—what?—set her alarm clock back an hour so that she'd miss her motion call? Now *that* was a ridiculous thought.

Wasn't it?

Come to think of it . . . the guy had snuck into her office, then sliced off and re-glued her heel so that she'd fall and embarrass herself in court. But they were past that now. Weren't they?

"Well, it's obvious that Chase's message changed something," J.D. said.

Payton finished buttoning her shirt and turned around. "This is all just so complicated."

"Because of Chase?"

"Because of lots of things," Payton said. "Because I need to be in court early tomorrow morning. Because of our history. Because of the fact that I should be focusing on work right now, and because, ironically, *you* are the reason I should be focusing on work right now." She paused. "I'd just like to be alone to think things through."

J.D. nodded, and Payton could see he was angry.

"Fine," he said tersely. He walked over, picked his jacket up off the floor, and headed to the front door.

As confused as she was, Payton hated for them to end the evening on such a bad note. "J.D., wait," she called after him.

He turned around in the doorway. "This is the second time you've thrown me out of your apartment. If you change your mind about things, you know where you can find me."

And with that, he was gone.

Payton stood there for a moment after he left. Then she picked up her briefcase and headed off to her bedroom.

An hour later, she fell asleep with her work piled around her and alone.

Twenty

ONE WEEK LEFT.

A mere seven days.

Payton entered the final stretch of her eight-year quest to join the prestigious elite of those fortunate few Ripley & Davis lawyers who had been elevated to the rank of partner by keeping two promises she had recently made.

First, she won her trial—thereby upholding her vow to the jury during her opening statement that she was certain that after hearing all the evidence, they would find her client not liable for sexual harassment.

As was tradition whenever one of the litigation attorneys had a trial victory, when she got back to the office after court the other members of the group dropped by her office to offer her their congratulations. All except J.D., that is.

He stayed in his office the entire afternoon, with the door shut.

"What's gotten into him?" Irma asked when she stopped by on her way out, with a nod in the direction of J.D.'s office. "Are you two fighting again?"

"I don't think he's talking to m—" Payton stopped, having caught the implication of Irma's question. "What do you mean, are we fighting *again*?" She and J.D. had always been so careful not to air their disputes in public.

Irma threw her a look. "The administrative staff is the eyes and ears of this institution, Payton. We know everything."

Payton sat upright in her chair. "You *talk* about us?"

Irma shrugged unconcernedly. "Yes."

Payton folded her arms across her chest. "Well. And what do you say?"

"Mostly now we talk about you two battling it out for partner."

"You *know* about that?"

Again, Irma shrugged unconcernedly. "Yes. We even have a betting pool on which one of you will make it."

Payton's mouth dropped open, shocked to find her arduous career struggles the subject of tacky, meaningless office gossip.

"I can't believe you're participating in this, Irma. It's so distasteful. Who's ahead in the pool?"

"It's pretty much falling along gender lines."

Payton smiled with satisfaction. "So I'm in the lead then. There's—what—like two male secretaries in the entire firm?"

"Well, some of the junior associates are in the pool as well. And by some, I mean all of them."

Payton rolled her eyes. "I suppose all the partners, too?"

"Strangely, no," Irma mused. "None of the partners seem to know anything about you and J.D. not getting along."

Payton scoffed at this. "It's not so strange, really. Half the partners here don't seem to know anything unless it's spelled out in a memo some poor associate had to sacrifice her entire weekend drafting."

Now it was Irma's turn to be surprised. "That sounded

awfully disgruntled for you." She nodded approvingly. "I like it." With a wink, she turned and left.

Payton sighed. *Note to self: bite tongue more frequently.*

And find out which junior associates had the audacity to bet on J.D.

If it was Brandon, she'd kill the kid.

THE SECOND PROMISE Payton kept was the one she had made to Chase, that they would sit down and talk as soon as her trial was over. The sit-down took place at Chase's apartment, but the talking was mostly on Payton's end.

Chase took the breakup well. He even laughed when Payton said she had his best interests in mind just as much as hers, seeing how she was thoroughly convinced she was far too difficult a person to ever make him anything other than utterly miserable.

In truth, any thoughts she still may have held that things could work with Chase pretty much ended the moment she kissed J.D. She had no idea what was happening between them lately, but clearly (as evidenced by their little tryst on her kitchen counter) she had no business dating anyone else until she figured it out.

The next day at work, she was on her way to see Laney to deliver the bad news that, alas, the Perfect Chase was no more, when she heard J.D.'s voice calling her name. She turned around and saw him halfway down the hallway, approaching her.

"Ben asked to see both of us, right away if possible," J.D. said. "Apparently there's been some development in the Gibson's matter."

Without further word, he coolly breezed past her and continued along the hallway to Ben's office.

Payton followed behind him, making no attempt to catch

up. If that's the kind of game he wanted to play, so be it. The two of them walked the entire way in silence.

When they got to Ben's office, they found him on the phone. He signaled that he was wrapping things up and gestured for them to wait outside. J.D. walked to the window at the end of the hall, turned his back to Payton, and checked out the view outside as he continued his silent treatment.

Payton was tempted at first to simply ignore him, but then she changed her mind. J.D. was beginning to seriously piss her off and she had every intention of letting him know that. She briskly walked up to him.

"Are you really not talking to me?" She kept her voice low, so that they wouldn't be overheard.

J.D. glanced sideways at her. "I'm just giving you your space, Payton." He turned back to the window.

"You're being an ass."

"And you're playing games. How's Chase these days?" he asked sarcastically.

"Fine, I guess. Chase and I aren't seeing each other anymore."

J.D. turned around to face her. "You broke up with him?"

"As a matter of fact, I did," Payton told him. "Contrary to what you apparently think, I *don't* like to play games with people. And by the way, you have a lot of nerve accusing *me* of playing games when you're the one giving me the silent treatment. Which reminds me, thanks for being the only person in our group not to congratulate me on winning my trial. Your actions lead me to believe that either (a) you felt awkward congratulating me, given that we are in competition with each other—in which case you can't possibly fault me for similarly struggling with the complications of our situation the other night, or (b) you were simply being a stubborn, spiteful jerk, in which case I'm not sure I'd want to be in your company anyway. Either way, if you're waiting for some big apology from me for asking you to leave the other night, you're going to be waiting a very, very long time because, as you see, clearly I was in the right." Payton put her hand on her hip defiantly. So there.

J.D. stared at her for a moment with that "amused" look on his face. "You really are an amazing lawyer, Payton," he said.

She poked him in the chest. "Don't try to flatter me now, Jameson."

He grinned. "You're angry with me again."

"I think this situation is difficult enough without you making it any more difficult."

This seemed to strike a chord with him. "Fair enough. Maybe I should make it up to you, then. What would you say—hypothetically speaking, of course—if I asked you out to dinner to celebrate your trial win?"

Payton hesitated. Not because she wasn't tempted by his offer, or quasi-offer. Quite the opposite, actually.

"Hypothetically speaking, I'm not sure I trust myself around you," she said. She could tell J.D. liked that answer.

He bent his head, lowering his voice further still. "Why? What are you afraid might happen if we're alone? Hypothetically speaking."

It was a dangerous game for them to be flirting in the office like this. Strangely, however, Payton wasn't sure she cared about the office right then. Sure, J.D. pissed her off like no one else could. But when he gave her *that look*, that look that was bold and intimate, but also slightly cautious—as if he was waiting and gauging her every move—she felt thrills of anticipation at the thought of where their little intrigue might go next.

So she leaned in, her smile blatantly coy. "Hypothetically speaking, I'm afraid I might—"

"There you two are! Sorry about that, I got stuck on a Rule 26(f) conference that ran a little longer than expected."

Interrupted by the sound of Ben's voice, Payton and J.D. looked over and saw him standing in his doorway.

"Shall we?" Ben gestured for them to join him in his office.

J.D. caught Payton's eye as they headed inside, seeming to find Ben's interruption as inconvenient as she. They had barely taken their seats in front of the desk when Ben got right down to business.

"So I got a call from Jasper this morning," he began. "Apparently they've had a little shake-up in the Gibson's legal department. He fired the general counsel—probably a smart move since the guy obviously didn't do a very good job of preventing this mess they're in. The new GC started on Monday and, not surprisingly, is eager to meet with some of the people at our firm who will be working on the case. Jasper specifically asked whether either—or both—of you might possibly be free to fly down tomorrow for a meet and greet with him and the new general counsel. He acknowledged that this was short notice, but said he thought that since tomorrow is Friday, there was a chance the two of you might be free in the evening from your other work commitments."

Ben cleared his throat. "Obviously, Jasper isn't aware of the situation here, that one of you will not be continuing on in this matter. And I think it's best that he not be made aware of that fact until the partnership decision has been announced." Leaning back in his chair, he sighed melodramatically. "Given the circumstances, I find it a little awkward to ask you two to do this. Although, with the decision being this close—"

"I'll go," J.D. said.

Ben stopped and looked over. He appeared pleased by the definitiveness with which J.D. had responded. "Good." He nodded his approval, then turned. "What do you say, Payton?"

She could feel J.D.'s eyes on her as she answered.

"I'll go, too."

Ben smiled. "Great. I'll call Jasper and let him know to expect you both." He glanced over at J.D. "You get there early enough, Jameson, you might even be able to squeeze in a round. Palm Beach has some great courses. I think the last time I was there was over three years ago. We went in May and it was nearly ninety degrees. And humid as all hell." He pointed. "You two better prepare yourselves. It's going to be a hot and steamy trip."

It took every ounce of Payton's strength not to react to that.

Twenty-one

THE FLIGHT ATTENDANT set Payton's meal down in front of her.

"And one vegetarian entree for you," she said efficiently before turning to serve lunch to the passengers across the aisle.

Seated next to Payton, J.D. didn't even bother to look up from his *Wall Street Journal*.

"Vegetarian? Now there's a surprise."

"About as surprising as you turning first to the financial section of the paper."

J.D. shrugged. "So? I have a few investments."

"I have investments. You have a *portfolio*," Payton emphasized.

J.D. felt the need to set the record straight. He put down his paper and turned in his seat to face her.

"Payton, I have to tell you something, and I know this is going to come as a shock, but it's better you hear it now." He leaned in consolingly. "*You* have money." He shook his head. What a shame.

Payton waved this off. "Please. *You* have money. I have a job that pays well. There's a difference."

"We make the same exact salary."

"But you have an extravagant lifestyle."

J.D. laughed at that. Did he now? Maybe in her eyes, he supposed. She was a walking contradiction and completely oblivious to that fact.

"*You* have five-hundred-dollar shoes," he pointed out.

"Not anymore."

J.D. cleared his throat. Probably best if they just moved on to another topic.

He watched as Payton picked at her sandwich, some sprouty/all-natural/no-taste concoction. Since they were flying business class, they had seats together, just the two of them. They could talk about anything and not be overheard, although so far Payton's conversation with him throughout the flight had consisted entirely of business-related talk and/or sass. Perhaps it was time to shake things up.

"So . . . you didn't say why you broke up with Chase."

"You're right, I didn't say."

"Are you avoiding the subject?"

Payton put her sandwich down and turned to face him. "Why don't we talk about you for a change?"

Realizing he really needed to refine his subject-changing skills, J.D. struck a nonchalant look. "What about me?"

"Well, you're thirty-two years old—"

"The same age as you."

"—and still single," she finished. "Aren't you supposed to be married by now to a Muffy or a Bitsy or some other society type with a brain as big as this pickle?"

J.D. peered over. "That's a pretty big pickle."

Payton smiled. "So? What gives?"

J.D. couldn't help but look as, while waiting for his answer, Payton crossed one high-heeled leg over the other, notably in his direction. Did she know the effect she had on him? He suspected she did. It was a little dance they did, the way they both conspicuously avoided talking about what had happened in her apartment the other night. He had a feeling that there was more behind her "innocent" questions regarding his love life than she wanted to let on. But he had no intention of cutting the game short. Not yet, anyway.

Seeing that she still waited for his answer, J.D. shrugged. "I guess I've just been focused on things at work." He watched as Payton nodded. This she could understand.

Now that the subject of work had been raised, the conversation drifted onto a safer topic: their upcoming meeting with Jasper and his new general counsel. In appreciation of the fact that Payton and J.D. had agreed to fly down to Florida on such short notice, Jasper had suggested, for their convenience, that they meet for dinner at their hotel. J.D. could certainly think of worse places to spend a Friday evening than at the Ritz-Carlton, Palm Beach. Putting aside all partnership/career advancement issues, one of the main reasons he had so quickly agreed to the trip was because he knew Payton similarly would never pass up the opportunity.

Payton asked him what information, if any, he had been able to uncover about the lawyer Jasper had hired to be Gibson's new general counsel. J.D. reached into his briefcase for the file he had thrown together earlier that morning when he stopped at the office before heading off to the airport.

Strangely, he discovered something in his briefcase that he had not put there.

A book.

Confused—and with the momentary thought that he was going to be really fucking pissed if this was some sort of South Florida drug-mule scam that would land him in jail and cut into his posh Ritz-Carlton relaxation time—J.D. pulled out the book.

Pride and Prejudice.

It bore a Post-it note, unsigned, that read:

In case of an emergency. Trust me.

J.D. rolled his eyes. Oh, for crying out loud. He had told Tyler about the trip with Payton and his "helpful" friend must have slipped the book into his carry-on when he'd stepped out of his office.

Just as he was about to stuff the silly girly tome back into his briefcase, Payton glanced over.

"Oh, you brought a book? What are you reading?" She leaned over, saw the title, then peered up at J.D. with an expression of unmistakable surprise. "*Pride and Prejudice*? Wow. I wouldn't have guessed that was your kind of book."

J.D. immediately went on the defensive. "Come on, do you really think . . ." His words trailed off as Payton leaned back languidly in her seat with a dreamy, faraway look.

"Mr. Darcy . . ." She sighed wistfully. She distractedly put her pen in her mouth—J.D. noticed a little flush to her cheeks—and without even realizing it, she slowly slid the pen in and out between her lips.

In and out.

"Fitzwilliam Darcy and his ten thousand a year . . ." she said, still dreamy.

J.D. had no idea what she was talking about, but he couldn't help but stare. The pen. The *lips*. In and out.

In and out.

Tyler was a fucking genius.

With a blink, Payton came out of her reverie. Most unfortunately.

"Sorry. What were we talking about?" she asked, a little breathless.

Clearing his throat, J.D. held up the book. "*Pride and Prejudice*?"

Payton smiled fondly. "Yes. It's one of my favorites."

"I caught that. Gotta love that"—J.D. quickly stole a glance at the back cover—"Elizabeth Bennet."

This seemed to wake Payton up. "Well, of course," she

said, not unlike Tyler, as if only a Neanderthal wouldn't be in the know. "Elizabeth Bennet is only one of the greatest literary heroines of all time."

J.D. could see she was beginning to get all riled up and lecture-y again. Not that he particularly minded. "Is that so?"

"Yes, that's so. She's clever, witty, bold, and independent. True, she can be a bit proud, some would say she's far too sassy for her time, and she's definitely judgmental, but still—that's why we love her."

J.D. cocked his head. "Well. I guess that settles that."

Payton grinned, a little embarrassed. "Sorry. I can get kind of carried away talking about that book." She paused, remembering. "Weren't you going to show me the information you pulled on Gibson's new general counsel?"

Back to business. J.D. handed Payton the file he had compiled and she began to read through it. But after a few minutes of working in silence, she cast a sideways glance in his direction.

"Still . . . it is kind of a wussy read for a guy, Jameson." With a sly half smile, she turned back to her reading.

J.D. didn't bother to dignify that with a response. But after a few minutes had passed, he subtly glanced over and watched Payton as she worked.

Proud and sassy, no doubt. And definitely judgmental.

But still.

PAYTON STOOD IN front of the closet in her underwear, scrutinizing her dress for wrinkles. She was relieved to see it had survived the plane trip relatively unscathed because (a) she had absolutely zero skill when it came to using an iron and (b) there wasn't time to iron anyway because she was supposed to meet J.D. in the hotel bar downstairs in five minutes.

This was business, she kept reminding herself. She and

J.D. were here, at the luxurious Ritz-Carlton, Palm Beach, just steps from the white-sand beach and the cerulean blue water of the Atlantic Ocean, on *business*.

She had stayed in nice hotels before, of course. Plenty of them. One of the perks of working for a top-tier firm was that its lawyers were expected to stay—for image purposes—at top-tier hotels when traveling. It also wasn't the first time she'd traveled on business on a Friday evening, and it certainly wasn't the first time she'd traveled with a male coworker.

But.

This time it didn't feel like business. Or at least, it didn't feel *entirely* like business.

After checking in at the front desk, she and J.D. had agreed to meet at seven, a half hour before their dinner with Jasper. This had been Payton's suggestion—it would've been her suggestion had she been with any other associate and she saw no reason to deviate from protocol. Work was still work, Gibson's Drug Stores were still the firm's most important new client, and the fact that she just happened to be spending the evening with J.D. was irrelevant.

Similarly irrelevant was the fact that she had snuck in a quick bikini wax after learning that they would be taking this trip.

And one should by no means construe anything from the sexy black lace underwear she had slipped on just moments ago. Honestly. Her fitted dress practically *required* her to wear a thong and low-cut plunge bra in order to avoid tacky panty and bra lines. And the sexy lacy part? Pure happenstance.

And yes, true, she may or may not have used a bit of dark liner that evening for a smoky-eye look, perhaps she did spend an extra ten or twenty minutes on her hair, and it was even possible that a few dabs of perfume—Bulgari Au Thé Blanc, her personal favorite—had made their way to her skin, a little here, a little there. But she'd only gone through these efforts because she'd had extra time on her hands and didn't see any reason to idly sit about in her hotel room. And that was her story and she was stick—

Shit!—she was late. Payton suddenly caught sight of the clock on the nightstand. She hurriedly slipped into her dress and slid on her heels. Because this was a *business* dinner, her dress was black and classic. But a dress nevertheless, and a slim-fitting one at that. She had decided earlier against wearing a suit—it was eighty-five and humid and she would be far too warm wearing a jacket.

And that was her story.

THE ELEVATOR REACHED the first floor and the doors opened. As Payton stepped out, she felt a momentary flutter of—excitement? Nervousness? She never knew what to expect from J.D.—at least not these days, anyway. Sure, they had flirted at times during the plane ride, but on the other hand, they'd talked a lot of business, too.

A question had been raised that night in her apartment, and Payton knew the time to answer that question was quickly drawing to a close. It was a simple question.

What did she want?

She cut through the hotel lobby and found the bar, called Stir, where she was supposed to meet J.D. *What did she want?* In court, she always trusted her instincts. Maybe she should apply the same philosophy here.

She walked into the bar and was surprised to see such a large crowd already gathered there. Her eyes quickly scanned the room, first the main bar, then the private tables, and found J.D. at neither. Then she spotted an outdoor terrace.

Payton headed outside and saw that the bar's terrace overlooked the ocean. It took a moment for her eyes to adjust to the low light provided by the softly flickering candles that adorned the tables. Through the crowd, she finally spotted J.D. near the back, seated at a table along the balcony ledge. She smiled—of course he would have the best table in the place.

J.D. had his profile to her as he looked out at the ocean. She headed over and—taking advantage of the fact that he had not yet seen her—took her time enjoying the way he looked in his dark gray suit and crisp blue shirt. She watched the ease and sophistication of his movements, the self-assured way he held the rocks glass as he took a sip, the subtle brush of his sleeve as he checked his watch. He certainly had style in spades, no doubt about that, and he was undeniably, incredibly good-looking. It struck her then how funny it was that *this* was the man she'd worked across the hall from—and fought with—for the past eight years.

As if sensing her approach, J.D. looked over. When he saw Payton, he turned in his chair and watched as she walked toward him.

"You look amazing." His eyes swept over her dress.

Payton stopped at the table and smiled. "Thanks. I figured it's too hot for a suit." Oh, the tangled web we weave.

J.D. watched her settle into the chair across from him. "You're also late." But his look suggested he didn't really mind.

"I'm sorry; I know," Payton said. She crossed one leg over the other so that the slit of her dress revealed a fair amount of her thigh. An old trick, but still a good one.

"Eager to get down to business?" she asked teasingly.

J.D. glanced down at her exposed leg, and when he looked up, his blue eyes bore right through her.

"There is some unfinished business I plan to get to tonight, yes."

Wow. Payton literally felt her breath catch at the way J.D. looked at her right then, a look that told her in no uncertain terms exactly what he wanted. No other man had that effect on her; no one else could make her heart race with just one glance and a few simple words. And it was in that moment that she knew without any hesitation exactly what *she* wanted.

"I guess the question I have, J.D. . . ." She paused lingeringly as she reached across the table and took his hand. She began to trace soft, slow circles with her fingers. ". . . Is how are we ever going to get through this dinner?"

She saw the flash of desire in his eyes as he took her hand in his.

"As quickly as possible," he said in a husky voice. He lightly brushed his lips against her fingers, his eyes never leaving hers, and Payton could tell that he wanted to kiss her as much as she wanted him to. But Jasper could walk through the door at any minute, and frankly, if she was already getting all hot and bothered from a few smoky gazes, she'd best keep J.D.'s hands, lips, and all his other parts as far away from her as possible until the business portion of the evening's festivities had officially concluded.

So she pulled back, eyeing J.D. across the candlelit table. "Perhaps. But for now maybe you should start by buying me a drink."

"That's awfully retro for you, isn't it?"

"Can't I be old-fashioned, too?" she asked. Even if she knew what she wanted, that didn't mean the games had to be over. *Yet.* After all, they had at least two hours to kill and she needed something to distract her through dinner.

But J.D. was on to her. He leaned back in his chair. "So, this is how you want to play this."

"Hmm . . . disappointed?"

With a smile of amusement, J.D. shook his head. "Not at all. Just remember, Payton, *two* can play at that."

More smoky blue eyes.

Damn. She really needed to devise a countermove to scorching hot sex looks.

But until she did, Payton planned to savor every moment of the possibilities that lay ahead.

"WHAT DO YOU say, Jameson? Another Scotch? Come on, Payton, you don't seem like the type of girl who'd let a man outdrink her."

Jasper was in rare form that evening.

J.D. watched in amazement as the CEO flagged down their waiter and ordered another round. He'd forgotten how much these good old Southern boys could drink. And Jasper—apparently oblivious to the fact that everyone else at the table still had untouched drinks from the previous two turns at "how 'bout another?"—showed no signs of slowing down anytime soon.

Richard Firestone, Gibson's Drug Stores' new general counsel and one of those—to put it delicately—tight-ass-style lawyers who gave all the others a bad name, leaned in his chair toward Jasper. "Don't say 'girl,'" he whispered under his breath.

"What's that?" Jasper asked loudly.

Richard glanced in Payton's direction. "'You don't seem like the type of *woman* who'd let a man outdrink her,'" he corrected Jasper's phrasing. "We don't say 'girl' anymore."

"You know what I say about all this political correctness these days? It's a load of steamin' bull crap." Jasper waved his glass around as he peered across the table. "Payton, you're my discrimination expert—can I still say 'girl'?"

"You can say anything you want to your lawyers, Jasper."

"Ha! See—you boys are too uptight." Jasper pointed at Richard and J.D. "And notice I said *boys*," he emphasized proudly, "lest anyone ever accuse me—or my company—of being unequal in opportunity." He polished off his whiskey on the rocks in one gulp and slammed down the glass with indignant emphasis. Then he glanced around the table. "Okay—so I guess this is as good a time as any—should we get down to business? Talk about this little case of ours?"

J.D. bit his tongue and fought the urge to check his watch. *Now* Jasper wanted to talk about the case? That wasn't a discussion they could've started, say, *two* courses ago?

He stole a quick glance at Payton, who sat to his left. She either had the best poker face he'd ever seen, or she was awfully damn nonchalant at the fucking tortoise speed with which this dinner was moving, because she actually appeared quite amused by Jasper's antics. And that, come to think of it, was beginning to piss him off, too. He'd told her earlier that two could play at her game, and indeed for the first *two* courses of their dinner he'd been as cool as she. But the truth of the matter was, he just wanted to be alone with her. Frankly, he was fed up with all the things that constantly came between them, like work and Chase Bellamy and client dinners. And clothes.

J.D. watched as Payton nodded along while Richard launched into his introductory take on their litigation strategy. Fine. Whatever. If she saw no pressing reason to hurry things along, then neither did he.

". . . So what I'm thinking," Richard was saying, "is that I'd like each of you to give me a short overview on how you plan to approach your part of the defense. Payton, since Jasper pointed out that you're the discrimination expert, why don't you start—tell me your thoughts on how we should attack the substantive issues presented in this case."

"Sure, Richard, I'd be happy to," Payton agreed. Then she chuckled. "You know, I can be a bit long-winded once I get going. I think I see our waiter coming—why don't we go ahead and order dessert now? Get that out of the way."

J.D. suddenly felt Payton's hand rest on his thigh underneath the table.

Interesting.

The waiter set dessert menus down in front of everyone. With her free hand, Payton picked up her menu and casually looked it over. "Now what am I in the mood for?"

She began lightly stroking her finger along J.D.'s thigh.

Very interesting.

"Come on now, Payton—this is Florida. Y'all have to try the key lime pie," Jasper declared. He took the liberty of ordering for all of them, and the waiter scooted off.

"In fact," Jasper said, "did you know that just last year, key lime pie was named our official state pie?"

Payton's fingers moved higher on J.D.'s thigh, now approaching Semi-Naughty territory. Two more inches and they would be officially within the limits of Outright Naughty.

"I didn't know that, Jasper," Payton said, never breaking stride. "In fact, I didn't know that states even had official pies. Did you know that, J.D.?"

"No."

He could give two shits about pies.

"Oh, absolutely," Jasper assured them. "It caused quite a stir in the senate, actually. There was a fairly large contingent that lobbied to name another as the state pie. Any guesses? Payton?"

Circle. Circle. Fingers. Thigh. Higher.

Payton cocked her head, thinking. "Hmm . . . some kind of pie with oranges?"

"Nope." Jasper smiled, clearly enjoying being the only one in the know. He turned to his right. "Richard?"

"Peach pie?" the general counsel guessed halfheartedly.

"That would be Georgia, sorry. How 'bout you, J.D.?"

At Jasper's question, three pairs of eyes suddenly turned and stared directly at J.D., who, in addition to not giving two shits about pies, had been busy concentrating on the fact that Payton had teasingly stopped her fingers right at the Semi-Naughty/Outright Naughty border.

"Are you okay, J.D.?" Payton asked with a mischievous grin. "You've been so quiet these past few minutes."

Ha. She was going to pay for that later.

J.D. paused. Then—

"Pecan."

Payton blinked, then smiled as Jasper smacked his hand on the table and shouted.

"Yes! With all the pecan farms in Florida, there was a push to make that the state pie. Good going, Jameson," Jasper said, impressed.

"What can I say? I work well under pressure," J.D. replied, with a smug look in Payton's direction. "Now—if we're through with the games . . . I think Payton was going to give us her overview on the substantive ways in which we should attack the plaintiffs' claims."

"Yes, I was—thank you, J.D."

"No problem, Payton—the floor is yours."

Three sets of eyes turned to Payton. Just as—underneath the table—one of J.D.'s hands moved to her knee. How convenient it was that the slit of her dress parted at her thigh, giving him easy access to her bare skin.

Payback could be such a devilish little bitch sometimes.

Twenty-two

SHORTLY AFTER TEN o'clock, Payton and J.D. stood in the lobby with Jasper and Richard, waiting for the valet to pull the car around front.

"I'm really glad we got a chance to do this," Jasper said, shaking their hands warmly. Richard did the same, saying how much he enjoyed meeting them.

"Didn't I say you'd be impressed with these two?" Jasper gave Richard a jovial slap on the back, nearly knocking the poor guy right into the heavy mosaic urn that sat atop the oak table next to them. J.D. had a sneaking suspicion the new GC wasn't going to last more than a month.

"Now normally I don't like lawyers," Jasper drawled with a chuckle, "and I definitely don't like it when somebody tries to sue one of my companies for two hundred million bucks, but with you two"—he squinted one eye, taking aim with his fingers at Payton and J.D.—"I've got a good feelin' here. I think I'm in good hands with y'all."

That had been the only negative part of the evening.

J.D. watched as Payton tried to keep her expression

impassive, but he could see it in her eyes. She hated not telling Jasper the truth just as much as he did, that because of the firm's—to coin Jasper's colorful phrasing—load-of-steamin'-bull-crap decision, one of them wouldn't have anything to do with his case in about five days. Not for the first time, J.D. resented Ben and the other powers that be for putting him and Payton in this position. That being said, he had to acknowledge his own shortsightedness; perhaps he had jumped too quickly at the opportunity to go to Palm Beach, before really thinking through the fact that going would also mean he'd have to be deceptive, in part, to Jasper. But candidly, it wasn't Jasper he'd been thinking of when he had agreed to the trip.

Not that J.D. regretted his decision to come to Palm Beach—far from it. True, the under-the-table hijinks between him and Payton during dinner had never crossed the Semi-Naughty/Outright Naughty border, but in reality, he never really believed they would. Without having to say a word to each other, they both knew exactly where to draw the line with the fun and games. Although at one point during dinner, J.D. had briefly worried that Jasper had seen something.

They had just finished dessert, and the waiter had finally brought the check. Payton and Richard had both excused themselves from the table to go to the restrooms and, after sliding his credit card into the check folder, Jasper turned to J.D. "Would you mind if I ask you a personal question, Jameson?"

J.D. grinned. "Sure, although I can't promise you that I'll answer. And remember that you're a gentleman, Jasper."

Jasper chuckled at that. "Fair enough. I'll put this in the most gentlemanly of terms: Are you courting Ms. Kendall?"

"That *definitely* is a question I'm not going to answer."

"Because I get a vibe."

"We can't have this conversation, Jasper. Sorry."

"Something about the way you look at her."

"Hmm."

When J.D. remained absolutely, firmly silent, Jasper laughed. "Wow—my whole life, I don't think I've ever seen a lawyer shut up so fast. You guys are normally happy to shoot your mouths off about anything. All right then—I know when to back off."

J.D. had simply smiled, and as quickly as possible, steered them onto another topic. Because if there was one thing he knew, it was to never make the same mistake twice.

WHEN THE VALET finally pulled Jasper's car around, J.D. couldn't help but give a low whistle of appreciation. Even the valet—who undoubtedly encountered many an expensive car while working at the Ritz-Carlton, looked giddily shell-shocked as he stepped out of the driver's seat and held open the door of the sleek admiral blue Rolls-Royce Phantom Drophead Coupé. Perhaps not J.D.'s first choice in color—he fancied himself more a jubilee silver kind of guy—but the car made quite an impression nevertheless.

Jasper killed the hush of respect that had momentarily befallen every man within sight of the Rolls by giving Richard another hearty slap on the back. "Thanks for offering to drive, Dick. I think that Baileys they put in my coffee musta done me in."

J.D. and Payton exchanged amused looks. Or maybe it was the eight whiskeys on the rocks, but who was counting? At least Jasper had the sense not to drive himself home in his condition, or at the very least, the awareness that the three lawyers surrounding him would never *let* him drive himself home in his condition.

Jasper handed the valet a tip—a generous one, J.D.

surmised, judging from the way the guy's eyes nearly popped out of his head when he saw the bill in his hand—and climbed into the passenger side of the Rolls-Royce. But just before he and Richard drove off, Jasper—being Jasper—rolled down the passenger window, unable to resist a few parting words.

"Now you kids be sure to enjoy the rest of your stay, y'hear?" he called out to Payton and J.D.

With a sneaky wink, Jasper rolled up his window and gave a decisive "let's roll" signal to Richard. Carefully, ever so carefully, Richard nudged the four-hundred-thousand-plus automobile out onto the hotel's circular drive, and—at a breakneck speed of at least six or seven miles per hour—they were off.

Payton turned to J.D. as the car pulled away. "Is there anything I should know about that wink Jasper gave us?"

"He fished around about us when you and Richard were in the restrooms," J.D. told her.

Payton stared him in the eyes. "You didn't say anything, did you?"

"You mean, like how all through dessert you could barely keep your hand off my c—"

"*Yes*, J.D.'" she bluntly cut in, although not without a smile, he noted, "did you say anything about that, or anything else about us in general?"

Now it was J.D.'s turn to give *her* a look. "Of course not, Payton. I know better than to mix business with locker-room talk."

Her slow exhale of relief reminded him just how narrowly he had dodged that bullet a few years back. Yes, he certainly did know better.

Now, however, was not the time to drag up unpleasant parts of his past. Right then, all J.D. wanted to do was focus on the present. He reached out and took Payton by the hand. "Come on. There's something I want to show you."

"I bet there is," she said with a laugh.

J.D. grinned. "I meant the beach, sassy. We've been here for eight hours and haven't seen it yet." He led Payton through the lobby, in the direction of the verandah. When he held the door open for her as they stepped outside, he caught her look.

"What?" he asked.

A light breeze blew her hair across her eyes. With her free hand, Payton reached up and tucked a long blonde strand behind her ear.

"Nothing," she said. "You surprise me sometimes, that's all."

Noticing that this came shockingly close to an actual compliment, J.D. led Payton down the stone steps that would take them to the walkway he had spotted earlier from the balcony of his hotel room. He liked the way her hand felt in his, liked the simple intimacy of the gesture and the way it said—without the need for words—that they were together.

Not that he particularly minded where her hands had been earlier that evening, of course. But there was plenty of time for that later. Although he certainly wouldn't kick up too much of a fuss if she wanted to forego the romantic moonlight stroll and started grabbing again for his c—

"What are you thinking about?" Payton cut into J.D.'s thoughts. He peered down and saw her studying him curiously.

"You have such a devious look on your face," she said, her dark blue eyes sparkling with interest.

J.D. laughed, pulling her closer to him. She really did know him too well.

THEY FOUND A gazebo, presumably one used for small weddings, at the end of the walkway. Payton made an executive decision that they should stop there—J.D. wasn't the only one running this show, after all—and led him to the railing that overlooked the ocean. There, she turned around to face him. Sure, the view was great, but that wasn't what she stopped for. Without so much as another word, she reached up to J.D. and kissed him.

His hand slid to the nape of her neck, demanding more from the kiss as his tongue met hers. Every part of Payton's body reacted—she wanted more, too, needed his hands on her, needed to feel him, and her breath caught and she nearly moaned out loud when J.D. pushed her back against the railing and slid between her legs. His mouth left hers and trailed down her neck and along her collarbone. Then he daringly went even further, to the dip in the neckline of her dress, and without any hesitation he pulled her dress and bra aside and lowered his mouth to her breast.

This time, Payton did moan. Only vaguely aware of the sound of waves crashing behind her, she arched her back and tangled her fingers in J.D.'s hair, giving into pure physical need. Wanting to touch him, she pulled his mouth up to hers and slid her hands along his chest, then down his stomach. She felt his abs tighten under her fingers as they came to rest on his belt buckle. She kissed him hungrily as she started to undo his belt. J.D. pulled his mouth away from hers. "Let's go up to my room," he whispered.

Payton could hear—and feel—how badly J.D. wanted her. The thought of making him totally lose it sent thrills running down her spine.

"Maybe we should walk a little farther. We do have all night." She took J.D.'s hand and brought it to her mouth. With her eyes on his, she kissed his finger and—while he watched—slowly slid the tip between her lips. From the look in his eyes, she could tell how much that turned him on. She may have been the first to moan, but she had a feeling she could quickly even the score right here, so she boldly flicked her tongue around the tip of his finger and gave him a look that unmistakably said how much more fun it would be if her mouth was somewhere else instead . . .

J.D. tangled his hand in her hair and stopped her. His eyes were dark and intense as he peered down at her. "Do you want to hear me say it, Payton? I want you. Now."

Payton felt her entire body go instantly hot.

Game over.

THEY HAD A minor disagreement in the elevator.

"What floor are you on?"

Fumble. Fumble.

"The top. Club level."

Zipper.

"My room's closer."

More fumbling. Gasp.

"My room's oceanfront. Fuck it—this thing keeps getting in the way."

Loud rip.

"Oceanfront? Hmm . . . I see somebody was a little presumptuous at check—"

Sharp intake of breath. "Oh, *yes* . . ."

Moan. Hands gripping rail. Heavy breathing.

"Screw it, I don't care . . . do it here, J.D. Now."

Wicked laugh.

"Not yet."

"You're gonna pay for this."

Devilish grin.

"I certainly hope so."

J.D. PRESSED PAYTON against the door to his room as he slid the key card into the lock. When he heard the familiar click, he grabbed Payton by the waist and pulled her into the room with him.

Okay, fine—at check-in, when she wasn't paying attention, he had asked to be upgraded to an oceanfront suite. He'd been feeling a little . . . optimistic.

And Payton didn't exactly look displeased with his decision. Still holding his hand, she walked around the room, checking out the oversized living room area, the separate master bedroom, the marble bathroom with a solid stone ocean-facing soaking tub, and, of course, the private balcony with a direct view of the Atlantic.

"You approve?" J.D. asked when she finished her perusal of the room.

Payton smiled. "Do I even want to know how much this cost you?"

In truth, he'd spent over a grand out of his own pocket for the upgrade. He debated what was better: to let her think this was all part of his so-called "extravagant lifestyle," or to tell her the truth. He decided to go with the truth. So far that evening, saying exactly what was on his mind had been paying off in spades.

"It's for you," he told her.

Payton seemed momentarily surprised by this. Then she pulled in close and wrapped her arms around his neck.

"It's perfect."

She kissed him. Before J.D. knew it, they had made their way into the bedroom. The hotel housekeeping staff had already turned down the bed and the lights were low and ambient. He peered into Payton's eyes and saw that familiar mix of daring and mischief. Seeing how the whole being-direct thing was working for him—

"Take off your dress," he said.

Payton gave him an "Oh, really?" look, and J.D. could tell that part of her wanted to get sassy again. But he could also tell that the other part of her really, really liked it.

She shrugged nonchalantly. "Easy enough. You already ripped the zipper in the elevator." With her shrug and the simple tug of one strap, the dress fell to the floor.

Interesting.

And here he'd thought she looked amazing *in* the dress.

J.D.'s eyes traveled from (black lacy) top to (racy thong) bottom. And she still wore her high heels.

This was going to be one long fucking night.

Gesturing to the black lace, J.D. gave Payton an "Oh, really?" look of his own. "It looks like somebody else was being a little presumptuous, too. Unless you wear that to all your client dinners?"

With a slight kick of her leg, Payton nudged the dress out of her way. She wrapped her arms around J.D., one hand at the back of his head, and threaded her fingers through his hair. She looked up at him and repeated his earlier words.

"It's for you," she said softly.

J.D. looked deep into those dark blue eyes.

This girl drove him absolutely crazy.

With a grin, he scooped her up and tossed her onto the bed.

Because tonight, she was his.

FOR NEARLY AN hour they teased one another, until Payton finally caved and grabbed a condom off the night-stand.

J.D. hooked one of her legs around his waist and grabbed her hand. "Put it on me," he whispered, nearly a groan.

So she did. Then she told him she needed to quickly check for polo ponies.

When J.D. threw her other leg around his waist and pinned her arms over her head, Payton decided to reschedule the pony-check for another time.

As he moved over her, J.D. told her to open her eyes and look at him, and she thought the moment couldn't get any better.

Then he held her face between his hands and whispered her name, and she knew it just did.

AFTERWARD, J.D. COLLAPSED on top of Payton, still tangled between her legs, his face buried in her neck as he tried to catch his breath.

His thoughts. ·

Deep, too.

Just.

Had.

Sex.

Sleepy.

He felt Payton suddenly stir beneath him and he perked up his head, instantly alert.

Ooh—again?

SOMETIME AFTER ROUND Two, they decided to open the drapes and the sliding glass doors so that they could hear the waves. They lay facing each other in the moonlight. As J.D.'s fingers traced lazy arcs along her hip, Payton couldn't help but grin.

"What?" He peered down at her while propped up on one elbow.

"Nothing," Payton said. "Just that . . . it's you."

J.D. bent his head to kiss her shoulder, seeming to understand exactly what she meant. "I know. We've said a lot of things to each other over these past eight years."

"I think we should've been doing this a long time ago."

J.D. laughed. "You hated me up until about a week ago, remember?"

Payton ran her hand along J.D.'s forearm, his shoulder, across the firm muscles of his chest. Had she really ever hated him? Funny, because now she couldn't keep her hands off him. She'd guessed that J.D. was in good shape because anyone who looked that great in a suit had to be in good shape, but . . . wow. There'd been a moment during Round Two when he'd lifted her off him and flipped her over onto her stomach like it was nothing. Et cetera.

A nagging question in the back of Payton's mind was whether J.D. was this incredible with the other women he'd slept with. She hated to think that what was undoubtedly the best sex of her life was just an average run-of-the-mill romp in the sack for him.

Payton decided she had better push her feelings aside. Since she didn't know what J.D. was thinking, it was best to keep things light and flirty.

" 'Hate' is such a strong word," she teased J.D. "And actually, when we first met, I didn't dislike you at all. Quite the opposite, in fact."

Payton pushed herself up on one arm. "Do you even remember the day we met? It was our first day of work, at the firm's welcome orientation."

J.D. toyed with a lock of her hair between two of his fingers. "Of course I remember. I saw you sitting at the table with the other litigation associates, and I walked over and introduced myself. You said—quote—'So you're the infamous J. D. Jameson.' "

Payton grinned. Before starting with the firm, she had heard things about J.D. from the associates and partners who had recruited him. "And you said, 'I've heard stories about you, too, Payton Kendall.' "

She still vividly recalled what had happened next. "Then they told us to take our seats, and you sat next to me, and just as they began welcoming us to the firm, you leaned over and asked if I was really as good as people said I was."

J.D. smiled as he remembered. "And in response, you gave me this sly little look over your shoulder and said, 'I guess you'll have to find out for yourself, J. D. Jameson.' "

Payton laughed. "It sounds so much more scandalous when you say it."

"I was intrigued. To say the least." J.D. paused. "But then you turned on me."

Payton studied him carefully. That was the second time he'd made a comment like that. "What do you mean, I turned on you?"

J.D. gave her a look. "How interesting that you don't remember *that* part . . . It was about a week later."

"Actually *I* recall that about a week later, I was still trying to flirt with you," Payton said. "Unsuccessfully, I might add."

J.D. sat up with an expression of pure skepticism. "Really? And when, exactly, was this alleged attempt to flirt with me?"

Now Payton sat up, too. "Not that I expect you to remember, but it was in the elevator. You jumped in right before the doors closed, and I noticed you were wearing glasses that morning."

J.D. jumped off the bed and circled around it. He pointed, as if to say she was busted now. Not that she was particularly intimidated, considering he was in his underwear. Then again, so was she.

"Oh—but I do remember that conversation, Payton. Every word. I had just gotten those glasses and you mocked the way I looked in them."

Now Payton was off the bed, also circling. "What are you talking about?" She turned on the light next to the bed to see him better. "I never made fun of the way you looked in your glasses."

J.D. pounced. "Aha! See—you don't remember. Allow me to refresh your recollection, Ms. Kendall. You looked over at me and said—and I can quote you directly here—'Nice glasses, Jameson. You look like Clark Kent.'" He folded his arms across his chest. So there.

Payton stared at him. "Yes, I know. That's exactly what I said."

J.D. held out his hands. "*Clark Kent?* The meek and awkward alter ego of Superman?"

Payton shook her head. "No, *Clark Kent*, the guy who seems all intellectual and restrained on the outside, but really he's got this . . . power and all these . . . muscles hidden underneath that tight, buttoned-up shirt that make you want to just grab him and muss up that perfect hair of his and find out how hard the Man of Steel can—"

J.D. held up his hand. "I think I get the picture."

Payton fanned herself. "Anyway, when I said you looked like Clark Kent with your glasses on, that was a compliment."

J.D. sat down on the edge of the bed. "Oh."

He had the strangest look right then.

Payton walked over and stepped in between his legs. She put her arms around him. "It doesn't matter now, J.D. That was a long time ago." She pushed him back onto the bed, straddled him, and slid her hands up his chest. "You don't happen to have those glasses with you, by any chance?" With a wink, she reached over and shut off the light.

Through the darkness, J.D. spoke. Still sounding troubled. "It's just—I thought you were insulting me, Payton."

"But now you know I wasn't. So what's the big deal?"

Silence.

"Wait a second . . ."

The light came back on.

Payton stared down at him. "Please don't tell me that's how this whole fight between us started."

J.D. sheepishly made an attempt to smile. "Um . . . the next day, I kind of gave you a hard time when you made your presentation at the group meeting about the new amendments to the federal discovery rules."

"I remember that!" Payton poked him in the chest. "You were a total asshole to me, asking all these questions about whether I had bothered to read the Advisory Committee notes and other bullshit like that." She poked him in the chest again, harder this time. "*That* was why? Because I said you looked like Clark Kent?"

"Um . . . yes?"

Payton climbed off him. "I don't believe this—that is the *stupidest* thing I've ever heard!" She grabbed her dress and shoes off the floor. "Eight years, J.D.! Eight years! At least *I* assumed we've been fighting for some legitimate reason, like politics, or socioeconomic issues, or at the very, very least because you're rich and my family is from the wrong side of the tracks."

J.D. laughed out loud at that. "Wrong side of the tracks? What is this, 1985 and we live in a John Hughes movie? I don't give a shit whether your family has money. That's almost as stupid as fighting over the Clark Kent comment."

Payton slipped on her dress. "Almost, J.D., but not quite. Definitely not quite." She stormed off into the living room.

J.D. followed her. "Where are you going?"

"I don't know. I need to cool down. I might say something I'll regret."

She was sliding one of her heels on when J.D. walked over, grabbed her hand, and pulled her away from the door.

"You're not going anywhere," he said firmly. He led her out onto the balcony. "If you need to cool off, you can do it out here."

"It's eighty-two degrees out here. Jerk. Ninety with the heat index."

"Well, then, the fresh air will do you some good." He shut the balcony door behind him and blocked her way.

Payton folded her arms across her chest and waited.

J.D. sighed. "Look—Payton—I understand that you're angry with me, and for once I understand why. I would, however, like to point out that you aren't entirely innocent in all this—you've lobbed more than your fair share of insults at me over the years, but notwithstanding that fact . . ." He ran his hand through his hair, then held his hands up. "What can I say? I fucked up. I'm sorry. Really sorry."

Payton softened a little at his directness. She knew how hard it was for him to apologize, especially to her. And he was right—regardless of how it started, once their fighting had begun she'd hardly been an innocent bystander.

"It's just that . . ." she bit her lip nervously. "I liked you from the start, J.D. I really wish things had been different, that's all."

J.D. stared her straight in the eyes. "You have no idea how much I wish that, too, Payton."

He looked so serious right then that it was impossible for her to stay mad at him. Plus he was still in his boxers and that was becoming a definite distraction. With a smile of acquiescence, Payton pointed. "Are you planning on blocking that door all night?"

J.D. relinquished his post at the sliding door and joined her at the balcony rail. "Not if you promise that you're not going to leave." He slid his arms around her.

"I'm not going to leave," she said, leaning back against his chest.

They watched the waves crash against the beach, and Payton laced her fingers through J.D.'s. "You know, I think that was the fastest, most rational way we've ever resolved a fight. We're so much better here."

"It's because we're away from the office," J.D. said. He sounded firmly convinced about that.

Payton closed her eyes. "The office . . . don't remind me." She hadn't thought about the partnership competition between them for the past several hours and wanted to keep it that way.

J.D. spoke softly near her ear. "I've been thinking— tomorrow is Saturday. Why don't we spend an extra night here? Frankly, if one of us doesn't go into the office tomorrow, then the other one doesn't have to, either."

Payton turned around to face him. "Stay here together?"

J.D. shrugged. Nonchalance or feigned nonchalance? It was hard to say.

"I figured you could move your things into my room in the morning," he said casually.

Payton thought for a moment. Or rather, she pretended to think for a moment. She shrugged as well. "Sure. Why not? I like it here."

"Fine. That's settled then," he nodded.

"Fine."

"Good."

"Okay."

Payton held up her finger. "But I pay for half of the room."

J.D. grinned. "You know what, Payton—you go right ahead. At fifteen hundred bucks a night, you won't get any argument from me."

Her eyes widened in shock. "Good god—*that's* how much you're paying?" She paused. "Hmm."

"Hmm, what?"

"Hmm, since the room costs that much, it's a good thing I didn't plan to do much sleeping."

J.D. laughed and pulled her close. "I really, really like . . . the way you think."

Payton smiled. She suspected there might have been a little slip and cover-up there. And the truth of the matter was, she really, really liked . . . the way he thought, too.

So she took the hand J.D. held out to her and followed him inside.

Twenty-three

THEY SLEPT IN the next morning.

Payton couldn't remember the last time she had slept past seven—she woke up with a start sometime after eight and nearly panicked when she saw the alarm clock on the nightstand. But then she saw J.D. sleeping next to her.

He stirred—he'd had his arm wrapped around her and she had thrown it off when she sat up after seeing the clock. Payton quickly nestled back in, hoping not to wake him. She wanted him to sleep. He *needed* the sleep—hell, they both did. And not just because it had been a very late night—although that probably didn't help—not that she was complaining one bit—but more because they'd both been through an exhausting couple of weeks.

And it wasn't over. True, by agreeing to stay in Palm Beach until Sunday, they now had only one more actual workday to get through. But the hard part would come on Tuesday, Decision Day, the day the firm chose one of them over the other. Decided who was better, in essence.

She and J.D. hadn't spoken much about the firm's

impending decision since they'd arrived in Florida. But it was a constant nag in the back of Payton's mind and she suspected he felt the same way.

It was kind of funny, the thought of spending the entire day and night with J.D. Not funny in a bad way, just new. A month ago, Payton never would've believed she'd be here, in an oceanfront suite at the Ritz-Carlton, sleeping next to the man who had been her sworn enemy for the past eight years. But now, it felt . . . right.

That was perhaps the scariest part of all—just how right it felt being with J.D. Because, whether they talked about it or not, they had a big, big problem facing them on Tuesday.

Payton snuggled into the crook of J.D.'s arm. These were things she didn't want to think about, at least not yet. For now, the most serious issue she wanted to tackle was whether the two of them were going to straggle downstairs for breakfast on the hotel's oceanfront terrace or simply order room service.

As Payton closed her eyes and began to let sleep retake her, she couldn't help but think: normally, it would've gone against all her principles and better judgment to spend fifteen hundred dollars a night on a hotel room, or even half that. On the other hand—and this was her justification and she was sticking to it—she'd barely touched any of the three weeks' vacation the firm gave her each year and she thought—*What the hell?*—she was allowed to have a little fun for one weekend.

Fun. Payton opened her eyes again and glanced at J.D. Was that all this was between them? Fun?

She knew, for her own good, that she probably should run right out of that hotel room, head straight for the airport, and get on the first plane back to Chicago. There was a definite danger in extending things.

But then she watched as J.D.'s eyes fluttered lightly, then relaxed again, deep in sleep. She'd never seen him look so calm.

Payton curled up closer to J.D. and yawned sleepily. Ah, screw it—she was staying.

If for no other reason, she was curious to see how the whole oceanfront-terrace-breakfast-versus-room-service dilemma turned out.

"SO WHAT WOULD you think about trying your hand at a round of golf this afternoon?"

Payton finished her sip of freshly squeezed orange juice, set the glass down, and looked across the table at J.D.

"I think that's not very likely to happen," she told him. But she sweetened it with a smile.

Room service had won out for breakfast. Actually, it had turned out to be the only viable option—while the hotel provided every toiletry imaginable for guests staying in their suites, the only clothing currently available to Payton was a black dress with a ripped zipper and a Ritz-Carlton bathrobe. And while the robe was perfectly acceptable for breakfast on the balcony with J.D., a more interesting question was what the hell she was going to wear to walk back to her own room to get her things.

Maybe she could borrow J.D.'s jacket or a T-shirt to throw over her dress when she headed down to her room. Sure, and maybe she could also just tack a sign to her ass that said, *Hello, rich people, I just spent all night in someone else's room getting fu*—

"But I was thinking," J.D. cut into Payton's thoughts, still on the golf thing, "that it could be fun if I showed you how to play."

Payton grinned as she buttered her blueberry muffin. "I'm sure that would be fun. For you."

"Come on, Payton," he baited her, "don't you want to broaden your horizons? Try something new? Get a little insight into 'my world' as you like to call it?"

She cocked her head. "You know what—you're right.

Let's both broaden our horizons. I'll learn how to play golf this afternoon and then you can, well, let me see . . ." She pretended to think for a moment, then pointed. "I got it: *you* can eat vegetarian all weekend." She shrugged matter-of-factly. "Seems like a fair trade to me."

J.D. thought about this. Then he grinned, holding out his hands.

"Or maybe we could just go to the beach." He picked a large piece of bacon off his plate, bit in with relish, and winked.

"Now that idea I like," Payton agreed, tucking her legs underneath her and leaning back in her chair to take in the view of the waves breaking against the sand. Yes, definitely—the beach sounded great.

A short while later, Payton walked down the four flights of stairs to her room. Not the most comfortable thing to do in heels, but she figured she'd run into fewer people in the hotel's internal stairwell than in the elevators, which in turn lessened the odds that anyone would notice the patch-work job she and J.D. had done on her dress.

Luckily, they'd found a safety pin to hold the zipper to-gether. When pinning her, J.D. had kissed her neck and his hands had begun to roam, and despite the fact that Payton knew she needed to check out of her room before the time expired, he pushed her against the wall and they were on their way to some serious mischief when the telephone rang. It was the travel company, calling back to reschedule their flights for the following day. Payton snuck out, leav-ing it to J.D. to explain that yes, they both wanted to change their flights but, no, only one of them needed to book an-other night at the hotel. Fill in the blank.

When Payton got to her room, she glanced at the clock and saw she had just enough time to squeeze in a quick shower before checkout. But first things first. She pulled out her BlackBerry and scrolled through her email. Luckily it was Saturday and things seemed relatively quiet. When she got to the end, she saw she had an email from J.D.—one that he'd sent about five minutes earlier. She opened the message and read:

Stop checking your email and get back here.

Payton laughed. Wow—for J.D. that was practically mushy. She showered, got ready, threw her things into her suitcase, and before she knew it, she was back on the "Club level," opening the door to J.D.'s room with the spare key he had given her.

Although now, she supposed, it was *their* room.

Given their history, it was kind of surreal that she and J.D. had a "their" anything. Payton shoved her suitcase into the closet, figuring she'd decide later where to put her stuff. She paused in the marble-tiled hallway, suddenly hesitating before entering the main part of the suite.

Maybe this was a bad idea.

Maybe she and J.D. should have left things on a high note. Last night was perfect, and maybe that's all they were meant to have together—just one great, crazy night, 95 percent of the details of which would have to be edited for content when she got back to Chicago and told Laney about it. Maybe now, in the light of day, things were going to be different.

Payton headed into the living room and could hear J.D. in the bathroom. From the intermittent splashing of water followed by pauses, it sounded like he was shaving. She peeked around the corner and saw that the door to the bathroom was open, so she knocked lightly. He told her to come in, so she did and—

—nearly did a double take.

"Hey, you," J.D. said with a smile, as he wiped his face with a towel. He had his shirt off, but Payton's shocked eyes were focused elsewhere on his body, a little farther south.

He was wearing jeans.

J. D. Jameson was wearing *jeans*.

He caught Payton's expression in the mirror. "What's with the look?"

Payton propped herself against the doorway, enjoying the view. "Nothing—I didn't think you owned jeans, that's all."

Now he gave her a look. "Of course I own jeans."

Payton stepped into the bathroom. "I didn't realize the Queen's tailors worked with denim," she teased. But the truth was, she loved it: very sexy-conservative-businessman-gets-down-to-earth-on-the-weekend chic. And had she mentioned that he was shirtless?

"Very funny." J.D. reached for the short-sleeved polo shirt he'd tossed onto the marble vanity before shaving.

Oh, hell, no. In two strides, Payton crossed the bathroom and put her arms around J.D.'s waist, stopping him from putting on his shirt. She stood up on her toes and kissed him.

"What was that for?" J.D. asked.

Payton smiled. "I don't know—I think I missed you."

Wow. That had just flown right out of her mouth before she'd had a chance to think about it. She quickly covered. "Or maybe I just really, really, like you in these jeans."

J.D. peered down at her. His eyes probed hers, and she had a feeling he was debating whether to call her on her slipup. But then he grinned. "In that case, maybe I should never take them off."

Payton inwardly breathed a sigh of relief. Banter. Flirtation. Good, this is what she knew—they were on equal ground again. She ran her hands along J.D.'s chest. Whether she admitted it or not, she *had* missed him. And it had only been an hour.

"I have a feeling I could get you out of those jeans if I wanted to," she said.

"You're certainly welcome to try," he replied. He leaned down to kiss her, and Payton knew that her earlier hesitation had been wrong.

Whatever this was between her and J.D., it most definitely was not over yet.

THE DAY FLEW by far too quickly.

It was after one o'clock by the time they finally stumbled out into the bright Florida sun. Although each of them had packed extra clothes, neither had a swimsuit, and while J.D. was thoroughly in favor of seeing Payton in a bikini, there was no *way* he was about to wear any swimsuit that came from a hotel gift shop. Payton laughed and called him a snob, but didn't seem at all disappointed when he suggested they walk the beach instead.

The walk led them to a nearby beachside café, which led to lunch and afternoon drinks—Payton looked as shocked when he ordered a beer as she had when she'd seen him in jeans—and by the time they headed back to their hotel they were both feeling good and warm and maybe just the slightest bit sunburned.

Partly out of convenience, partly due to laziness, and frankly because there was no beating the view, they had dinner on the hotel's oceanfront terrace. The "scene of the crime," Payton called it as they ordered a bottle of wine. In one sense, J.D. agreed—that was where things had all started. But not really. In truth, things had started eight years ago, at a welcome orientation, when he walked up to the most beautiful woman he'd ever seen and introduced himself.

J.D. never would've described himself as a particularly sensitive or romantic guy—and even if he did have any tendencies of that sort, he definitely would've hidden them far, far beneath his rational-minded lawyer exterior—but he was in touch with his emotions enough to know that, simply stated, everything about his weekend with Payton had been perfect and he wanted more time with her.

The problem, of course, was that he had no clue whether she held a similar opinion on the subject. He sensed that she was holding back, and he understood that better than anyone. Possibly his favorite part of the weekend had been earlier in the day, the moment in the bathroom when she said she'd missed him. It was a rare thing for him to see her let down her guard like that.

J.D. realized that, sooner or later, he and Payton were going to have to have A Serious Talk, and if she didn't initiate it, then he would. If he had learned anything from the Clark Kent Stupid-Fuck-Up-Beyond-All-Stupid-Fuck-Ups, it was that he wasn't about to waste any more time wondering or assuming what Payton Kendall might be thinking.

"ADMIT IT—YOU were a little spitfire in law school, weren't you?"

Payton grinned at J.D.'s question, shaking her head no. "By the time I got to law school, my rebellious, instigating days were pretty much over. My freshman year of college, per family influence no doubt, I joined protests over . . . well, everything. But by my junior year, I guess I just got tired of being so . . ." She searched for the right word. ". . . angst-y all the time."

They lay in bed, again with sliding glass door open, so they could hear the crashing of the waves on the beach. This being their second night together, they had a routine now, a way "they" liked to do things. They had drifted into the airy, sentimental kind of conversation that lovers do after eight years of wanting to throttle each other and then realizing—oops—maybe we should just have sex instead.

"I wish I could've seen you back in your angst-y college days," J.D. said.

Curled in the crook of his arm, Payton couldn't see his face, but she could hear the smile in his voice. "You really don't," she assured him. "You've met my mother—picture her scaled down just a notch or two."

"Considering that we're lying here naked, I think I'll pass on picturing your mother doing anything, thank you." J.D. tilted her face up toward his. "Although I am kind of curious—did she hate me as much as I think she did?"

"My mother generally dislikes everyone I introduce her to," Payton said evasively.

J.D. gave her a pointed look.

"Okay, fine—you weren't exactly her favorite person," she conceded.

"Does that bother you?" he asked.

Payton thought that was kind of a curious question. "No, it doesn't." Along with her angst-y days, her attempts to follow in her mother's footsteps had ended long ago.

Payton noticed that J.D. relaxed again after her response, and while she had suspicions where he might have been going with his question, she wasn't 100 percent positive. Which meant, once again, that she went for a light and teasing tone.

"Does this mean we can now talk about what you were like in college?" she asked him.

"No."

"No?"

In one smooth move, J.D. suddenly rolled Payton over, tangling them both in the sheet and trapping her beneath him. He stared down at her with sort of a half-coy, half-serious expression. "I want to talk about what's going to happen when we get back to Chicago."

Payton met his gaze. Okay. Good. Frankly, she was relieved they were finally going to talk about this.

"I don't know," she answered him truthfully.

Now *that* answer he didn't seem as pleased with.

"I've been thinking about this," Payton continued. "A lot, actually."

"And?"

"And I think this has probably been the most amazing two nights of my life," she told him. "I'd love to figure out a way for this to work back in Chicago. But I'm worried about what's going to happen after Tuesday."

She saw the acknowledgment in J.D.'s eyes.

"I'm worried, too," he admitted.

"I can't hate you again, J.D." Payton touched his face gently.

He took her hand in his. "I thought you said it was never hate." He said it lightly, but his expression remained serious.

"The problem is that we're both in this race to win," Payton said. "What's going to happen to the one of us who the firm doesn't choose—the one who has to leave, who has to go out and interview and start all over again somewhere else? I'd like to tell you that I won't be resentful if they choose you—that I could swallow my pride and not be angry or embarrassed—but honestly, I'd be lying. I know myself too well. And I know you, too."

She searched J.D.'s eyes, trying to gauge his reaction. He was quiet for a few moments. Then he rolled off her and lay on his back with one arm folded behind his head.

"So are you saying this is it?" he asked.

Payton felt something tug at her. "I'm saying . . . that I think we need to see how things go on Tuesday. Then we take it from there." She moved next to him, wanting him to look at her. "Don't be mad at me," she said softly.

J.D. turned his face toward hers. "I'm not mad at you. Just mad at the situation."

Not knowing what to say, Payton kissed him while holding his face in her hands, hoping the gesture at least somewhat conveyed the way she felt. And when he wrapped his arms around her and pulled her closer, with his chin nestled against the top of her head, Payton closed her eyes to savor the moment and forced herself not to think about what might lay ahead.

J.D. MADE UP his mind: Payton had given her answer and that was that.

Truthfully, he wasn't sure he disagreed with her concerns. Come Tuesday, one of them might very well resent the other for making partner, and—given the animosity that had been the cornerstone of their eight-year relationship—who knew where that could take them?

While it was true that J.D. had some definite reactions to Payton's "wait and see" approach—to put it bluntly, he hated it—he didn't want to have to *tell* her that. And he certainly didn't want to spend any part of their remaining time together arguing. So for the rest of the night, he said nothing.

Similarly, the next morning, when he woke Payton up by sliding over her, when he laced his fingers through hers and kissed her neck, not wanting to waste another moment with sleep, he said nothing.

During breakfast, as they joked about whether they could bill their time for the weekend, and about how Ben and Irma and Kathy and everyone else back in the office would react if they only knew what they had been up to, he said nothing.

During the airplane ride home, when Payton leaned her head against his shoulder and kept it there nearly the entire flight, J.D. may have reached over the armrest to take her hand, but he still said nothing.

And finally, when the plane landed at Chicago's O'Hare Airport, and Payton gave him a sad, regretful smile, J.D.'s heart sank because he knew he was losing her.

But even then, he said nothing.

AS THE TOWN car pulled to a stop in front of her building—and despite the fact that it was only mid-afternoon—it finally struck Payton that the weekend was over. She turned to J.D., not having a clue what she was going to say, and was surprised to see him already getting out of the car. He took her suitcase from the driver and asked him to wait, saying he would only be a few minutes.

Once inside her building, J.D. carried her suitcase upstairs and deposited it on her doorstep. But when Payton unlocked her front door, he didn't follow as she stepped inside her apartment.

"I should get back to the car," he said.

She nodded. "Thanks for helping me with my suitcase." Lame. They had been home for all of about thirty seconds and she already hated the way things were between them.

She leaned against the doorway. "I don't want things to be strange between us."

"I don't want that, either," J.D. said. He hesitated. "There's something I've been wanting to say, Payton, something I need you to understand, and that is . . ."

Payton caught herself holding her breath.

". . . that I'm not going to chase you."

Payton blinked. Whatever she thought J.D. was going to say, that hadn't been it.

"You've made your decision," J.D. said. "You want to see how things turn out once the firm makes its decision, and I get that. And while I'm not angry, at the same time I don't know what you expect me to do in response to your decision. So I just felt like I needed to say, for the record, I guess, that—"

"You're not going to chase me," Payton finished for him. "I got it. We're all clear." She tried to decide how annoyed she was with J.D. for thinking she might be the type of girl who *wanted* to be chased. Then she tried to decide how annoyed she was with herself for secretly thinking that maybe she did.

J.D. gave her a half smile. "Okay. I just didn't want you

to be expecting me to show up outside your window blasting Peter Gabriel from my car radio or anything."

Payton couldn't help but laugh at that. The thought of J.D. standing in front of the Bentley holding a boom box over his head was just too priceless. "Are you too proud for that kind of thing, J.D.?" she teased.

She'd meant it as a joke, but J.D. suddenly turned serious.

"Yes," he said softly. He gently touched her chin. "With you, Payton—actually, *only* with you—I am."

As he held her gaze, Payton realized that he might have been trying to tell her a lot more than she'd initially thought. But she didn't get a chance to do anything further, because he turned and headed down the steps and out the front door.

Payton shut her door, walked over to the window, and watched as J.D. stepped into the town car that waited below for him. For a long while after the car had driven off, she continued to stare out the window, running through his words again and again.

She knew she was in over her head. After a weekend like the one she'd just had, she needed input. Guidance. She needed someone with an objective eye with whom she could review the past two days, someone with whom she could conduct the proper analyses of tone and facial expression, someone whose skills she trusted in that nebulous and precarious art known as Reading Into Every Word. She needed someone who not only understood her, but the enemy as well.

In short, things were going to get tough and she needed her wartime consigliere.

So she picked up the phone and called Laney.

Twenty-four

LANEY OPENED THE front door to the town house she shared with Nate. Payton quickly stepped inside, eager to get out of the rain that had set down upon her as soon as she'd jumped in the cab to come over.

They had decided to skip the coffee shop, their usual meeting place, since Nate was out with some friends and because Payton was already wired and could probably do without the additional buzz of caffeine.

She had been vague on the phone with Laney—saying only that she needed to talk—because she wanted to say this in person. But unable to wait any longer, she had barely stepped foot into her friend's immaculately designed *Martha Stewart Living*–esque home before she got right down to it.

"I have something I need to tell you about this weekend," Payton said, setting her purse on the console table next to the front door, never again making the mistake of tossing it onto the couch as she might have done at her own home, because—as Laney had most helpfully noted the one and only time Payton had done so—this was, indeed, *not* her home.

"And I know this is going to come as a shock," she continued, "so I'm just going to come right out and say it." She stopped. "Wait—I just realized that I never told you that I broke up with Chase."

"No, you didn't," Laney said pointedly as she oversaw Payton's efforts to dry her shoes on the mat next to the door. "I had to learn about it through Nate."

"I know, I know, I'm sorry about that—everything's been happening so fast these days, and I meant to tell you, but then the trip to Florida came up." Payton tentatively stepped one shoe off the mat. When Laney said nothing, Payton took this as an indication that she had been granted access to the town house proper.

She stepped into the living room. "But if it makes you feel any better, you are the first and only person who I've told this to." She turned and faced Laney.

"I slept with J.D."

Laney's mouth dropped open, stunned.

"I know." Payton smiled. "Holy shit, Laney—I slept with J.D."

Laney shook off her shock. "Where? When?"

"This weekend. Palm Beach. We flew down to meet Jasper Conroy and the new general counsel of Gibson's." Payton looked her friend in the eyes. "Laney—it was incredible."

Payton pointed down the hallway, in the direction of the kitchen. "Do you mind? I'm gonna grab a glass of water." Hell, she was already getting flushed, reliving the weekend in her mind. As she headed down the hall, she began the postgame analysis. "I barely even know where to start—"

"Actually, Payton, you might want to—"

"—I mean, we had sex, like, a billion times. And I'm talking *everywhere*—in the bed, on the floor, on the desk, in the shower—I'm sure the unlucky people in the room next to us heard that one—which reminds me: Do you and Nate have one of those bench thingies in your shower?"

"As a matter of fact, we do, but—"

"Good—because I've gotta tell you about this trick I figured out that makes it a helluva lot easier to—"

"I really don't think you want to get into that at this particular moment—"

Payton waved over her shoulder. "Fine, later then—anyway, I had no idea how ridiculously hot J.D. is—and I don't only mean his body, which, yummy—the things I *did* to that man, that's all I'll say there—but also the way he looked at me and, ho-ly shit, some of the things he said were so sexy they blew my mind, like this one time when he pinned me against the wall and told me he wanted to—" She stopped as she turned the corner into the kitchen.

Nate and five other guys were standing around the counter.

Having just heard *everything.*

The six men stood motionless with their mouths agape as Laney came next around the corner.

Payton glared at her. "I thought you said Nate had a softball game."

Laney gestured to the window, at the rain falling steadily outside. "Canceled."

Payton's mouth formed an O. Canceled. Bugger.

Suddenly finding *his* voice, Nate turned to his wife with a question of his own. "Is *this* how you talk?" He gestured between the two women.

Laney shrugged. "Yes."

Nate and his friends whispered nervously amongst each other at this.

Men.

If they only knew.

Payton glanced over at Laney. "Maybe we should go to the coffee shop after all," she suggested, with a raised eyebrow that spoke volumes in code. Me: Embarrassed. You: Deep shit. Next time. Try harder. To warn.

"In light of what I've heard so far, I think I'm going to need something stronger than coffee," Laney said. She grabbed her keys off the organizer that she and Nate had built into the wall, then walked over and gave her husband a chaste kiss on the cheek. "I might be late. There's a lasagna in the fridge."

Nate nodded. "Okay—call me from the cab on your way home." Then he paused, glanced briefly in Payton's direction, and lowered his voice as he whispered in his wife's ear.

"And find out what the trick is with the shower seat."

GIVEN THE RAIN, they decided not to go far and took a cab the short distance to 404 Wine Bar. The intimate atmosphere of the bar suited Payton's confessional mood. She and Laney sank into a leather sofa in front of the fireplace. When the waitress arrived, Payton ordered one of the red wine flights, thinking multiple drinks spread out all at once was the right way to go that evening. Laney ordered the same.

Payton threw her a look. "By the way, I nearly had a heart attack when you said those guys were from Nate's softball team. I was waiting for Chase to come out from around the corner having heard what I said about J.D."

"Actually, Nate mentioned that Chase had a date tonight. That's how I knew you two weren't seeing each other anymore," Laney said. "I'm guessing—in light of everything that's happened with J.D.—that you're okay with that?"

Payton nodded. "Definitely okay. I'm glad to hear it, actually." She liked Chase. And maybe if the circumstances had been different . . . well, probably not even then. But regardless, she still thought he was a good guy.

The waitress arrived with their flights. After she set four glasses down in front of each of them and explained the wines, Payton decided it was time to tell Laney everything. Or at least, the PG-13 version of everything. Laney listened carefully, then finally jumped in with a question that was surprisingly blunt for her.

"So was this all about sex?" Laney held up her hand, her expression softening. "That sounded like I was judging. I'm not judging."

Payton shook her head. "No, it wasn't only about sex." She knew that much was true. "That's just the part that's easier for me to talk about." She hesitated, then decided to come out with it. "I think I've had feelings for J.D. for a while."

Laney laughed at that. "Oh, really? You think?"

Payton sat upright. "Well if you knew so much, why didn't you ever say anything?"

"I did. For years I've urged you to get along with J.D."

"I thought that was some weird Republican loyalty thing."

"No, it's because I've always thought you and he just needed to get back on the right track." Laney took a sip of the second wine, a South African pinotage. "By the way, while you two were bonking your brains out, did you happen to figure out how your feud even started?"

"You wouldn't believe me if I told you." Payton threw Laney an amused look. " 'Bonking our brains out'? Really?"

"It's as tawdry as we Republicans get."

Payton thought back to certain portions of her weekend with a certain Republican that had been cut out of the PG-13 recap. "Oh, I don't know about that," she said. "I didn't get to tell you about the time on Saturday night, when we got back to the room after dinner and J.D. pushed me up against the desk and said—"

Laney held up her hand. "Don't. I can't know these things—I'll be blushing every time I see the guy. I have to work with him, remember?"

She'd meant the comment in jest, but it had an immediate sobering effect on Payton.

"Do you think you'll still work with him after Tuesday?" she quietly asked.

Seeing the look on her face, Laney fell serious, too. "I honestly don't know who they're going to choose, Payton."

Payton swirled her glass, pretending to study the legs of the wine running down its side.

"If they don't choose me, I'm not sure I can ever look him in the face again," she said. "I couldn't stand it if he felt sorry for me." She took a sip of her wine. "Of course, if they do choose me, then that's exactly how *he* will feel, and I'll probably lose him anyway."

Laney sighed. "That is a predicament."

"You have to give me more than that, Laney. You're my wartime consigliere." Payton saw her friend's clueless look. "It's from *The Godfather.*"

Laney folded her hands in her lap. "Oh. Never saw it. Too much violence. But remind me—who, exactly, are you at war with?"

"It's just an expression."

"An interesting one. I think my first piece of advice as your wartime counsel-whatever is to stop thinking of J.D. as the enemy."

Payton thought about this. Good point.

Laney pressed harder. "Seriously, how do you feel about him? You've already slept with him, Payton—I think it's okay to admit it now."

Payton took in her friend as she considered the question. After a moment, she smiled. "I'm crazy about him." She saw Laney's grin. "And in many ways, I mean that literally, you know. There are times—many, many times—when he drives me absolutely nuts. But still."

"Are you in love with him?" Laney asked.

Payton blushed. "That's a little personal, don't you think?"

Laney threw up her hands. "Oh, my god—we finally found the one word that makes Payton Kendall blush. Love." She pointed. "It's because your mother didn't let you read fairy tales when you were a kid."

"And just when I thought I understood all the levels at which she messed me up, a new issue emerges."

Laney chuckled. "So, do you want my second piece of advice?"

"Don't listen to anything my mother says?"

"Okay, maybe my third piece of advice."

Now it was Payton's turn to laugh. "Sure, go ahead."

Laney's expression was matter-of-fact. "If you're as crazy about J.D. as you say you are, then, well, don't you kind of have to try to make it work? Who knows what will happen after Tuesday? Maybe he'll surprise you. Maybe you'll surprise yourself."

Payton thought about this. *Maybe*, just maybe, Laney was right. She eyed her friend with faux suspicion. "Are you sure you're not just saying this because you want to start making plans for Sunday couples barbecues?"

"Well, yes," Laney said. "You're my best friend, Payton. Of course I want you to find that one person who really makes you happy."

Touched, Payton reached over and hugged her. "Thanks, Laney." When she pulled back, she squeezed Laney's hand sheepishly. "I've been so caught up in everything, I didn't even ask how you're doing. Although I did notice you're drinking wine tonight."

Laney sighed wistfully. "Yes, it didn't happen this month." Then she perked up. "That's okay. The fun is in the trying."

"Wow—you're almost approaching a PG-13 rating yourself with that comment."

Laney sat up and smoothed back her hair, seemingly pleased. "Me? PG-13? In that case, since we've already crossed the line, I suppose we should just get this out of the way. No, wait—"

Payton watched in amusement as Laney quickly downed the rest of her drink. Then she set the glass down and peered over.

"The shower trick. Let's hear it, Kendall."

Twenty-five

ONE DAY LEFT.

Payton's worries over what to say the first time she ran into J.D. at work on Monday had been needless. While things may have changed for the two of them over the weekend, life at the firm remained constant, business as usual, which meant that she barely had time for lunch, let alone a stroll across the hall for a tête-à-tête.

It didn't help that Irma was uncharacteristically anxious and jumpy. As if suddenly realizing it could be their last full day working together, Payton's secretary had dropped by her office every fifteen minutes, asking what else she could do to "help."

"Seriously, Irma—you're making me nervous," Payton said after the tenth drop-in.

"Don't you need me to get started on your travel reimbursements from the weekend?" Irma wore the I'm-worried-but-trying-not-to-show-it expression someone had when distracting a friend who'd just had serious medical tests.

"Yes—thanks for the reminder. Here you go." Payton handed her the pile of receipts from the weekend—the ones she was seeking reimbursement for, that is.

Irma nodded, appearing appeased by the busywork, and left Payton's office.

She was back in five minutes.

"These reimbursements don't make any sense." Irma leafed through the receipts. "The receipt from the airline says that your return flight was Sunday, but you've only submitted a hotel bill for Friday night."

Pesky industrious secretary. Sitting at her desk, Payton tried to keep her expression indifferent. "I decided to stay an extra night. I'm not billing the client for that."

"An extra night?" Irma asked, confused.

"I . . . decided to relax for a day."

At first, Irma looked surprised, then she nodded approvingly. "Really, Payton—whatever's gotten into you these past few weeks, I like it." She pointed, suddenly remembering. "I forgot your time sheets. I'll be right back with them."

"That's okay," Payton said, getting up. "I can sign them at your desk." This was code for setting up a potential just-happened-to-be-walking-by drop-in on J.D.

Payton followed Irma to her desk, where she skimmed through her completed time sheets. She was on the last one when she heard Kathy call out from the desk next to Irma's.

"Oh, good, J.D., you're here. Do you have a minute?"

When Payton heard J.D.'s reply coming from behind her, she willed herself to be cool and casual. After all, they had been performing for audiences for years. This shouldn't be any different.

She glanced over her shoulder and saw him standing next to her. Shit—it was *totally* different. Wehadsexwehadsexwehadsex.

"Hello, Payton," he said.

"Hello, J.D.," she replied in the same innocuous tone.

Kathy riffled through the papers she held, thankfully paying little attention to their awkward interaction. "I'm confused about these travel receipts," she said to J.D., "particularly the receipt from the hotel. I know you said that I should submit a reimbursement for Friday night at the regular room rate, which I did, but don't you need to be reimbursed for two nights? You didn't come back until Sunday."

Certain she was blushing, Payton didn't dare look up from the time sheet she was reviewing at Irma's desk.

"The second night was personal travel. I'll take care of that myself," J.D. said.

"Personal travel?" Kathy repeated, surprised.

Out of the corner of her eye, Payton could see that Irma was listening intently to their conversation. She decided that now would be an extremely good time to return to her office.

"I decided to stay and golf," she heard J.D. say to Kathy. "You know, take a day to . . . relax."

"Oh. My. *God*."

Payton stopped in the doorway to her office, turned around, and saw Irma staring at J.D. with her mouth hanging open in shock.

Irma's wide eyes darted over to Payton. She covered her mouth. "Oh, my god," she repeated, giggling.

Payton crossed to her secretary's desk. "Irma, can I see you in my office? *Now?*"

Nodding, still with the Cheshire-cat grin, Irma followed Payton into her office. She kept her hand over her mouth as if fearing what might come tumbling out.

Payton closed the door behind them and turned to face Irma. "Whatever you think you just learned, I need to ask you to keep that information to yourself."

Irma took her hand away from her mouth. "At least I know what's gotten into you lately. Literally."

"All righty then," Payton said in response to the not-at-all-subtle innuendo. "Wow, I really don't know where to go from there."

"You and J.D. did the *deed*." Irma lowered her voice to a conspiratorial whisper. "Oooh . . . was it *angry* sex?"

"I'm going to pretend I didn't hear that."

"Does that mean it's serious between you two?" Irma asked.

But Payton remained firm on this. "Irma, I need you to do this favor for me. Please—don't ask me any more questions, because you know I can't answer them. And please don't say anything to anyone about what you heard. You know how bad office gossip can get."

Seeing how important this was to Payton, Irma sighed. "*Fine*."

Payton smiled. "Thank you." She knew how difficult it was for her secretary to bite her tongue about anything, let alone something as juicy as this.

Irma nodded, sizing Payton up with a look. "Boy, you two really decided to go out with a bang, didn't you?"

"Irma—"

"Sorry. It was just too easy to pass up."

AT THE END of the day, Irma dropped by Payton's office on her way out. She held a midsized box in her hands.

"The mail room sent this up while you were on your conference call," she said. "They needed someone to sign for it, so I went ahead and took care of that." She set the box on Payton's desk. "Can I see them?"

Distracted, Payton glanced over from her computer. "Can you see who?"

Irma gestured to the box. "The shoes you ordered."

"I didn't order any shoes."

Irma pointed to the return address label. "Tell that to Jimmy Choo."

Payton picked up the box and opened it. She sifted

through about twenty pounds of tissue paper, which of course led to another, smaller box. When she opened that, she discovered a new pair of black heels.

Irma leaned over to inspect them. "Don't you already have a pair like that?"

"I used to. I broke one of the heels," Payton said.

"Oh, right . . . when you ripped your skirt in court. A friend of mine works in the clerk's office, and she said everyone talked about that for weeks." Irma looked Payton over. "That must've been really embarrassing."

"Yes, thank you, Irma, it was."

"She also said that the thing they talked about most was how well you handled it. She called you a true professional." Irma's expression turned proud. "Whatever they tell you tomorrow, Payton, you can walk out of here with your head held high. I couldn't have asked to work with a better lawyer these past eight years."

Payton found herself a little misty-eyed. Everyone was getting so damn mushy these days. "Thanks, Irma."

"Of course, if you could somehow manage to walk out of here with your buns still in your skirt, that probably would be best."

Payton laughed. With a quick wave good-bye, Irma turned and headed out the door.

Once alone in her office, Payton picked up the box and pulled out the small envelope that had been tucked inside with the shoes. She opened the card and smiled when she read it.

You already know who they're from.

PAYTON WAITED UNTIL the secretarial staff had left for the evening before she made her way to the office across from hers.

She knocked on J.D.'s door and was surprised to find him packing up his briefcase for the evening.

"You're leaving?" she asked.

J.D. nodded. "I'm done. For once, I want to leave this place while it's still light outside."

Payton pulled the door shut behind her. "I got the shoes. I can't accept them, J.D."

He grabbed his briefcase. "Of course you can." He peered down at her on his way out the door. "Besides, they were my favorites."

"J.D.—"

"There's nothing you need to say. Really." He reached around, and at first Payton thought he was going to kiss her, but instead he opened the door. He stepped out into the hallway.

"Good luck tomorrow, Payton." His eyes met hers, then he turned and left.

Payton stood in J.D.'s office, alone. Message received. Loud and clear. It brought to mind another time, not all that long ago, when he had left her apartment on a similar note. She hadn't gone after him then.

But this time she would.

Among other things, she'd be damned if she was going to let J. D. Jameson get in the last word.

AS J.D. REACHED for the handle on the driver's door of the Bentley, he heard a slightly pissed-off voice call out from behind him.

"You're a real pain in the ass, you know that?"

He turned and saw Payton striding across the parking garage, coming from the direction of the elevators and heading straight for him. She carried her purse and jacket over one arm.

"Is that what you came down here to say?" he called back.

"Yes, that is *one* of the things I came down here to say." Payton stopped before him and folded her arms across her chest. "I also came here to say that, contrary to your belief, I don't need to be chased."

"Oh?"

"Don't give me that look—in fact, it's probably better if you don't say or do anything. I need to get through this."

J.D. watched as Payton took a deep breath.

"This situation between us is totally messed up," she began. "Frankly, I haven't changed my mind in thinking that whatever decision the firm makes tomorrow is going be a problem for us. A big problem."

She took a step closer to him. "But here's the thing—the alternative means not being with you. And I've been *not* with you for years, J.D. I don't want that anymore." Payton peered up at him, her blue eyes dark and expressive. "I think we can get past this partnership thing if we go into it together." She paused, then blushed and laughed nervously. "Now would be a really good time for you to say something."

J.D.'s mind raced with the thousand things he wanted to say to her. Was it time? He thought maybe, finally, it was.

"Payton, I—"

But he stopped when he saw something—or someone, rather—over her shoulder. "*Shit.*"

Payton cocked her head. " 'Payton, I shit,' " she repeated. "That's good to know. I'm glad we cleared that up."

J.D. had to bite his tongue not to laugh. "No, it's Ben," he told her under his breath. "He just got off the elevator."

Payton's smile turned into a frown. "Crap. I don't want to deal with him right now."

"He's walking straight for us."

"You know what? Since you two are such good buddies, *you* deal with him. Just figure out some way to get rid of him. Quickly."

J.D. watched as Payton hurried off, careful to never look in Ben's direction, and headed over to a stairwell just a few feet away.

"Jameson!" Ben called out to him from across the parking garage.

As J.D. waited while Ben approached, he was struck by a sudden fear: What if Ben—either purposefully or accidentally—said something about the one of them the firm had decided to make partner? And in that moment, whether J.D. wanted to admit it or not, he began to wonder if Payton was right in thinking the two of them could get past the firm's decision.

Pushing this aside, J.D. smiled as Ben walked up to him, hoping to play it casual and innocent-like. "Ben, hello."

"Where did Payton run off to?" Ben asked.

"Payton?"

"Yes, Payton. She was standing here, talking to you, just a second ago."

So much for casual innocence.

"Oh, *Payton*," J.D. said. Bad dinner theater threatened to rear its ugly head again. "She forgot her key card upstairs. She saw me and asked to borrow mine so that she could go back up and get it." *Not bad*, J.D. thought. That actually sounded plausible.

Ben nodded. "Right, right, her key card." Then he cocked his head. "You don't really think I'm that stupid, do you?"

"What do you mean?"

"I saw how close you two were standing, the way she was leaning into you." Ben winked. "I guess you decided to go back to that well one last time, huh?"

J.D. felt his heart stop.

"I'm not sure what you're talking about, Ben."

The partner grinned slyly. "You can drop the charade, Jameson. It's just the two of us here. It's not like I'm going to call Human Resources and tell them that you're banging Payton again." He lowered his voice. "Did you two at least make it out of your office this time?" Chuckling, he gave J.D. a little slap on the shoulder.

J.D. closed his eyes.

Five fucking minutes.

If he had left his office just five minutes later, he would've been in the clear.

"All right, fine," Ben was saying. "You keep the dirty details to yourself this time. It's probably better that I don't know." With a wink, he told J.D. to have a good evening, then headed off in the direction of his car.

J.D. waited, watching as Ben rounded the corner and finally disappeared out of sight. Then he waited some more, trying to decide if there was any chance Payton hadn't overheard their conversation. He walked slowly to the stairwell where she had hid to avoid Ben. As soon as he turned the corner, he knew there was zero chance she hadn't overheard absolutely everything.

Payton's mouth was set in a grim line. "Tell me I misunderstood."

More than anything, J.D. wished he could tell her that. "It was a long time ago, Payton," he said quietly.

Her eyes darkened with anger. "It was a long time ago that you—what?—*lied* and told Ben that we slept together?"

"Yes."

She pulled back in surprise, and J.D. knew that part of her had hoped there was some other explanation for what she had overheard. She looked him over with an expression of betrayal. "Tell me what you told him."

"It's not important," J.D. told her, even though he knew that wasn't true.

"I heard Ben ask if we at least made it out of your office this time. Whatever lie you told him, I want know. I think you owe me that at least," Payton said coldly.

J.D. had to look away, unable to meet her gaze. When he hesitated, he heard the panic creep into Payton's voice.

"Oh, god, J.D. He's my *boss*. What did you say to him?"

J.D. turned to face her. She was right; she should know exactly what had been said. And he needed to own up to his mistakes. So he steeled himself for the inevitable.

"I told him that we had sex on top of my desk one night after everyone left."

Payton blinked. "Why? Why would you do that?"

J.D. hated that he was the one who put that hurt expression on her face. He tried to look away from her, but she was having none of that. She stormed over, confronting him. "You know what gossip like that can do to a person's reputation—particularly a woman's reputation," she hissed. "Why would you say something like that to Ben? To help you get ahead? Look at me, J.D. *Tell me.*"

When J.D. peered down at her, he saw all the familiar anger and distrust in her eyes once again. He clenched his jaw. "I don't know, Payton. Maybe I am the asshole you always thought I was after all."

It was a cop-out, he knew. But the alterative was the truth, and the truth—at least with the way she was looking at him right then—did not appear to be the most viable option.

Payton stared at him with an expression of disbelief. "That's it? That's all you're going to say?"

"Is there really anything I could say that would make a difference?" J.D. was pretty certain he already knew the answer to that.

And here he'd thought her eyes couldn't get any colder.

As Payton backed away from him, her gaze was absolutely icy. "I guess we'll never know," she said in a flat, emotionless tone.

Then she turned and walked away.

Twenty-six

"WHY THE HELL don't you have your cell phone turned on?"

Outside Wrigley Field, J.D. stormed over to the will-call booth where Tyler waited, too angry to bother with a greeting.

Tyler didn't appear to notice the frustration in J.D.'s voice. He pulled out his phone and looked at it matter-of-factly.

"Would you look at that—the battery's dead. I must've forgot to charge it. Oh, well."

J.D. could've strangled him. Three weeks ago, Tyler had suggested they catch a game the night before the partnership decision, as a distraction. At the time it had seemed like a great idea. But now, after everything that had just happened with Payton, baseball was the last thing on his mind.

" 'Oh, well?' " he said. "I've been trying to call you for the past hour."

"Sorry." Tyler cocked his head. "What'd you want?"

"To tell you that I wasn't going to make it tonight."

"You came here to tell me you're not coming?" Tyler asked.

"Yes," J.D. said, exasperated.

"But if you're not coming . . . then how are you *here*? Wait—is this a time-travel kind of thing? If so, you've got to tell me how that works, because I would really love to go back to Saturday night and tell myself not to bring home Ms. Looney Tunes, because that girl has—"

"Screw this." J.D. whirled around, cutting Tyler off. "I should've let you sit out here all night waiting." He began walking back to his car. Normally, he could take all the shit Tyler wanted to dish out. But not tonight.

"Hey, J.D.—come on," Tyler said, following him. "I'm just messing with you. Hold up a second."

J.D. slowed down, then finally turned around.

Tyler saw the look on his face. "What happened?"

J.D. looked up at the sky, shaking his head. He still couldn't believe it himself.

Seeing his reaction, Tyler took a guess. "The firm. They told you their decision," he said in a somber tone.

J.D. laughed bitterly. "I wish that was it." He was struck by his choice of words. That was quite a statement to make.

Tyler seemed less surprised. He stepped over and put his hand on J.D.'s shoulder. "So, then. Do you want to tell me what happened with Payton?"

J.D. didn't know where to start. He ran his hand through his hair. "I . . . wow, I totally fucked it up."

Tyler nodded. "I'll tell you what—we're both here, and I've already got the tickets. Let's go inside, have a beer, and you can tell me everything."

J.D. knew that Tyler had sprung for club box seats, just five rows back from the dugout, and felt bad letting his friend's money go to waste. Plus, the part about the beer didn't sound like a bad idea. He was going to need something alcoholic—probably several somethings alcoholic, in fact—just to get through this conversation.

"Okay," he agreed. He followed Tyler inside the stadium.

STAYING TURNED OUT to be a surprisingly good idea.

It was easier for J.D. to talk while pretending to keep an eye on the game. Discussing his emotions wasn't exactly something that came naturally for him, and the game gave him the opportunity to look away from Tyler during certain key parts of the conversation.

He told his friend about the weekend in Palm Beach, about Paytons's hesitations concerning the partnership decision, and what she had said to him in the parking garage just a couple of hours ago.

Which then brought him to the conversation Payton had overheard between him and Ben, and more important, to the lie he had told Ben several years ago.

It was here that J.D. stopped. As much as he might've wanted to gloss over that particular part of the story, he knew that wasn't going to happen.

Tyler, who had been relatively quiet up until this point, ran his hand over his mouth, and then exhaled loudly. "J.D. . . . that's pretty bad."

"I know."

"How did Payton react when you admitted what you'd told Ben?"

"Not well." J.D. peered over at Tyler. "She wanted to know why. So I told her that I'm an asshole."

"I'm guessing that didn't go over any better."

"No, it did not."

Tyler looked at J.D. expectantly. "So? Are you at least going to tell *me* the truth?"

J.D. took a moment, then looked back toward the game. "It was a few years ago, at the firm holiday party. Payton had brought a date, some writer she'd met at the gym or something, and they were standing at the bar getting a drink. And I remember, as I watched her . . . I guess it was the way she smiled at the guy. The way she laughed at something he said. It made me think, it made me wonder what it would be like to . . ." He cleared his throat. "Anyway, Ben caught me staring at her, and he cornered me the next day at the office and made some jokes about it. I panicked, thinking he might say something in front of Payton, so I made up a story that I thought would get him off my back. A story that would . . . make things seem like less than they were."

"Make things seem like less than what?"

J.D. paused. Then he slowly looked over and stared Tyler straight in the eyes. He didn't say a word. He didn't have to.

"For how long?" Tyler asked, shocked.

J.D. considered this. "About eight years now, I guess."

"You're kidding me." Tyler's expression was one of disbelief. "All this time."

"Pretty much, yes."

"This *whole entire* time."

"What do you need to know, like, the exact moment?" J.D. asked.

"Well, now that you mentioned it, I am kind of curious. Wait, let me guess—from the first moment you met her," Tyler joked.

"Actually, no, smart-ass." J.D. paused. "It was the second moment." *I guess you'll have to find out for yourself, J. D. Jameson.* Yep—he had spent years trying to deny it, even to himself, but that sly little look of hers had pretty much done him in for good.

Tyler laughed. "No offense, J.D., but isn't that a little deep for you?"

"I've managed to remain remarkably shallow in pretty much all other aspects of my life. I figure it balances out."

Tyler nodded. "Good point."

The crowd around them suddenly roared and things

turned ugly as people began booing the umpire. For a few minutes, J.D. and Tyler were distracted, swept up in the game. Then the fans quieted down, satisfied that their indignation had been properly expressed, and everyone went back to their beers, hot dogs, and peanuts. They were Cubs fans—they got over disappointment quickly.

Tyler and J.D. ordered another round of beers from a vendor passing by. After they shuffled their money down the row, and the beers made their way back, Tyler settled into his seat.

"You have to tell her, you know."

"I knew you were going to say that," J.D. said. "I don't think she'll care. You didn't see the look on her face as she walked away."

"But before that, she came after you to tell you she wanted to be with you. There's hope in that."

J.D. took a sip of his beer. "Even if she could forgive me for the thing I told Ben, I think she's right. At the very least, it's going to be awkward between us after the firm's decision. And there will be tension, lots of it. Maybe even resentment." He switched his beer back and forth between his hands. "I don't want to start something with her that's destined to fail. That would be worse than not being with her at all, I think."

Tyler shifted in his seat. "Have you considered . . ." he trailed off, uncertain whether he should even suggest such an idea.

"Yes." J.D. had already considered the possibility, even though he couldn't say it out loud. He raked his fingers through his hair. "I, uh . . . whew." He took a deep breath. "I really don't know that I could do that. *Maybe* if I knew it would make a difference. Maybe."

"There's no way of knowing that, J.D."

"I've grasped that, yes."

Tyler grabbed J.D.'s shoulder. "I wish there was more I could say, buddy. But I think you're just going to have to ask yourself what you're willing to risk for a chance to be with her. That's really what it boils down to, isn't it?"

J.D. took a moment to consider his friend's words. "It's not just the job, you know," he finally said. "I'd like to at least walk out of there tomorrow with my pride. I'm not exactly good at putting myself out there."

Tyler laughed. "You don't say?"

"Do you have any advice that's actually constructive? Don't get me wrong, I enjoy trite commentary and rhetorical questions as much as the next guy, but can you at least throw me a bone with *something* helpful?"

Tyler turned serious. "Listen—I can't give you any advice on what to do about the thing you don't know if you can do. Only you can make that decision. But in terms of whether you should put yourself out there, I'll tell you this: If *I* was Payton, and I had overheard what you'd said to Ben, I wouldn't even have bothered to give you the opportunity to explain yourself. I would've pulled out my white glove and slapped you across the face and walked away."

"I just want to clarify—in this scenario, are we also in a Bugs Bunny cartoon?"

"It's a metaphor, J.D."

"I would guess so."

"Fine, I'll be more blunt: You don't like to put yourself out there? Well, too bad. Fuck your pride—it's the only chance you've got."

"You're asking me to sacrifice the two things that have probably most defined my entire adult life," J.D. said.

"I'm not asking you to do anything," Tyler told him. "I'm just telling you what I think has to happen if you want any chance of making things work with her."

J.D. nodded and fell quiet. There really wasn't anything else to say on the subject.

Like it or not, he knew Tyler was right.

Twenty-seven

PAYTON STARED OUT her office window.

She had just discovered that she had a view of the lake.

True, it wasn't a good view. In fact, it wasn't even a mediocre view, but if she looked to the right, there it was: breaking between two black skyscrapers, a narrow sliver where the crystalline water of Lake Michigan met the brighter, lighter blue of the summer sky.

Strange that she had never noticed that before. Then again, maybe not so strange—she hadn't exactly spent a lot of time in her office gazing out the windows.

Laney had called and offered to wait with her, and though appreciative, Payton had declined. This morning was something she needed to face on her own. Besides, she wasn't exactly good company right then.

As she'd already done several times, Payton checked the clock on her desk. She closed her eyes. Ten o'clock. Finally.

It was time.

As if on cue, she heard a knock on her door. Payton turned around, saw Irma through the glass, and nodded.

Irma stepped inside. "Ben said you can come down to his office now."

Payton couldn't help it—she glanced across the hall. She saw Kathy leave J.D.'s office, presumably having just told him the same thing. She could see J.D. through the glass and noticed that he appeared to be hesitating.

If he was waiting for her, thinking they would walk down to Ben's office together, he was going to be waiting a long time. In light of what had happened yesterday, she had absolutely nothing to say to J. D. Jameson.

After a few moments, Payton saw him leave and turn down the hallway toward Ben's office. She gave him a moment's head start, then not wanting to delay any further, strode out of her office with what she hoped was an expression of optimistic confidence. Even if she didn't feel it, she was determined to look the part.

When she got to Ben's office, she found not only the head litigation partner there but also the other six members of the firm's Partnership Committee. They sat in chairs flanking Ben's desk, forming a semicircle with him in the middle. Two empty chairs had been placed in front of the partners, presumably for her and J.D.

"Come on in, Payton," Ben called from his desk.

Surprised to see both chairs empty, Payton looked around and saw J.D. standing off to the side of the room. He looked up as she entered and for a moment, Payton was tempted to avert her gaze. Then she thought—*The hell with that*—and stared him straight in the eyes. With her head held high, she took a seat in one of the chairs in front of Ben's desk.

Ben glanced over. "J.D.?"

Payton kept her gaze fixed on the partners as J.D. took the seat next to her.

"Payton, J.D.—you obviously know why we brought you here," Ben began.

Out of the corner of her eye, Payton could see J.D. glance in her direction.

"We know how important this is to both of you, how much dedication each of you has shown to the firm. All of us on the Partnership Committee deeply regret the circumstances that have forced us to make this choice."

Payton could feel J.D.'s eyes rest on her as Ben continued.

"You're both very talented lawyers, and that has made our decision extremely difficult. Nevertheless, it was a decision we had to make, and we have done so."

Payton could see J.D. shift again in his chair, and she noticed that he bounced his leg nervously. Finally, unable to resist, she looked over.

As if he'd been waiting for just that, J.D. held her gaze. His eyes searched hers, and he had an expression on his face that she had never seen before. One of uncertainty.

Then something happened. Payton saw a flash in his eyes, and he clenched his jaw.

"All right, Payton," he said. "Fuck it."

He turned to Ben.

"I quit."

Payton's mouth dropped open. "What?"

That was the collective reply from pretty much everyone in the room.

J.D. stood up from his chair. "I resign. Effective immediately."

"Oh, no, you don't," Payton told him.

J.D. looked down at her. "Yes, I *do*."

Now Payton stood up, too. "No, really, you *don't*." She turned to Ben. "Ignore him, he doesn't know what he's saying. Anyone who knows J.D. knows he's willing to do anything to get this."

J.D. moved to her side, speaking in a lower voice. "Can I talk to you for a second?"

"No."

"Thanks." Without further ado, he took her by the elbow and led her to the corner of the room.

When they got there, Payton folded her arms across her chest and lowered her voice so that only he could hear. "How dare you even think about trying this," she hissed. "I told you before, I won't win by default."

"I'm resigning, Payton," J.D. said firmly. "Even if they did choose me, I couldn't accept it. Not after what I said to Ben."

"Fine, I get it. Mea culpa. I don't care—I'm ready to accept the firm's decision, whatever it is. At least after today, I'll never have to see you again. So can we get on with this?" She turned back toward her chair, but J.D. grabbed her by the elbow again.

"No. I want to talk to you."

"Sorry—you had your chance to talk yesterday. Now I'm focused on more important things."

"What happens between us isn't important to you?"

"Are you kidding me with this shit?" Payton gestured to the row of partners who were staring at them in utter confusion. "Seriously, J.D.—you want to talk about this *now*?"

"Yes. *Now*," he said.

"Oh, in that case . . . sorry—still no." Payton pointed. "And by the way—I forgot to tell you this last night: you're an asshole."

Over at his desk, Ben sat upright in his chair, obviously having at least caught that part.

"Whoa—Payton, J.D." He looked between them, confused. "When the hell did you two start fighting?"

A thousand snide retorts came to Payton's mind. She was quickly scrolling through the list, debating whether she could get away with any of them, when she felt J.D.'s hand on her arm.

"I want to talk to you, Payton," he repeated. "We can either do this here or somewhere more private. You decide."

From the determined look on his face, Payton could tell he was serious. She turned and saw seven pairs of stunned

and extremely curious Partnership Committee eyes on
them.

She smiled politely.

"Would you excuse us? We'll only need a moment."

PAYTON AND J.D. stepped out of Ben's office and
turned the corner into the main hallway. They both stopped,
surprised by what they saw.

A crowd—it had to be at least half the office—had
gathered in large, gossiping groups. Attorneys, secretaries,
legal assistants, everyone. They all fell to a hush as soon as
the two of them came around the corner.

J.D. noticed a particularly tight group huddled around
Irma and Kathy's desks that included a very sheepish-now-
that-I've-been-busted-looking Tyler, the Brandon/Bren-
dan kid, and what looked suspiciously like the top of
Laney's head peeking out from behind the plant on Irma's
desk.

Everyone was silent, staring at them.

J.D. felt compelled to say something. "We're on a
break."

He heard the confused whispers.

Thinking it was best to keeping moving, J.D. guided
Payton toward an empty office. Once inside, he shut the
door behind them and locked it.

Payton moved away from him, toward the vacant desk.
"Thanks. Do you think you could possibly draw any more
attention to us?"

"I think I probably could, sure."

She turned around. "Haven't you pretty much lost the
right to be sarcastic with me? Or maybe you think I'm supposed to just stand here while you—"

J.D. put his hand over her mouth. "Normally, Payton, I
would love to do this with you. But I've got several things
I need to say, and you're not making this any easier. So for

right now, I need you to just sit down and *shut up*." With his hands on her shoulders, he pressed her down into the desk chair.

Payton stared up at him. "Well, I never," she said in her most indignant tone.

But interestingly, J.D. noted, she said nothing further. Although she really didn't need to—the look in her eyes said more than all the choice profane words out there.

Not particularly encouraging.

He began pacing the room. He felt Payton's gaze on him as he moved back and forth.

"All right, let me start with the thing I told Ben. I know that was inexcusable—I regretted it the moment I said it. I panicked." J.D. glanced over at Payton. "Apparently, I have this *way* of looking at you that gives it away."

He stopped before her. "Maybe you could just nod your head yes or no if you understand what I'm saying."

Payton shook her head no. Still with the glare.

J.D. went back to his pacing. "You drive me crazy, you know. The way you snap around here in your heels and your little skirt suits and your sassy quips and comebacks and the way you always, always have to challenge me on everything I say and do, and for *eight years* I have tried to get ahead of you, I've tried to break away from you, Payton, and I can't."

He stopped before her hopefully. Again. "Now do you see where I'm going with this?"

And again Payton shook her head no. But she dropped the glare at least.

J.D. nodded. Crap. He took a deep breath.

"I'm in love with you, Payton."

Her mouth fell open. Then shut again.

J.D. figured there was no turning back. "I've been in love with you since the very beginning. You asked why there isn't anyone else in my life, and the reason . . . is you." He cleared his throat. "I know I've acted otherwise.

I know I've been terrible to you at times. That's just a defense mechanism. Because the truth is, every single day for the past eight years I've wanted you to look at me the way you did when we first met."

He waited for her to say something. "If this strikes any sort of chord with you at all, feel free to jump in."

Payton nodded. She seemed shell-shocked, and for J.D. the silence was agonizing.

Then the unthinkable happened.

A tear ran down her cheek. She laughed in embarrassment and wiped it away. "Sorry. I just keep thinking"—she looked down at her hands—"how we've wasted so much time." She glanced up at him. "Why didn't you ever say anything?"

The tear totally did him in. J.D. got down on one knee before her. "I know, Payton—I wish I could go back, I wish I could take it all back." He wiped the tear from her cheek. "But I'm saying it now. Don't tell me it's too late."

Suddenly there was a knock, and Ben's voice called through the door. "Payton? J.D.? Is everything okay in there? This is extremely unusual."

J.D. watched as the door handle turned. He heard Ben call to someone in the hallway. "Call maintenance. Find out if they have a key to this door."

Realizing he was running out of time, he turned back to Payton. "You were right when you said that this partnership decision would divide us. Letting the firm choose will never work—we're both too proud for our own good. That's why I'm resigning."

Payton shook her head. "Too proud or not, I don't want to make partner that way."

"I know. So instead . . . I was hoping you'd want to come with me."

Her eyes went wide at the suggestion. She bit her lip anxiously. "I really don't know that I could do that, J.D."

There was another knock at the door, firmer this time.

"All right you two—I'd like you to open this door. Whatever this is, it's getting ridiculous."

J.D. held her gaze. "We can do this, Payton. We don't have to let them separate us—that was their decision, not ours. The best part of this job is that I got to spend every day with you. I don't want to lose that."

"What are you saying, that we try to go somewhere else? Do you really think we could find a place that would take us both on as partners?"

"Yes. *Our* place. I want us to start our own practice."

Payton laughed. "That's ridiculous."

J.D. shook his head. "No, it's not. Just look at the Gibson's case—we work great together. And do you honestly want to go someplace that's going to be more of the same thing? The same lifestyle? The same hours? Wouldn't you rather work for yourself and control your own schedule? Maybe even be able to take a vacation for once?"

"Sure—those things all sound great. But it's too big of a risk," Payton said.

"Is it really? You and I are pretty damn good lawyers. Starting our own firm is probably the smartest move we could make."

Another knock. By this point, Ben sounded extremely pissed as he shouted through the door. "I just thought I should let you two know that a maintenance man is on his way up to open this door."

J.D. turned back. "We're out of time, Payton. You said it yourself: the only way we'll make it is for us to go into this together. I *know* we can do this. But I need you to believe it. You need to believe . . . in us."

Payton didn't say anything for a long moment, and J.D. could literally hear his heart beating.

Then she finally answered.

"It would have to be called Kendall and Jameson."

It took J.D. a moment to catch on. Then he grinned. "No way. Jameson and Kendall. It's alphabetical."

"You told our boss that you banged me on top of your desk."

"Kendall and Jameson sounds *great*."

Payton smiled, victorious.

"So we're really going to do this?" J.D. asked.

She stuck out her hand. "Should we shake on it?"

He took Payton's hand and stood up, pulling her with him. "I want to hear you say it, Payton. Are we really going to do this?"

She nodded. "Yes."

"Good. Then you should know that starting today, I never, ever want to spend another day without you."

Payton's expression changed, and the lighthearted smile turned into something deeper. She moved closer to J.D., taking his hands in hers.

"Done," she said softly.

J.D. brought his hand to her face and kissed her, more gently than ever before, more lingering, because for the first time he felt absolutely nothing hanging over their heads, nothing standing between them. They had all the time in the world to themselves.

Except for the angry man banging incessantly on the door, that is.

And the crowd of at least a hundred people waiting impatiently in the hallway outside.

With all the rumblings coming from the other side of the door, Payton pulled back. "I think we should probably go out there."

J.D. grinned slyly. "Actually, there's something I'd like to do first."

"Is that so?" she asked. "Oh, I see . . . did the empty desk give you some ideas?"

"Just so I have a sense, how long is that going to be held against me?"

"Longer than a day, I can tell you that." But she sweetened it with a smile.

"Well, *your* mind may be in the gutter, but I had been thinking of something else." J.D. pulled his cell phone out of his suit jacket pocket and scrolled through to find a number. He held out the phone to show her. "What do you think?"

Payton looked at the number on the screen. "If we do that, there's no turning back."

"I know."

She grinned. "I really like the way you think, J. D. Jameson. Let's do it."

Twenty-eight

WHEN THE DOOR opened and Payton and J.D. stepped out, the crowd that had gathered in front of the office immediately quieted down.

Front and center stood Ben, who walked over to them with a look that said he was thoroughly annoyed. "Are we done with the theatrics now? Can we finally finish this?"

Payton nodded. "Actually, Ben, we are finished with this. Because I resign, too."

She could've sworn she heard several people gasp.

Ben's eyes narrowed. He glanced between her and J.D. "What sort of bullshit is this? You're *both* resigning?"

"Sorry, Ben. But you forced our hand," J.D. said. "Payton and I have decided to stay together."

Payton heard an "awww" come from the crowd behind her in a voice that sounded suspiciously like Irma's.

But Ben was not ready to be outplayed yet. He held up a sealed envelope. His trump card. "I've got a letter offering partnership that I think will change one of your minds."

Neither Payton nor J.D. moved.

Ben looked between them, stunned. "Don't you at least want to know who we chose?"

Hell, yes. Payton wouldn't deny that part of her was tempted to grab the envelope out of Ben's hand and rip it open right there.

But.

She glanced over at J.D., who glanced over at her, and she knew he was thinking the same thing.

Some questions were better left unanswered.

Realizing that neither of them was going to bite, Ben shoved the envelope into the inside pocket of his jacket. "You're both fools," he snapped.

"Yes. But only for not doing this earlier," J.D. said.

"You shouldn't have let it come to this, Ben. J.D. and I both deserve this," Payton said. "And if this firm values strategic leveraging over the commitment we've shown over the last eight years, then, frankly, *you* don't deserve *us.*"

J.D. peered down at her with that "amused" look. "Nice speech."

"Thanks. I worked on it while you were on the phone."

J.D. cocked his head in the direction of the hallway behind them. "Shall we?"

"Yes." Unable to help herself, Payton's eyes went to the pocket of Ben's jacket where he had stashed the envelope.

J.D. laughed and held out his hand. "Come on, cupcake— let's go."

Payton threw him a look. "I can't *believe* you just called me that in front of the entire office."

She took his hand, and side by side they walked through the office corridor, past their offices, to the elevators and the exit.

J.D. smiled. "I told you, it's endearing."

"No, it's paternalistic and quasi-sexist. I can't think of one comparable name a woman can call a man."

"I know. That's what makes it so great."

Et cetera.

AS SOON AS the doors shut, the office broke into complete pandemonium. Of primary concern, of course, was the betting pool, and how to address the issue of the double forfeiture.

The Kendall camp, led by Laney, duly noted that Payton's statement to Ben had been "I resign, *too*," evidencing that J.D. had, in fact, resigned first, thus making Payton the de facto winner, even if only for a few brief moments.

The Jameson faction, however—headed by Tyler and relying upon secretly procured hearsay testimony from one of the members of the Partnership Committee who had been inside Ben's office—argued that although J.D. had *attempted* to resign first, Payton had demanded that said withdrawal of employment not be accepted, thus her statement to Ben of "*I resign*, too" was, in fact, the first and only official resignation, making J.D. the winner.

In the midst of the chaos, Marie, Ben's secretary, walked up to him and whispered that he had a phone call.

"Take a message," Ben barked. Whoever it was, it could wait.

Marie looked uncertain. "He insisted on speaking with you immediately."

Ben wasn't in the mood. "Deal with it, whoever it is," he said, brushing past her.

"It's Jasper Conroy."

Ben stopped in his tracks.

They couldn't have.

He nodded to Marie. "I'll take it." Not wanting to waste another minute, he headed into his office. He saw the blinking light on his phone and immediately picked up the receiver.

"Jasper! Good to hear from you. How are things down in Palm Beach?"

Jasper's drawl came over the other end of the line. "Ben—glad I caught ya. Listen, I've been thinking lately about doing a little restructuring of Gibson's trial team . . . I'm concerned that we're leveraged a little too heavily on the *lawyer* side. So I've decided to take my business elsewhere, to a smaller firm."

Ben looked up at the ceiling. "And who might that be?"

"A new outfit, actually. Just got the call today, sayin' that they're open for business."

"Jasper, you can't seriously be con—"

"Loyalty, Ben—I wouldn't have gotten where I am today without it. That's something you might want to look into."

"Don't be an idiot just to prove a point, Jasper. You can't hand them over a two-hundred-million-dollar case."

"Oh, I think I can," Jasper said. "I told you, I've got a feelin' about those two. I think you're gonna be seeing big, big things from them." He chuckled. "Catch you around, Ben. Oh, yeah—and thanks for the introduction."

Ben heard the click as Jasper hung up. He set the phone back in its cradle and stared at it.

They really did it.

Son of a bitch.

AS SOON AS the elevator doors shut behind them, Payton faced J.D., rubbing her hands together eagerly. "So. We're going to have to hire associates right away. How many do you think we need to start? Five?"

"Ten."

"Hmm . . . you're probably right," she mused. "I certainly don't plan for Jasper to be our only client for long. As soon as we file a motion to substitute counsel for Gibson's, people will want to know who we are."

J.D. leaned back against the elevator railing. "We can release a short press statement with our contact information."

"Which means we also need office space and an administrative staff," Payton noted.

"I'm sure we can get Irma and Kathy to come over—they'll be enough to cover us for the short term."

Payton nodded. "Yes. Good. Okay." She took a deep breath and smiled. "I can't believe we're doing this."

J.D. raised an eyebrow. "Any second thoughts?"

Payton shook her head definitively. "None." A lot had happened in the last few minutes and she was still trying to process it all. She reached up and tugged the lapels of J.D.'s suit. "You're so calm."

"And I plan to stay that way, at least for the next few weeks. Not that I think that will be particularly difficult, considering where we're going."

"Where we're going?" Payton repeated. "Ooh . . . where *are* we going?"

"Have you forgotten?" J.D. asked. "You made partner—albeit of a different firm—but you said it's what you wanted."

Payton had to think. Then it clicked. "Bora-Bora?"

J.D. grinned. "And I'm laying down the law right now: there will be absolutely no voice mail, email, BlackBerrys, or laptops."

"Wow. What are we going to do with all that free time?"

J.D. gripped Payton's suit jacket and pulled her closer. "I'm sure we'll come up with something."

Payton slid her arms around his neck. "As long as we actually make it into the water this time."

"I'm sure we can manage that." J.D. said with a grin. "I hear those overwater bungalows are very private."

"An overwater bungalow?" Payton asked. Criminy, she had forgotten about the Jameson style of doing things. "I don't think I even want to know how much something like that costs per night."

J.D. pulled back and looked her in the eyes. "All right, Payton—let's just deal with this now, get it out of the way. You know the estimates as well as I do—Gibson's legal fees for the first year alone are expected to be somewhere around twenty million dollars. And now, thanks to our brilliant maneuver—which was, for the record, initiated by me—there are only *two* partners who will split those fees. You and I." He took her by the shoulders. "Which means that you are going to be a very, *very* rich woman, Payton Kendall."

Payton stared at J.D. as this sank in. Of course she had known that landing Gibson's as a client was a coup for the two of them. But she'd been so caught up in what was happening between her and J.D. that she hadn't stopped and done the math on just exactly *how* great a coup it had been.

She and J.D. would be splitting nearly $20 million in legal fees in the first year alone.

Sure, there would be business expenses, associate and administrative staff salaries, office overhead, et cetera. But still.

Twenty million in legal fees.

Twenty million.

J.D. grinned. "Say something, Payton."

She closed her eyes and groaned. "My mother's going to kill me."

J.D. laughed at that. "Buy her a thousand carbon credits. She'll get over it."

The elevator came to a stop, and as the doors opened, he took Payton's hand and stepped out. They cut across the parking garage to J.D.'s car. "And if that doesn't work, then *I* will talk to your mother and smooth things over," he said assuredly.

They stopped at the Bentley. J.D. unlocked the car and opened the passenger door.

Payton grinned as she started to climb in. "I love you

for your confidence, J.D. As misplaced as it might be in this particular situation."

J.D. suddenly blocked her with his arm.

Payton looked back, surprised.

He cocked his head. "What did you just say?"

Payton tried to think. "What? What did I just—ohhh . . ." She covered her mouth. "I said it, didn't I?"

"I'm not sure," J.D. said. "There was a lot of other rambling going on there. Could you repeat it?"

Payton feigned nonchalance. "Is that necessary? I mean, don't they say that actions speak louder than words?"

With a look—probably the one that was constantly getting him in trouble—J.D. took a step closer to her. "And what actions might those be?"

Payton was suddenly aware that she was trapped between J.D. and the Bentley. This was typically the part where *both* of them got into trouble.

"Well, for starters, I wouldn't have walked out of the firm if I didn't have at least *some* feelings for you," she pointed out.

"You could've done that because it was a smart move for your career," J.D. said.

"True, true," Payton conceded. "But I'm going to Bora-Bora with you—that says something, doesn't it?"

"Maybe you're just using me for sex."

"That is a possibility . . ." Payton mused. She held out her hands. "There has to be *something* I can point to. Wait, I know—"

She touched J.D.'s face. "What about the fact that, through the good and the bad, you are pretty much the only man I've thought about for the past eight years? Does that say anything?"

J.D. gently tucked a strand of hair behind her ear. "I think it does."

"Good. Or instead, what if I just told you that I love

you?" Payton gazed into his eyes. "What would you say, J. D. Jameson, if I told you that?"

J.D. smiled. He touched his forehead to Payton's, closed his eyes, and answered her with one word.

"Finally."